Seas the Day

**Seafood Capers Mystery Series
by Maggie Toussaint**

SEAS THE DAY (#1)

Seas
the Day

A
Seafood
caper
MYSTERY

MAGGIE
TOUSSAINT

HENERY PRESS

Copyright

SEAS THE DAY
A Seafood Caper Mystery
Part of the Henery Press Mystery Collection

First Edition | April 2020

Henery Press, LLC
www.henerypress.com

Trade Paperback ISBN-13: 978-1-63511-583-3
Digital epub ISBN-13: 978-1-63511-584-0
Kindle ISBN-13: 978-1-63511-585-7
Hardcover ISBN-13: 978-1-63511-586-4

Printed in the United States of America

For my siblings, near and far

ACKNOWLEDGMENTS

No book comes to print by itself. I'm grateful to many in my writing community who have encouraged me and cheered me on over the years. Thanks to Jill Marsal of the Marsal Lyon Literary Agency who took a chance on this new series and also to Henery Press for loving it too.

No list of thanks would be complete without mentioning my critique partner Polly Iyer, whose sharp eyes always bring more shape and zest to my words.

The nucleus for *Seas the Day* sprang from an anthology call I received from author Beth "Jaden" Terrell for romantic mystery short stories featuring Carolyn Haines's black cat Trouble. The couple from my "Trouble with Horses" short story kept nudging me for a series, so I began the Seafood Capers Mysteries with a new black cat.

I am very thankful to the men and women in law enforcement who were so kind to answer questions: Georg Trexler with the McIntosh County Sheriff's Office, Wesley Harris and Wally Lind of Crimescenewriters, and Lee Lofland's Writer's Police Academy.

Also, I'm blessed to have family who know how to cook and greatly appreciate their tips and suggestions. Any mistakes in this book are my own.

Chapter One

"My Chili's gone," Estelle Bolz sobbed in my ear. "You gotta help me, River. You can find anything. Please, please find my son."

"Gone?" Oh, no. I needed his fresh fish for tonight's Holloway Catering client. Still holding the phone, I stepped away from the pie crust bowl, moved to the kitchen window, half-expecting to see Chili sauntering across my lawn. "I don't understand. He left town?"

"You tell me. His keys are on the hutch. His truck was parked at the house until the cops took it. His boat's in the slip. He hasn't called me since Tuesday morning. I can't lose another son."

My heart went out to this woman who'd been through so much. Her youngest son perished at sea last year. Having another missing son was my late mother's bridge partner's worst nightmare.

I switched the phone to speaker and reached for pen and paper. "When did you last see him?"

"Monday. Around dinnertime."

"Did you notify the cops?"

"I did. A deputy is looking for Chili, but he's made no progress all week. I rode over to the Law Enforcement Center for three days in a row. They say there's no sign of foul play and he's an adult. Meanwhile, Chili hasn't called in three nights. This is not right."

Today was Friday. "I ordered sea bass from Chili on Tuesday morning, right after I booked a catering job. Nobody's heard from him since Tuesday?"

"Nope. He wouldn't take off like this and leave me to worry about where he is. That's why he calls every night. I'm tied up in knots." She sniffed loudly into the phone. "You've always been like a daughter to me, and I know this is a lot to ask. Please help me find Chili."

I felt uneasy being asked to find a missing person. That was much different from finding misplaced keys or a lost dog, but Chili was my friend. He must be in trouble if he wasn't calling his mom. Estelle's rapid breaths filled my ear like a huffing freight train. "I'll help you. First, sit down and breathe deeply. We'll sort this out together."

"Thank you," Estelle said. "I just didn't know where else to turn."

"That' s it. Deep full breaths. In and out." My breathing calmed too. I started with the easy questions: "Have you tried his friends? Did he find a new girlfriend after he and Trina broke up?"

"After his brother died at sea, Chili kept to himself. That no-account Trina lasted six minutes past Kale's funeral. Chili's all I got left in the world. When I consider possibilities of why he's missing, my gut aches so bad I can't stand up straight. Something's horribly wrong. I'm terrified he's hurt or worse, and I need to do something. *We* need to do something."

I felt for her, I truly did. Mr. Bolz died of a heart attack long before the family moved here. Estelle supported her family with a dry-cleaning business, with only her sons and friends for companionship. My mother died last year, a few months after Kale was lost at sea. It was hard enough to lose one relative, but to lose two so close together would be devastating.

Estelle needed an advocate. Without her boys, she was all alone. Mom's friend needed an insider who knew her son. However, there must be a reason the cops weren't getting anywhere.

"Chili needs your help," Estelle continued while I mulled things over. "I'm begging you. Find my son."

I stated the obvious. "If he left Shell Island, I don't have the resources to find him. The cops do. Convince them to expand their search. I'll go with you to the station if you like."

"Don't get me started on the po-lice. The sheriff has his eye on reelection and that new deputy thinks I'm an alarmist. It's so frustrating."

Estelle paused for so long I thought she must be crying, then she began again. "Your mother, bless her heart, used to brag on you all the time, especially how good you were at solving puzzles. I trust you, River, not the people who hand out speeding tickets. Those outsiders don't know my family. They don't understand why Chili wouldn't leave. Not on purpose. We rely on each other. I-I-I can't make it without him. Please, River."

I'd known the Bolz family most of my life. Chili was two school grades ahead of me, Kale a school grade behind. Like in my family, the children worked several jobs to make ends meet because money was scarce here.

"I'm flattered by your faith in me, but I'm not a detective. I don't have a network of professional investigators like the sheriff does. If I ask around, will you keep the pressure on the cops? They can put out a notice that he's missing, and it will go all over the state. Did you think about going to the newspaper, radio, or TV with your story?"

"Heavens, no," Estelle shrilled. "Chili doesn't want everybody and his brother spying on him. He's a private person. First, I thought he must've fallen off the wagon and gotten tangled up with Mr. Jim Beam again." She sighed. "I looked, and there's not a drop of booze in his place or in his trash. He isn't on a bender. I want somebody I trust on the case. I'll pay you too."

"I won't take your money. I'm hesitating because if he's in dire straits, you need more than me helping you."

"Tell you what, I'll keep the pressure on Sheriff Vargas, if you'll question the younger crowd," Estelle countered. "They're more likely to talk to you than a stranger anyway."

I was relieved she sounded calmer. "I am very concerned about Chili and wish I could drop everything and start searching right now. But my livelihood depends on successful catering events. Tonight I'm booked for the Robertson's anniversary dinner. I'll be busy all afternoon prepping the meal. They eat at seven and it will be after nine before I get home."

"Do what you have to do, and ask everyone about Chili. We have to find him."

"I'll do my best. If I learn anything, I'll call you. When you spoke to him on Tuesday, what did he say?"

"He cancelled on our regular lunch at the Sunset Buffet. It's unlike him to miss the meatloaf special. That boy loves his meatloaf. If I'd'a known that when I had him, I'd've named him Meatloaf."

"Did he say why he cancelled?"

"Nope. Said something came up. I didn't actually speak to him. He left me a message."

"Did you play it for the cops?"

"Deputy Hamlyn said it wasn't helpful. I'm out of my mind worrying about Chili. You'll find him, won't ya?"

"I hope so."

Estelle ended the call. I glanced at my notepad. At the top of the page I'd written "no fish." I'd also written "Chili missing." With no fresh fish coming off a deep-sea fishing boat today, I needed another fish source pronto.

A few calls later, I struck gold and headed to Neptune's Harvest over by the new marina. Except for the high traffic weeks before and after Easter when most schools took their spring break, springtime was slow on the island. Sunshine dappled the two-lane road, creating radiant pools of light beside dark shadows on the oak-shaded pavement.

I loved the centuries-old live oaks here, and the bearded look they had from the moss-draped limbs. Mom always rolled down her windows as she drove across the causeway toward the island. At first, I thought it was to catch a sea breeze, but she didn't relax until we crossed that last bridge. She always said the island smelled like home.

I agreed with her. Shell Island's warm, moist salty top notes hit me first on that same causeway drive, followed by the fragrant heart notes of seasonal azalea, jasmine, and honeysuckle, and infused with woody bass notes of oak, pine, and cedar. This fragrant symphony permeated my life and emotions, forever anchoring my memories here.

Memories. So many of my childhood memories included the Bolz brothers. Now Chili was missing, and Kale was dead. Everything about this felt wrong, only I didn't know why. I navigated a bit of congestion around the airstrip and made a right.

When I pulled into the seafood market's parking lot, Dasia Allen waved me inside the store. Dasia and Jerry married right out of high school, and thanks to his father's life insurance policy, were able to open Neptune's Harvest two years ago. Dasia was ten years younger than me with jet black hair and a lithe body, a knockout.

Display cases held fish, shrimp, crab, and scallops on ice. The shelves were lined with colorful seasonings and sauces. "Jer's in the back finishing with the filets," Dasia said. "I'm so glad you called. We were going to run the whole lot down to Jacksonville. With selling half of them to you, I can push the rest out the door today and tomorrow. And we get a larger slice of the pie that way."

"I hear you about pie slices. Every dollar counts in a small business." I cleared my throat. "Thanks for helping me out on such short notice. I had arranged to buy fish from Chili today, but he's missing."

"I know Chili. What's going on?" Dasia asked.

"He disappeared on Tuesday, but I learned about it a few minutes ago. I assume he sells fish here if he doesn't already have a client on the hook."

"Yes, we buy his fish. He calls as he heads to shore with his catch."

"I'm trying to find him. Does he have a regular fishing buddy?"

Dasia snickered. "Not since that sucky Loretta gal threw up all over his boat. He said chicks weren't allowed on board unless they were paying customers."

"No guys as first mates either?"

"He used to take his brother, but that can't happen, not unless he takes Kale's ghost."

I winced at her poor choice of words. "Still. Seems dangerous to head offshore alone."

"Lotta guys do it."

Jerry sauntered in with a bag of sea bass filets. His tall, lean physique mirrored his wife's. "How're you fixing these, Ms. River?"

"If I told you, I'd have to kill you."

"Seriously. We talking broiled, baked, sautéed, grilled?"

"Seriously, how I prepare my food is proprietary information. All I'll say is there's a marinade, parchment paper, and spicy veggies."

"My mouth's watering just thinking about it."

"Good. Hire Holloway Catering, and you'll have the most delicious seafood meal ever."

"I hear you." Jerry snuck a quick glance at Dasia who was helping another customer. He lowered his voice. "Maybe we can work out a deal. I'll catch up with you later to share my idea."

A deal? He had seafood, and I cooked seafood and other foods. If he'd discount seafood to me for a specialty meal here or there, I would agree to that in a heartbeat.

I dug out a business card and passed it to him as I paid for the fish. "I'll wait to hear from you."

Dasia laughed at something her customer said, and Jerry leaned forward as he handed me the receipt and whispered, "It's the opportunity of a lifetime."

Chapter Two

The Robertsons loved my arugula and pear salad with citrus vinaigrette so much they asked for seconds. I was tempted to remind them to save room for the main course, but I knew better. The simple truth about keeping my business afloat had nothing to do with the quality or quantity of food I provided or my appearance, none of which I ever let slide.

My ultimate success depended on customer satisfaction. Therefore, whatever they asked for, they received. The customer was always right.

Unless they asked for me. The few times that happened, I made it clear I wasn't on the menu. Tonight, I brought out more of the extra salad from the kitchen. Since the Robertsons were repeat customers, I knew their kitchen layout in advance and had pressed their double oven into service. The smaller top oven kept the pre-cooked parchment-wrapped sea bass warm, while the lower oven roasted onions and sweet potatoes, perfuming the air.

As the Robertsons and their four friends enjoyed dinner, I prepped the decaf coffee they liked and plated slices of lemon meringue pie. During the dessert course, I loaded their dishwasher, refrigerated leftovers, ate a few bites of fish from the packet I made for myself, and packed my catering van.

A thin black cat mewed plaintively from the yard as I came and went. He sounded hungry. The poor thing. I placed some fish on a stepping stone. The cat blinked its golden eyes at me, then skittered over and inhaled the fish.

"You must've been starving," I said. "What's your name, kitty? You remind me of my friend's cat, Trouble. He stayed with me not long ago."

The feline scampered a safe distance away and watched me steadily. It felt like he or she wanted me to understand something, only I wasn't getting it. I bid the kitty goodbye, drove the van home, unloaded everything, and checked the time. Ugh. Nine thirty. I thought longingly of the sofa. My usual MO after catering involved putting my feet up and falling asleep in front of the TV.

But I'd promised Estelle to ask people about Chili's whereabouts, so that was my plan. The hour wasn't late for island nightspots, only for me. I locked the commercial kitchen and hurried next door to my home. After a quick pass through the shower, I donned clean jeans, a flirty top, and strappy sandals and headed out.

Creekside Grill was packed to capacity as I threaded through the crowd to the bar and ordered a soda. Then, I asked everyone if they recognized Chili's photo on my phone. I struck out, so I drove to the Wine and Dine, known to locals as the wine bar. Surely, I'd have better luck here.

The animated conversation from the outdoor tables drifted over to my catering van. The last time I came here was with the love of my life, Pete Merrick, before he left Shell Island, Georgia, for California. Even though we'd reconnected recently, he didn't understand how demanding catering was or how long it took to establish a caterer's reputation. I was equally at fault for not mentioning this, but at the time I'd assumed he knew since he specialized in business. Love and divergent careers put blinders on both of us and now we had to take them off, whatever the cost.

That memory was bittersweet. Bitter for the geography still between us and sweet because we had a shot at a future. As I approached the bar, my gaze flitted to the table where we'd had that momentous discussion. I wished Pete was here to help me find Chili.

I elbowed my way to the counter where Reg the bartender asked me which red wine I wanted. His trademark navy bandana around his bald head added a splash of normal to this night.

"Surprise me," I said.

Vivian Declan swept me into a hug. Two inches taller than me and easily twenty pounds lighter, she wore her bleached blonde hair big and her shorts short. The scents of beer and honeysuckle sweetness clung to her. We'd been buds in elementary school, but our adult friendship fell victim to busy schedules.

"River Holloway, as I live and breathe," Viv said. "You're a sight for sore eyes. What gives, girlfriend?"

"Hey, Viv. I'm hitting the hotspots tonight. FYI, it's standing room only over at the Creekside Grill."

"Hmm. Are you back in circulation? How odd. I heard you patched things up with Mr. Hunkmeister."

"Just a sec." I paid for my wine and stepped away from the two men arguing loudly beside me. "Whew, is it always this noisy out here?"

"This is nothing. We drink enough firewater, and everyone's true self shows. You're not the barfly type, so you got dumped or something is going on. Tell me, is Pete a free agent?"

My ears rang. If I'd accepted Pete's proposal on Valentine's Day, we'd be engaged. "We're together again, but we have details to address."

"Like the sleeping arrangements? You leaving Shell Island?"

"Working those details out." My face felt tight and so did my voice. I chugged half of my wine without realizing it. Viv was direct about men and she didn't care who knew it. I couldn't bear to think of Pete with anyone else.

"So your relationship is okay," Viv said, speculation rife in her eyes. "Must be curiosity bringing you out at night. Are you on a secret mission, like our golden Nancy Drew days?"

"Something like that. You still work at the paper mill?"

"Yeah. I'd love to marry Mr. Right, but he doesn't work out there. Trust me, I'd know by now." She shot me a sheepish glance. "Pete's a good guy. When are you gonna put him out of his misery and marry him?"

Maybe it was the wine. Candor welled in my throat. "We're

getting there. Like I said, logistics are an issue."

"Wowser. Must be hard having that hanging over your head." Viv whistled at the bartender and pointed to our glasses. "Drink up. A few more glasses of wine and you'll have the secrets of the universe at your fingertips." She greeted Reg the bartender who'd brought us another round.

"Thanks," I said, reaching for my wallet.

Reg brushed aside my money as he left. "You're good. Deputy Dawg bought this round for you ladies."

"Who?" I glanced over the crowd and saw a familiar face. Deputy Lance Hamlyn. My fingers tightened on the wine glass. Great. The cop who arrested my brother a few months ago. Across the bar, he raised his beer glass to me. I mouthed thank you and wished I could slip through a crack in the pavement.

"You're a guy magnet," Viv said. "Even the hot deputy likes you. What perfume do you use?"

"I don't use perfume."

"Right. I forgot. You always smell like cookies from grandma's oven." Viv sniffed the air. "A compelling mixture of savory and sweet. Every man in this place is calculating his odds of going home with you tonight."

Her flip remark had me tugging on my top that fit just right. Why hadn't I worn something blousy? "Should I stand on the table and announce I'm not here for a hook up?"

"Nah. They'd take that as a challenge. Spill the beans. Why are you here?"

I savored another sip of wine. It felt perfect in my mouth. I'd have to ask Reg for the brand name so I could share it with Pete on his next visit.

"I'm trolling for information. Chili Bolz is missing. His mom made me promise to look for him. Have you seen him?"

"Missing? Oh, no. That's awful. Lemme think. He was here last Friday night. Maybe we hooked up, I can't remember. Anyway, I haven't seen him since then."

Oh, dear. Too much information. The casual-sex singles scene wasn't for me. I was such a dinosaur. *This isn't about you*, I reminded myself. "Who are his friends?"

"Chili works too much to have close friends. He's serious about his charter fishing business and his mom. Losing his brother at sea nearly did him in. For a while, I hoped he'd get serious with me, but he cried himself to sleep after we got busy. That was hard on my ego. If I was such a bad date, why'd he bother? But we had a steady Friday night thing for a few weeks."

I glanced at the growing crowd. "You know the people here?"

"Sadly, I do."

"Will you introduce me around? I need to know if anyone knows Chili's whereabouts."

"Sure. That'll give me a few moments of innocence by association."

"You're not worried about Chili?"

"Heck no. He's a grown man. He's got a head on his shoulders too, unlike some of these goobers. He'll come home when he's ready."

I flashed my the-client-is-always-right smile, and she bought it. I felt like a fraud. I was using her, but she was using me too. What a pair we were. Viv led me to clusters of men and women, and I asked about Chili. As Viv suggested earlier, several men shot me calculating glances. Not wanting to inadvertently encourage someone, I tried to appear friendly without making direct eye contact.

The answers I received about Chili's whereabouts ranged from shacked up with a supermodel to meditating in the woods, and everything in between. After I spoke to everyone, we circled back to the bar.

"I appreciate your help," I said, wistfully eyeing the exit. "I grew up here, but these people are strangers to me. Thank you for opening those conversational doors for me. I wish we'd found a lead."

Viv beamed. "You struck out, but I got four invites for a sleepover, my pick. Let's do this more often."

A herd of overly loud women stumbled into the bar. Viv turned away from them and grimaced. "Bridal shower alert."

My focus narrowed to the tiara-clad blonde in the center of the boisterous group. "You know her?"

"You do too. Melanie Walker stole my only serious boyfriend in high school. It pissed me off that she singled George out because he was tall. She thought she'd have the nicest prom photos with a man his height. I liked George before he took up with her. Afterward, I wanted nothing to do with him even though he assumed we were still a couple. Men. Anyway, back to Melanie. She thinks her family money allows her to have any man she wants. Better hope she never sets her sights on Pete Merrick."

"Pete wouldn't go for her. He likes stability in a woman." I snorted. "He's not into flashy or flighty. Come to think of it, that makes me sound dull."

"At least he's not reshaping you into the image of his mother." Viv shivered. "Some men fixate on that. Makes me wonder what went on behind closed doors."

I let that remark slide. I needed purposeful gossip, not idle chitchat.

Viv stiffened beside me and swore softly. "Shoot. She's coming this way."

"River Holloway, you're just the woman I need to see," Melanie said. "I want you to cater my wedding."

Melanie wore a sequined top, skintight black leggings, and gold sandals. The rock on her finger sparkled and caught the light as she gestured with her hands. She seemed outgoing until you looked at her blue eyes. The wide pupils told a different story, one that likely involved pharmaceuticals. I sincerely hoped she wasn't driving.

"Hi, Melanie," I said. "Congratulations on your engagement. Who's the lucky guy?"

"Malcom Conway, a businessman out of Savannah. Together we're Mal and Mel."

She sounded unnaturally perky and young. "How'd y'all

meet?"

"He visited the island on business before Thanksgiving. His company wants to expand into Riceland County."

"Did he buy commercial property here?"

"They postponed the expansion, but he couldn't walk away from me. It was love at first sight for both of us. He wants to get married as soon as possible, but I'm doing it up right. I have six bridesmaids and the biggest, fluffiest gown on the market."

Melanie had been married twice before, so while I was surprised at her making a big to-do of this, I accepted her antics. Growing up, she'd gotten everything she wanted. If someone had a pony and Melanie wanted it, her mother got her that pony.

Though I didn't grow up a Walker, I recognized a sterling opportunity when I saw one.

I handed Melanie a business card. "Sounds delightful. Give me a call when you set the date. If I have availability, we can sit down together."

Melanie took my card. "Great. I'm so glad you can do it. I'll call soon."

I started to correct her because I didn't agree yet, but the gaggle of laughing girls moved to a table that had opened for them. I met Viv's gaze. "That was intense."

"It's always intense around her."

"You know her fiancé?"

"Nope. She snagged him right away. Rumor is that man has stamina."

"He'll need it with her."

"See how easy this was? You should hang out with me more often," Viv said. "I haven't had this much fun in years."

"It wasn't as bad as I thought, so thanks. Now, I need to go home. I've got a busy morning ahead."

"Okay. It was good to see you. And here's some advice. Beware of men buying you drinks."

"What?"

She pointed with her beer glass. Deputy Lance Hamlyn's dark

brown eyes had a bead on me, and he headed my way, cutting off my exit. I gulped. "Oh, dear. What now?"

"River, wait," Hamlyn called. "We need to talk."

Chapter Three

"Deputy Hamlyn, thanks for the drink." I tried to strike the right note between polite and no thanks. "I'm headed home."

He fell into step alongside me and we walked to the parking lot. "Thought so. I need a word in private with you."

Since he was only an inch or so taller than me, his stride easily conformed to mine. His sturdy appearance suggested composure, but the air around him churned with intensity. How'd he do that? I gave him a sideways glance and somehow missed a step, causing me to career into him. To make matters worse, we were directly under a streetlamp, so he saw my cheeks glow with embarrassment. "Oh! I'm so sorry. I wasn't paying attention."

He steadied me with both hands on my hips before releasing me. "Happens when people drink."

The calculating look in his dark eyes put me on defense as did the heavy-duty aftershave aroma. "I had exactly two glasses of wine. You knew that since you bought my second drink."

He grinned. "Guilty. Like I said, I hoped to speak with you, but you gadded around the bar talking to everyone. I didn't know you and Vivian Declan were close friends."

Where was he going with this? "We went to school together. She offered to introduce me around. I was surprised at how few people I recognized. This community is really growing."

"You were asking about Chili Bolz."

Busted. Wine made me bold. "He's my fish supplier, and he didn't show up with fish for me today. I'm concerned."

"His mother called you, didn't she?"

I ignored his question. This was starting to feel like an

interrogation. "I also went to school with Chili. What's your point?"

A couple who'd been very handsy on the dance floor strolled past, laughing and flirting. The woman glanced over at us and my cheeks stung with heat again. Did they think I was dating this cop?

"Chili's disappearance is a police matter," the deputy said. "I'm heading his missing persons investigation. This is an active case."

"His mother doesn't think it's very active. She asked if I could find any information. If you don't want people asking about Chili, find him."

"It's not that easy."

"Then you need more help."

His face clouded, and he groaned. "Old timers, and no offense, but I mean people like you who grew up here, won't talk to me. They see the badge and clam up."

He sounded more confused than I was. I dug my car keys out of a pocket. "What do you expect? Riceland County has a storied history of iron-fisted lawmen who ran this county for two generations."

"Times have changed. That corrupt regime ended fifty years ago. No one with that bloodline is left on the force. Sheriff Vargas is a straight shooter and he hires only the best, as he's fond of saying."

Old news. I let a yawn slip out. "Is there something else, Deputy? I've been on my feet for hours and I want to go home."

"You're good at investigating. In ninety minutes, you interviewed thirty people and got more feedback than I gathered in two days. People talk to you."

"People who are drinking like to talk."

"To you. I tried to strike up several conversations, but I got nowhere. Figured I'd keep an eye on you and ask what you learned."

"Seriously? I got nothing. Everyone had a guess, like Chili's status was a game show question on TV. Not one of those people knew where he was. They made up answers to entertain me."

"Welcome to the world of police investigation. We get dead ends and lies all the time. The trick is sifting out the noise and finding the facts."

"Fact is, Chili wouldn't disappear because of his mom. He knows her mental state is fragile."

Lance gave a terse nod. "She came across as emotional."

My spine stiffened at his snide tone. "Estelle Bolz is a loving mother who provided for her sons, one of whom is dead, the other missing."

"She stormed into the station raving about Chili. We had to wait twenty-four hours until he could officially be called a missing person."

"She's upset and rightly so. Estelle filters information differently, but she's a good person."

He held up fingers pinched nearly together. "The sheriff was this close to sending her for a psych workup."

"Everyone is a little crazy here on Shell Island. It's how we roll. Nothing wrong with crazy, and if you don't like crazy, you should work elsewhere."

His lips quirked up momentarily. "No need to be defensive. I like it here, and I want to do my job. Tonight, I admired your natural ease with people. Would you collaborate with my investigation?"

Another yawn slipped out as he spoke. "What? Sorry, I missed what you said."

"Collaborate, as in bar hop, only together and pool information."

I hoped I'd misheard him. "A few minutes ago you warned me about encroaching on your investigation. Now you're encouraging me to continue?"

"I'm asking to align forces. You can help me rule out places where Chili isn't. Once we find him, you'll have your fish supplier back."

"I covered two hot spots tonight, Creekside Grill and the wine bar," I admitted. "Tomorrow I'm hitting the Top Cat Lounge, Molly's Brew House, and the American Legion. If that's where you're headed, I see no reason we couldn't visit them together and compare notes."

"Glad you see it my way," Lance said. "The Chief Deputy is making noises about retiring soon, and I'm angling for a promotion. If you collaborate, you'll have a friend for life in the department."

Oh, joy. "Whatever. Can I go now?"

"Sure. I'll pick you up at six tomorrow. We'll start with dinner at the brew pub."

I did a mental head shake. "Dinner? I thought we were questioning bar patrons."

"Might as well eat while we're out. My treat."

"It's not a date. Let's be very clear about that."

"Message received."

"Great. Now, get this message in your head. Good. Night."

He nodded. "I'll follow you home, for safety reasons, and then I'll swing by tomorrow evening at six."

I didn't live far from the Wine and Dine, five minutes tops. As promised, the deputy followed me. Once I sat in the van, the weight of the busy Friday settled heavily on my shoulders. Sleep was my immediate goal. When I pulled into the driveway, Lance waited until I unlocked the door and stepped inside before he drove away.

I changed into pjs and crawled into bed. Nothing else I could do tonight for Chili, except start fresh in the morning.

Chapter Four

A ringing phone jarred me awake. I glanced at the bedside clock in the thin light, saw it was seven, then read the caller ID display. I sat up and answered the call. "Good morning, Estelle."

"You find him yet?"

Wow. She expected a report already? Sleep clouded my thoughts. I needed coffee. On autopilot, I rose and padded to the kitchen. "I checked two night spots last night. No one's heard from him. I'm checking the other three clubs tonight."

"Nobody knew anything?" Estelle's voice cracked. "You sure one of them didn't hurt my boy?"

"I'm uncertain of anything except Chili is missing. I wish I had better news. I'm worried about him too. Did you call hospitals in Brunswick and Savannah?"

"I called the hospitals and the morgues. He's not in either place. I got this gut feeling he's hurt and it's tearing me up that we can't find him."

My mom used to get gut feelings about Doug too, and they were always right. "I wouldn't have thought to check the morgue, but it's good to know he's not there. I feel like I'm going into this blind. Other than talking to Chili about fish for my business, I haven't kept in touch. I wish we hadn't drifted apart. I have happy memories of riding bikes with Chili and Kale all over the island. Chili taught me how to hold a fishing pole on my bike."

"Those were happier times. Everything seemed simpler. Now life seems harder, uglier, and I'm going to die alone."

"We'll find him, Estelle. I trust your gut feeling that he's alive."

"He's gotta be hurt bad if he can't pick up a phone and call me.

I'm worried sick about him."

"We're searching for him and so are the cops. We'll find him."

"None of those people at the bar spoke to Chili on Tuesday?"

I started the coffee machine and debated taking headache meds. Nope, caffeine would clear out the cobwebs and the dull ache from a late night. "Far as I know, I'm the last people to talk with him, and I called him around ten Tuesday morning."

Estelle sniffed a few times. "Anybody take a special interest in what you were doing?"

"Just about everybody I met." I sighed. "Vivian Declan introduced me around the wine bar. That was my next stop after the marina restaurant. Viv knew everyone there. Anyway, I spoke to the twenty- and thirty-somethings at both places, and no one knew Chili's whereabouts."

"That Viv tried to get her hooks in Chili once and I told him he could do better."

Vivian did us a favor, and Estelle was trash-talking her? "Viv was nice to me, and I appreciate her help. Because of her kindness, I made excellent progress."

"The wine bar rings a bell. What about that bartender fellow?"

The scent of brewing coffee strengthened me. I drifted to the kitchen window to gaze out. To my surprise, a lean black kitty perched on the deck bench seat, staring my way. What was that about? I didn't have a cat.

Was it possible the stray at the Robertsons knew where I lived? Not likely, and yet I had a black cat in my yard looking like it expected breakfast. I turned away from the cat to finish the conversation, vowing to focus on the feline mystery later. "Reg made a very nice wine selection for me last night. He's a good bartender."

"A few months ago, before Reg got hired at Wine and Dine, he was Chili's first mate."

Estelle could've told me that earlier. "Reg didn't mention their association. How many people worked for Chili's charter business?"

"Not people, hon. Men. Only men crewed for him on the *Reel*

Fine."

Guess she didn't know about the vomiting gal. I poured coffee and sipped it. "Women are as good at fishing as men. Seems to me a woman has a lot more patience at waiting for a fish to bite."

"But not the upper body strength to help customers land the bigguns."

"Good point." An idea sparked in my barely caffeinated brain. "Say, getting back to his former crew members, is there anyone he fired that might hold a grudge?"

"Heavens. I don't know. Most guys work a few trips, then they move on, no hard feelings either way. Not steady money in crewing. Chili takes the fuel, rigging, and bait cost off the top then he gives a crew member twenty-five percent of what's left over. Considering he doesn't usually have more'n three charters in a week, the money isn't regular enough for most folks."

"How'd Chili make ends meet?" I wondered aloud.

"Odd jobs here and there," she said vaguely. "Sometimes he picks up a shift at the dry cleaners. He sometimes helps his friend who moonlights as a handyman. It all works out."

I knew the feeling. One day I'd have enough catering customers to stay afloat. Until then, I picked up extra work too.

"Which handyman is it?" I asked. "I'll add him to my query list."

"Darry Declan."

"Viv's brother?"

"Half-brother. He's a good six years younger than Chili."

"Interesting. Also very interesting that his sister latched onto me last night. I thought her kindness was about doing a good deed, but I don't trust coincidences. I'll talk to Darry and Reg. If you think of anyone else connected to Chili, let me know. There must be an explanation for why your son is missing."

"He better have a darn good explanation after all this."

I ended the call and dressed for the day. Back in the kitchen, I refilled my coffee cup.

What to eat this morning? I decided on a microwave-poached

egg. You'd think being a chef that I loved to cook all the time. Not so much. I enjoyed cooking for others. I often cooked meals for myself, but it wasn't fun to cook for one person. Early on as a business promotion, I invited people over on Wednesday nights to sample my meals.

Though they raved about my food, very few of them hired me so I stopped the free-meal train. Instead, I targeted community functions and fundraising auctions people with money attended, donating a dinner for four or a specialty dish. Little by little the word spread, and I finally gained traction. At first, the Garden Club and the Bridge Group asked me to bid on their catered functions. Then they told me they were hiring me whatever the cost.

The microwave dinged, and I removed my perfect egg. When I turned to eat at the table, I noticed the cat again. It was still here, crouched in a pool of sunshine and staring at the window. Did I want to risk feeding it? That's how they hooked you into caring for them. They showed up, ate, and moved in.

As if in answer to my thoughts, the kitty yowled, demanding my attention. My heart softened. If I was a cat and I had no food, wouldn't I do the same thing? This cat sure sounded hungry. I grabbed a foil pack of tuna from the pantry and plated it. Then I carried the tuna and a dish of water outside for my furry guest.

The black cat watched me with unblinking eyes and then scampered to the far steps at my approach, so perhaps it was shy. Or maybe it had one foot out the door if things went awry. I'd dated guys like that.

He wouldn't approach the food with me outside, so I returned to the kitchen to eat my egg. Even so, the kitty finished first and darted into the woods.

I cleaned up and checked my schedule. Saturday was clean the house, mow the lawn, and buy groceries day. Oh, joy.

But I didn't have to start right away. I could search Chili's house first. Maybe I'd see something Estelle and the cops missed. The more I thought about it, the more I wanted to do it. I had his address in my phone, so I could be in and out quickly. No one would even know.

Mind made up, I dressed and motored to his place, about a mile past the marina. I'd come here once before to pick up fish, and I'd stepped inside the two-bedroom bungalow while he retrieved my fish from his fridge. So I already knew how his house looked on a regular day.

With the stoplights and traffic circles, it took me ten minutes to get there. The outside of his wooden clapboard house looked the same as before. An outboard motor hung on a board nailed between two pines. Four commercial crab traps graced his porch, and a barren concrete planter on one side of the steps showed that his mother had tried to soften the masculine edges of this place at one time.

The door was locked when I tried the knob, but I knew the Bolz family secret. There was always a spare key under the planter on their porches. The dirt-filled concrete planter weighed a ton, but I lifted it and retrieved a key. It snicked in the lock and I opened the door cautiously. "Chili? It's River," I called out in case he'd returned home. "I came to check on you."

No answer, as I'd expected. His truck wasn't in the yard, but Estelle said the cops had it. His place looked messier than the last time I saw it. Could be something, could be nothing.

A couple of unmatching chairs and a large leather recliner populated his living room. Some laundry was strewn around. One shirt smelled fishy, so the clothes weren't clean. Belatedly, I realized I should've worn gloves for this expedition. I didn't bring any, so I hurried to the kitchen, thinking he might have a pair under the sink.

Using my shirt tail, I opened the cabinet. Nothing. Not even a bottle of dishwashing detergent. How did bachelors live without all the cleaners, sponges, and dish towels I required in a kitchen?

Carefully, I unrolled the paper towels so that I held one in each hand. That way I wouldn't leave any prints. I opened all the kitchen drawers and cabinets. A tall stack of paper plates sat atop his real plates, plasticware covered his eating utensil tray. His fridge had a pack of half-used hot dogs, three kinds of hot sauce, and the largest jar of mayonnaise I'd ever seen. The freezer was packed with fish.

But there were no notes, indeed, no pens or pads or paper, not even any bills. What kind of person had zero paperwork at home? There wasn't even a stack of junk mail and his trash can was empty. How odd.

The bathroom was tidy, though his sink, john, and shower looked like they should be power washed. A smattering of toiletries littered the medicine cabinet. Two spare rolls of toilet paper topped the back of the john.

His bedroom reflected the same bachelor mentality. Dust bunnies ran amuck and a cloud of dust triggered a coughing fit when I moved the heavy drapes. The spare bedroom had four sets of weights and a treadmill. Two suit coats hung in the closet.

Chili had no washer or a dryer, and there were no mowers or tools outside. I didn't get it. This place seemed like a temporary haunt instead of a home. I realized there'd been no pictures on the walls. No TV and no landline phone.

I called his cell phone and listened for it, in case he'd left it behind.

Nothing.

Only one thing stopped me. His Georgia Bulldog hat sat upside down in the recliner. He never went anywhere without that hat. But he'd left it behind now.

Discouraged, I drove home and hoped I had better luck tonight. People couldn't vanish into thin air. There must be a clue somewhere.

As I scrubbed, dusted, and vacuumed my place, I thought about my boyfriend. If Pete lived on Shell Island, this morning would've gone much differently. My daily activities would revolve around him, and his would revolve around me. I wanted that synchronicity and so did he, but the geography issue was tricky. I loved coastal Georgia and felt rooted here. Pete loved changing jobs and seeing the world.

Was it possible that two people who loved each other couldn't make it work?

No matter where Pete and I ended up, our future seemed bright compared to Estelle's. It was hard to bury a loved one. I couldn't imagine what Estelle went through putting a headstone on Kale's empty grave and now to have her remaining son go missing. I had to find Chili for her, but I was stumped. He didn't go far without his truck or boat. I hoped and prayed my bar hopping tonight would yield a lead.

Chapter Five

Lance arrived promptly at six holding a bouquet of mixed flowers. I stared at them and retreated into my house. "This isn't a date," I said. "I shouldn't take flowers from you."

"These are thank-you flowers," Lance said, following me in and closing the door. He clutched the bouquet to his heart like a little boy would. "I understand we have a professional relationship, and I promise you are safe with me. If you don't like the flowers, I'll throw them away."

They were pretty and exactly the vibrant colors I preferred. Not wanting them to go to waste, I reached for them. "Don't do that. I like them, but flowers are a traditional date gift. You're a nice person and all, but I have a boyfriend."

The concern in his dark eyes faded. "Understood. I won't thank you with flowers in the future."

I winced. "Gracious, my apologies for misinterpreting your gift. Thank you for the flowers. They are beautiful. Give me a minute to put them in water."

"Sure." He followed me back to the kitchen. "Nice place."

With my head inside the under-sink cabinet I didn't quite hear him. I grabbed the vase I wanted and stood. "What?"

"I said nice place. I like how you've blended old with the new. Seems homey and contemporary at the same time, like you."

"Oh, thanks." Not sure what to do with the offhand compliment, I fussed with the flowers and set the arrangement on the center of my table. I turned and he was standing at the back door, looking through the top window panel.

"Do you have a cat?" he asked.

"That one followed me home yesterday, so I fed it."

His gaze narrowed. "You make a habit of taking in strays?"

My skin prickled. Was this collaboration a cover for an interrogation? He was a police officer, and I was the last person to talk to Chili. I'd better watch what I said tonight. "I like to help people and cats. I have a helping nature."

"Does this one have a name?"

"Don't know yet. If the cat stays, I'll figure out something." I shouldered my purse. "We should get going."

He guided me out to the high-end black sports car he'd been driving last night. As we got underway, I said, "Nice ride. You had it long?"

"Bought it a few months back."

Lots of shiny chrome and gauges on the dash, creamy, like-new leather everywhere else. How'd he afford this on a cop's salary? "Seems fancy."

"I got a sweet deal on it."

"Oh?"

"At the annual sheriff's sale on the vehicles we've impounded. This one belonged to a drug kingpin we pulled off I-95. He's doing time, and I bought his wheels on the cheap. A fine example of karma if you ask me."

Fancy cars equated with high maintenance costs, which reminded me that my economy van was overdue for an oil change. "Must cost a fortune to upkeep. Every time I take my van to the shop, they always find other things to be repaired."

"I'm a gearhead. I do most of my car maintenance."

"Huh." Lucky him. He probably saved a bundle on car repairs every year.

We arrived at Molly's Brew House, bypassed the loud bar, and were seated in the dining room. I ordered a house draft with my barbeque sandwich for dinner. Lance encouraged me to order a meal, but I wasn't that hungry. He had ribs with a side of barbecue, fries, and slaw, along with a dark ale. When we finished, Lance refused my offer of payment for my dinner, saying it would go on his expense report. After the scuffle over the flowers, I didn't protest.

We drifted into the bar. Lance hung back while I approached patrons and asked if they knew Chili. All but one person denied knowing him. Trevor Murray wasn't wearing his hearing aids. He thought I'd asked if he wanted a bowl of chili, and it took fast talking to convince him I didn't work here and chili wasn't on the menu.

Next, Lance and I cruised over to the American Legion and ordered another beer. "Put your money away," Lance said when I tried to pay for our drinks.

"I'm giving you a gift," I said, throwing his words back at him.

"Guys don't let women buy their food or drinks. It's against the code."

I didn't believe him, but I got the message. His reputation as a man would be tarnished if I paid for my drink or his. Women didn't have this ego problem when we went out together. It felt weird to be out with a man, especially when I wanted that man to be Pete.

Stop thinking about Pete and stick to finding Chili Bolz. I recognized Florrie the bartender as a longtime resident of the area, but I didn't know her other than by sight. The sparse crowd here offered no new information about Chili, though most folks knew he was Estelle's son. With this place a bust, we quickly took our leave.

As we motored over to the Top Cat Lounge, I turned to Lance and said, "It's frustrating when you come up empty. How do cops handle the disappointment?"

"Easy. We ask more questions and chase leads until we find something."

He sounded so serious. "I thought it was always the spouse who did someone in."

"We don't know that Chili's dead, only missing, and he isn't married. Far as I know, he wasn't dating steadily." Lance pulled into the parking lot, careful to park away from the other cars.

Music thrummed through the walls of the building, and I hoped I didn't leave this place with a permanent hearing loss. I suppressed a groan. I'd become my grandmother in my preference for quiet.

Maybe we could wrap up quickly and minimize our time in the Top Cat. It was worth a shot. "Let's split up in here to get finished in half the time. From the looks of the crowded parking lot, its wall-to-wall people inside."

"We stick together. This can be a rough place. I don't want anything to happen to you."

"Okay." We entered, and the bass notes vibrated in my fillings. I glanced around the shadowed room, relieved when my gaze landed on a familiar face. I hurried over to Vivian. Her face lit up, and she hugged me like a long-lost friend.

She whispered in my ear. "Thank you. This guy is creeping me out talking about stalking his last girlfriend. You still searching for Chili?" At my nod, she said, "I'll help you. Different crowd here."

I looked around at the clusters of people talking and dancing. "Who are these people? I don't recognize a soul."

"Believe it or not, the folks here are mostly from out of town. Top Cat has a reputation for being a place to score."

"Drugs? Sex?"

"Yes," she said. "I've come here for both."

I shook my head, unable to turn off my judgmental thoughts in time. "One of these days I hope you'll tell me what you're running from."

"That's easy. The past. The present is all about escaping the past."

The caretaker in me wanted to take her outside, hear her story, and fix her with good food and sisterly love. "I appreciate your help, Viv. Would you come over to my place for lunch soon? It's hard to have a real conversation here."

"I'd like that," Viv said. She linked elbows with me and dragged me from one clique to another, Lance scowling in our wake. Between sets of people, she asked, "What is it with Mr. Hot Cop?"

After nearly three beers, I felt no pain. "We joined forces for tonight's investigation. He was impressed with how many people we reached last night."

We circled the lounge and struck out. "Want a ride home?" I asked Viv.

"No thanks. I'm working on a happy ending for this evening. Hand me your phone."

I watched as she entered her name in my contact list and then texted herself. "Slick. I wouldn't have thought of that."

"You haven't been on the singles market as long as I have," Viv confided in my ear. "You two go ahead. I'll be fine."

"We're not on a date," I said. "I have no interest in Lance."

"Gracious, gal. Get your vision checked. That guy is sexy and he can't stop looking at you. One come-hither look from you and y'all could be heating up the night sky."

"Not going to happen. Thanks again for your help. Oh, wait a sec. What's your brother up to these days?"

Viv snorted. "Nothing good. Darry moved to Alaska in November. Ain't been home since and still hasn't sent for his wife or kids. I'm angry at his irresponsible behavior."

There went that possible lead. Estelle thought Darry Declan was a possible suspect in Chili's disappearance, but it would be impossible to do anything all the way from Alaska. Whoever made Chili vanish had to be local.

Lance played soft music on the drive home. The adrenaline buzz faded, and I yawned. I covered it in time, or so I thought. "Viv was so helpful tonight."

"Um hmm," Lance said.

"We could still be trying to get those people to talk to us."

"I'm glad we're done too, but let me be clear. You asked everyone about Chili and got no answers. There should be no repercussions, or I wouldn't have allowed you to do it. But, if you feel someone is bothering you after tonight, tell me."

I laughed out loud. "Really?"

"I'm serious."

"I can tell you're serious. I didn't think anything would come of asking about Chili."

Lance negotiated a right turn and accelerated. I snugged into my cushy leather seat. What would it be like to live like this? To have luxury at your fingertips instead of wondering which bills to pay.

"Which brings me to my second point," Lance said. "Your part in this investigation is over."

My head swiveled his way. "What?"

"It's dangerous for civilians to stick their noses in police business. I made sure you were safe tonight, and my presence with you should've sent a strong stay-away signal to any guys looking for trouble."

Okay, this conversation was veering into strange areas, ones I wasn't sure I could adequately address in this relaxed frame of mind. "Are you saying someone might've been upset by our questions and try to harm me?"

Lance slowed for a turn onto my street. "You took a risk to help a friend. I did what I thought was expedient in offering my protection by appearing to be your date."

I hated it when people talked down to me. "You're making too much of nothing. We didn't get a single lead. No one knows where Chili is, least of all, me. And I'm not looking for a boyfriend or a protector. This is Shell Island, for goodness sake."

The fury in my words resonated around in his fancy car until he parked in my drive. I knew I'd overreacted as soon as I spoke, but I couldn't help myself. It was one of the reasons I didn't drink much. In the last two days, I'd consumed more alcohol than I had in the previous five years.

"I apologize for snapping at you," I said. "Your comment implied I wasn't capable of taking care of myself, and I've been doing that for years."

Lance didn't say anything, but his fingers kept squeezing the steering wheel. His knuckles gleamed in the dash light.

What a mess. I'd let my guard down, blurted out things I shouldn't, and now there might be repercussions. Would Lance retaliate by tightening the scrutiny on my brother? With Doug already having a police record, anything as much as a speeding ticket could be big trouble for his future.

I took a deep breath and prepared to make amends. "I do have manners, and other than these last few minutes of exchanging cross words, I had a good time tonight. Thank you for the flowers, dinner, and drinks."

He shifted the car into park. "I'll walk you to your door."

The thought of what usually happened at the door after a date threw me into a tizzy. "No, thank you. If you want to make sure I'm safely inside, please watch from here. I'm a big girl, and I don't need a protector."

He slanted me a glance. "You always so frank?"

I shot him my eat-crow-and-die smile. "It's my best feature."

Chapter Six

My phone began ringing before I put my purse down. I glanced at the display and felt happiness well up from deep within. Pete Merrick, my fiancé, wanted to connect via a video call.

I eagerly accepted the call. "Hey, Pete. How's it going?"

"You're the first ray of sunshine I've had all day. What's your day been like?"

His pale face concerned me. His dark hair was a bit too long and lank. Oh, dear. California did not look good on him. Maybe my amateur detective work would cheer him up. "I'm fine, though I'm dead tired after helping look for a friend these last two nights. Chili Bolz is missing."

"Who is this Bolz guy?" Pete asked.

"You met him a long time ago." I pulled off my shoes and padded to the bedroom. "He's my fish supplier for Holloway Catering, but he's also the only surviving son of Mom's bridge partner, Estelle Bolz. Her other son, Kale, was lost at sea six months ago."

"That must feel awful to lose two sons so close together. Did Mrs. Bolz go to the police?"

"First, we hope Chili is alive." I flipped on hall lights as I walked, turning them off when I entered my bedroom. "Second, she told the deputies he was missing, they tried to brush her off because he's an adult. Finally, she convinced them Chili isn't the leaving type. Now she doesn't trust them to do a thorough job. She's upset, Pete, and her anxiety is off the chart. She said Chili always calls every day. Here it is Saturday, for a few more minutes at least, and he's been missing since Tuesday. I may've been the last person to talk to him."

"I'm sorry your friend is missing, hon. I wish I was there to help you find him. Were you questioned about his disappearance?"

"The cops contacted me about it, but not in the way I expected."

"How?"

I clicked on my bedside lamp, cut off the overhead light, and dropped my shoes in the closet. "The deputy who arrested Doug after Mom died, Deputy Lance Hamlyn, was at the second bar I visited last night. He convinced me to combine forces and then followed me home, for safety. Tonight we hit three more bars together seeking news about Chili."

Pete's emerald eyes filled the screen of my phone, suddenly flashing gem bright. "It concerns me that he singled you out. Are you okay with it?"

"Far as I know, I'm the only other person on the entire island besides Estelle asking questions about Chili Bolz. Deputy Hamlyn said people weren't opening up to him, but he noticed they spoke readily to me, that's why he wanted to join forces. I didn't do it all on my own, though. A friend from elementary school, Vivian Declan, helped me ask twenty-somethings if they'd seen Chili."

Pete looked thoughtful. "Learn anything?"

I smiled at the spark in his eyes, the fresh color in his cheeks. He looked much better now than a few minutes ago. I pulled down the covers and cozied up in a seated position against the pillows, phone resting on my bent knees. "Nope, and so far, no one I've met harbors a grudge against Chili. He's had many charter clients through the years, but none ever lodged an official complaint about him or downgraded his online five-star rating."

"He have a first mate on the boat?"

"Heard he had several over the years. I compiled an anecdotal list of names and passed along the scant information to the deputy."

"Good. A trained police officer can follow those leads. I know you love finding things, but there's a part of me that wants to keep you safe forever."

"You're sweet, but I need to do this. I promised Estelle I'd look for Chili, and that's what I did. I wasn't in any danger at the bars or afterward because I had a police escort home. Estelle has no one else, and she's all alone in the world. I can't turn my back on her. Besides as Mom's long-term bridge partner, she's practically family to me."

"Let's think this through for a moment. If her son is missing, it's bad news. If he's a screw up and zoned out elsewhere on booze, drugs, or sex, that's also bad news. And before you protest what a great guy he is, let me assure you that people change. There's a reason he can't be found, and whatever it is, it isn't good."

Protests about Chili's good character automatically sprang to my throat, but they also died there. How well did I know Estelle's adult son?

I knew him as a boy, as a man, not so much. Even so, I was Estelle's only lifeline. "Driving a car can be dangerous. So what?"

"I understand your need to help others, and I fully support it. I only wish I wasn't so far away."

"Message received. I'll be careful." I sighed. "I enjoy helping people. And finding lost things stimulates me in a way I can't explain, other than it's necessary."

"I'm not trying to put constraints on you. I understand we both have passions. Mine is turning businesses around. North Merrick turned out to be a bad choice, but we both make important choices every day." He took a slow considering breath and then nodded slightly as if he'd come to some resolution. "I didn't know how much I'd miss you when I came out to California and then I didn't make much headway turning this business around. Now I want to walk away but I can't afford to lose my total investment."

"You'll figure it out. I have complete faith in you. I can hop on a plane if you want company."

"A great idea, but I feel like I have to constantly watch my back here. These are not good people and I don't trust any of them. I won't put you at risk like that. You're safer at home in Georgia." He cleared his throat. "As for our other shared passion, starting our family, any luck in that regard?"

When we reconnected a few weeks ago, both of us wanted to make up for lost time. Both of us wanted to put down roots and start a family. I wanted to have a baby, Pete's baby, and my biological clock kept ringing in my ears. "No news on that front. I sure hope I didn't wait too long to try for a baby."

"Are you disappointed?"

I dithered over my answer, not wanting to offend him or sound too self-centered, and then spoke the blunt truth. "Yes."

"We'll keep trying." He let out a deep breath. "I want to see you in person. I wish I could hold you in my arms right now."

"I want that too, but I've had too much to drink tonight to be good company. Soon as we finish talking, I'm falling asleep with my clothes on."

His voice roughened. "You'd sleep better if you undressed."

A goofy smile filled me from the inside out. We may not agree on everything, but we had each other. That's what I'd always liked about Pete. He wouldn't let conflict or geography split us up.

"You may be right," I said.

"Will you undress for me, River?"

"Yes, I will."

Chapter Seven

Sunday passed in a flurry of church, laundry, and baking for the upcoming Chamber of Commerce awards dinner. Some of my desserts froze quite well, and it helped to make things ahead of an event. I spoke with my brother at his trade school briefly, and Doug promised to come home soon for a visit. Though he'd been gone six weeks, it seemed longer.

Every time I passed the kitchen table with Lance's flowers I died a little inside. It felt wrong with them in my home, as if I wasn't honoring my commitment to Pete. I threw the flowers away and felt better within minutes.

Throughout the day, I thought about Chili's disappearance. He wouldn't walk away from his life. His tie to his mother was too strong for that. If Pete was right, then Chili had crossed some bad people or maybe been in the wrong place at the wrong time. I had to consider those possibilities. Speaking of Chili, I needed to question his former crew member, Reg.

I texted Viv for Reg's number and caught up with him at the beach. I sat down in the sand beside his beach chair. He wore a low-crowned hat, swim trunks, and nothing else. "Hey, Reg."

"River, I was surprised to get your text," Reg said, thumbing his hat up over his eyes. "What's up?"

"In the course of asking questions about Chili this weekend, I learned that you crewed for him a few times."

Reg nodded. "That's right."

"I'm trying to figure out what happened to Chili and I hoped you could shed some light on his life."

"He and I fished together a few times and that was it."

"You ever hear him get in an argument with anyone?"

"Nope."

"Did you get in an argument with him?"

"No. Where are you going with this?"

"Trying to learn if he had enemies."

"We parted on good terms. I liked the job, but I didn't make enough money to pay my bills."

"Who are his friends?"

He rubbed his clean-shaven chin. "You and Viv. Between working and keeping his mother calm that was all he had time for."

"I already spoke to Viv, and I haven't had a real conversation with Chili in years. I wish I knew what happened to him. You got any theories?"

He pulled his hat down over his eyes. "Nope, but I'm an optimist. If he ain't dead, he must be alive."

On Monday morning, my friend Rosemarie called at seven thirty. "You got time to help with a cleaning today? The rental on Rude Dog Lane is clearing out by noon and the owners insist I clean the day someone leaves."

An afternoon of my time, forty dollars in my pocket. I didn't think twice about it. "Sure, I'll meet you there. One o'clock, right?"

"Yes. And why are you fooling around with Deputy Dawg when you've got the real thing on the hook?"

"No fooling around, promise. I'll tell you more this afternoon."

"You're killing me."

"Suspense makes any story better. See you later."

After ending the call, I showered, dressed, and headed for the kitchen. With a big afternoon ahead of me, I thawed chocolate chip pancakes for breakfast and then made egg salad wraps for Rosemarie and me to nibble on later.

A glance out my window made me smile. The kitty was back, and he had a very compelling way of staring at my window. Good thing I'd picked up cat food at the grocery store yesterday. I emptied a whole can onto a saucer before carrying the food and a bowl of water outside. I set the containers on the deck and then settled in the farthest chair.

The black cat approached the food cautiously, as if I might serve him bad food, sniffed a time or two, and then inhaled the food like a vacuum cleaner. After drinking most of the water, he retreated to a pool of sunshine near the steps.

"Who are you, kitty?" I asked. "What's your name?"

The animal regarded me steadily as if it were sending me a subliminal message, only I was dialed into the wrong channel. After a bit, the cat lay down and groomed itself. As it changed positions, I discovered the cat was indeed a male.

I listened to the sounds of nature around us. Insects and birds chittered as our Southern spring got started. After a few weeks of moderate temps and rainfall, we'd feel the heat of summer. Easter would be here soon. How would my life change by then? I could be carrying a child, married, or living on Shell Island with nothing changed. I liked knowing what came next, so it was frustrating not knowing where Pete and I would live.

Better not to dwell on it. I should live in the now and focus on the people and the cat I could help. Finished with its facial grooming, the cat rested. I wouldn't say it was comfortable around me, but it tolerated my presence and was making the effort to get to know me. That counted.

"You remind me so much of my friend's kitty, Trouble. He had that same intense way of looking at people. He saved me too. My boyfriend thinks I might be in danger because of this case, but maybe if I had a kitty like you at my back, I'd be all right."

The cat didn't answer of course. "Are you a Blackie?" No twitch of recognition. I tossed out some more traditional cat names. "Tigger, Midnight, Taz, Whiskers, Shadow, or Inkie?"

The cat looked away, and I got the message. He hated those names. "Okay, boy, we'll figure out what suits you soon enough."

I checked the time. Hours to go until I helped my friend with housecleaning. I could work on finding Chili, but what would be most fruitful? Cops were looking for him. Not much point in my burning gas driving all over the island. What did TV cops do when they got stumped? They went back to the beginning.

Estelle phoned me to ask for my help in the beginning. That call led to two nights of barhopping, no progress on the case, and a stay-out-of-it from the deputy. Chili had been gone six days now. A lot could happen in six days.

Speaking of Estelle, I didn't hear from her yesterday. She'd called on Friday and Saturday, but not on Sunday. I called her. When she didn't pick up, I left a message. I waited for a few minutes, but she didn't return my call.

How odd.

Estelle was practically attached to her mobile phone. She would've taken my call regardless of where she was because I might have news about Chili.

A stray thought triggered an involuntary shudder. Could my "where's Chili" questions at the bar have brought trouble to Estelle's door? Once that thought rooted, I couldn't shake my unease. I hurried inside, grabbed my purse, and sped to Estelle's place in the historic district.

Her SUV slumbered in the drive. She must be home. I knocked on the door. No answer. No sound at all coming from the house. "Estelle," I shouted at the door. "Are you okay in there? This is River Holloway. I didn't hear from you, and you didn't return my call. Do you need help?"

No answer. I turned to leave, but the prickly silence weighed on me. I walked around the house, calling her name, looking for anything that might rate a call to the police. The windows were intact, wicker chairs and a table perched on her porch, the garbage can stood upright. Nothing indicated foul play. She didn't appear to be home.

I tried her mobile number again. This time I heard it ring inside the house until it clicked over to messaging. This was starting to feel like very bad déjà vu. Chili had been here one moment and gone the next. I walked up the front steps again and banged on the door, yelling loudly, not caring who saw or heard me.

Nothing from inside and nothing from the neighbors.

How very strange.

I tried the doorknob and it turned easily. My blood ran cold. Opening the door wide, I shouted her name with increasing dread. "Estelle!"

The sound of my voice died to nothing, and I heard a ragged gasp. "Estelle?" I left the door ajar, punched in the digits of the emergency number with my thumb poised over the call button, and stepped inside.

Several items dotted the foyer floor. Two jackets and a hat had fallen off the coat tree hooks. In the living room, the coffee table was upended, magazines on the floor, and a lamp tipped over. Something happened here.

I prayed whoever grabbed Chili hadn't come here and harmed his mother. If I rejected that explanation, then sudden illness, like the flu, might have felled her. If so, I could improve her health with hydration in the hospital.

First, I had to find her. She must be close for me to have heard her from the door.

I headed down the narrow hallway to the kitchen, where I'd heard her phone ring before.

"Estelle! Where are you? This is River Holloway. I'm looking for you."

My heart beat so loud in my ears, I could barely hear anything else, but I stopped to listen. There it was again. That rasping noise. Definitely coming from the kitchen.

Summoning my courage, I kept going. I saw a bloody handprint on the white refrigerator. Dishes had fallen off the counter and broken. Then I noticed a black heel poking out from behind the island.

I turned the corner, saw a bloody, battered mess on the floor, and froze.

Chapter Eight

"What's your emergency?" the 911 operator asked.

I clutched the phone lifeline. "Estelle Bolz is hurt, bad. She needs help. Send an ambulance."

"Is she conscious?"

"Her eyes are closed and she didn't respond to my voice. I don't know CPR. I'm afraid to touch her. Everything is bruised."

"What's the address?"

"Two hundred Beachview Drive, Shell Island. Please hurry."

"Stay on the line."

A few moments later, the woman returned. "EMS and the sheriff's office are on the way. What's your name and contact information?"

I told her, adding, "I feel so helpless."

"You're helping her by calling us, River. Is there a pool of blood or a bleeding wound?"

"No puncture wounds that I can see. No pool of blood." I tried to be objective, but I couldn't breathe until my body forced air into my lungs. I sagged against the center island. "I don't know how long she's been lying here. Her hands, face, and clothes are caked with dried blood." I sniffed back tears. "None of it looks fresh."

"You're doing fine. Stay on the line until help arrives. Is anyone else in the house?"

"No one's on the ground floor. I didn't check upstairs." I gulped air and glanced around, feeling alone and vulnerable. "The house is quiet, and I left the front door open when I entered."

"Tell me what happened."

"I came to check on Estelle. She didn't answer calls or knocks on the door. Her door was unlocked, so I came inside, shouting her name. I found her in the kitchen, on the floor. Her face and arms are black and yellow and puffy. I thought she was dead, but she's breathing, barely."

"How old is Estelle Bolz?"

"Not sure. Her sons were my age, so she must be in her fifties. I don't know."

"Her sons' names?"

"Kale Bolz. He died at sea six months ago. Chili Bolz vanished last week. Far as I know she has no other immediate family."

Estelle's eyes fluttered when I said Chili's name.

I gasped and fell to my knees beside her. "Estelle!"

"What's wrong?" the operator asked. "Are you in danger?"

"Her eyes opened. Her pupils are big as saucers." I set the phone down on the wooden floor and leaned over her. "Estelle, can you hear me? It's River. Who did this to you?"

"River," Estelle said. "The bridge. Check bridge."

Her eyes fluttered shut again. I took her cool hand gently in mine. "I'm here with you, Estelle. Hang on, help's on the way."

The phone squawked beside me. I reached for it. "Estelle was awake briefly, but her eyes closed again."

"Stay on the line. What did she say?"

I repeated the four words and added. "Estelle was my mother's bridge partner. I don't understand what she meant. Maybe she wants me to check the bridge calendar to get a sub for her. That was always a big deal for my Mom, even on her deathbed." I realized what I'd said. "I didn't mean that, Estelle. Hang on. You can't die on us. Chili needs you."

"Do you hear a siren yet?" the operator asked.

I listened. A high-pitched warble reached my ears. "Yes."

"Help will be there soon. Secure any pets in the home for their safety."

I didn't need to look for fur balls or animal bowls. Estelle was allergic to animal dander. "No pets. Just me and Estelle." I prayed silently as I held the phone and Estelle's hand.

Behind me I heard car doors open. "Sheriff's Office," a man called.

I recognized Deputy Hamlyn's voice. "Lance. Back here. In the kitchen."

Footfalls thudded on the wooden floor. Lance knelt beside me. "She alive?" he asked.

"She's still here. Where's that ambulance?"

The air roiled around him. "On the way. They just finished a call at the other end of the island. Takes a while to drive to this end with the traffic circles."

"I hate those things," I said. "Can I hang up the phone now?"

"Yes, I'll discharge the operator."

Placing my phone in his gloved hand, I leaned close to Estelle. "Keep breathing, Estelle. You can do this. I know you can."

Another ragged breath heaved from her chest. EMS and firefighters arrived. In a few short moments, they loaded Estelle on a gurney and drove her over the causeway to the hospital.

A female officer escorted me to Lance's SUV, tucking a blanket around my shoulders. I clung to it while investigators scoured the house. My breathing evened out, and my hands quit trembling. I may have dozed once I warmed up because the clock showed an hour had passed.

Deputy Hamlyn strolled out and joined me. "Talk to me," he said. "Why'd you come here this morning?"

"I gave all that to the 911 operator."

"Humor me. What brought you to Estelle's house this morning?"

The vivid memories slammed back, front and center, in my thoughts. I hugged the blanket tighter. "You were right."

"Come again?"

"Asking questions was a bad idea. You said somebody could get hurt, and somebody did. Estelle."

"We don't know that her assault is connected to questioning people."

"I feel terrible. My actions drew attention to the Bolz family.

For all I know, Estelle is the last of her line. I could've been the final straw in their family's extinction. I brought death to her doorstep."

Lance handed me my phone. "No need to be melodramatic. Go home and rest. If you're too upset to drive, I can take you."

"I got this." Wearing the blanket like a shawl, I exited his SUV, walked over to my catering van, and drove to the nearest ice cream parlor. I ordered mocha chocolate chip, two scoops. The sweetness cut through my guilt and made me feel a little less like crying. Halfway through the first scoop, my hands stopped trembling, and by the time I'd scraped the bowl clean, I felt strong enough to power through an afternoon of house cleaning. I felt a pang of guilt for not heading straight to the hospital, but I wasn't family, and it wasn't likely I'd be allowed in to see Estelle anyway. Not until she woke up and could ask for me. In the meantime, I'd promised to help Rosemarie and cleaning would give me something to do besides worry.

Chapter Nine

Even though I made it to the rental on Rude Dog Lane a little before one, Rosemarie arrived first. A pile of sheets and towels lay on the laundry room floor, and the washing machine and dryer were humming, so she'd already done one of my jobs. That meant I had to hustle to get in the groove.

"Rosemarie, I'm here," I said as I entered the five-bedroom ranch style house. Nothing fancy about this place, except for the panoramic marsh view. That kept renters coming back year after year. Well, that and the gleaming state of cleanliness my friend consistently delivered. You could literally eat off any surface in this house.

She hollered at me from the back bedroom over LeAnn Rimes belting out how could she possibly live. Rosemarie loved ninety's music. "Great. You know the drill."

Indeed, I did. I collected trash and moved items back to their proper places as Toni Braxton sang about wishing her heart was unbroken. I wiped down the kitchen cabinets and counters, knowing full well Rosemarie would go over them again. Mariah Carey sang about her vision of love as my friend emerged from the bedrooms.

"I've dusted all the bedrooms and cleaned three of the bathrooms," Rosemarie said. She looked energized and perky with her trendy white and purple striped hair. "You can vacuum the floors back there now. By the time you hit the living room, I'll be finished with the sleeping quarters, and we can polish the floors."

"Sure. You got here early. You're way ahead of me."

The music changed and Ace of Base sang jauntily with a

personal question about belonging I couldn't answer. Where did I belong? I was rooted in Shell Island, Georgia, but my heart was in California. I had two allegiances. How could I choose?

I snapped out of my mental lapse to realize Rosemarie was talking a million miles an hour, as she was apt to do. I rewound the conversation and hoped I caught the gist of it.

"The renters left early, so I swung by at noon to start a load of sheets. One thing led to another and I didn't leave. We should have the linens done before we finish." She studied me closely. "What's wrong? You don't look like yourself."

"Rough morning. A friend of mine went to the hospital."

"Estelle Bolz?"

"How'd you know?"

"Heard it on my police scanner. What happened?"

"Someone beat her nearly to death. I hope she makes it."

"We'll call the hospital when we're done, okay? They need time to stabilize her. That must've been quite a shock. Estelle and your mom were good friends."

Estelle's battered face surfaced in my mind, and I tried to shake it loose. "Yes. I can't wrap my head around it."

Rosemarie patted my shoulder. "I can finish this if you need to leave."

Her compassion sparked my energy. "No. I need the work. I can do this."

"You sure?"

I reached for the big vacuum. "Definitely. I can compartmentalize for now."

When we finished, Rosemarie whipped out two canned lemonades from her car cooler and invited me to sit on the porch with her. We settled in the padded rocking chairs, eating the egg salad wraps I brought. She called her cousin Herman who worked in billing at the hospital. She hit the speakerphone button so that I could hear the conversation.

Rosemarie leaned close to the phone. "Hey, Cuz. I'm with my friend River Holloway, and we're concerned about Estelle Bolz.

They hauled her to the hospital a few hours ago. How is she?"

"Rosie, you can get this information from the front desk." Herman sighed heavily. "It interrupts my flow when you make me think about patients."

"I do it because I love you. Too many numbers aren't good for you, Cuz. You need to connect more with living people."

"Speak for yourself. People always want something from me. Uh-oh."

"What-oh?" Rosemarie asked.

"I, uh, have bad news for you. Ms. Bolz didn't make it. She's listed as DOA at the hospital."

"Dead? That can't be right," I blurted out. "She was alive when she left in the ambulance."

"Must've been her last moments," Herman said. "I'm sorry I don't have better news for you. Oh..."

"You're killing me, Herm," Rosemarie said. "What'd you find?"

"Ms. Bolz was a frequent flyer at the ER. Seems she was beaten two months ago, and there are visits stretching back over the last eight months. Someone beat the crap out of her on a regular basis. Repeated head trauma is too much for a person's brain. I'm sorry for your loss."

I was sorry too. And steaming mad. "Why didn't she report the assaults to the police? Why didn't the hospital report her recurrent injuries to the police?"

There was a painful silence, then Herman dropped his voice. "You didn't hear it from me, but we recently changed hospitalist services."

I glanced at Rosemarie who shook her head. How strange to clearly hear the words someone spoke but to utterly lack in comprehension. "I have no idea what that means."

"The group we contracted with previously treated each patient visit as a single occurrence. They didn't flag repeated visits. They treated whoever presented that day according to their symptoms and then forgot about it. We have a different team now and much better patient oversight."

My blood simmered. "Excuse me? Estelle's death was preventable?"

"No, and if you tell anyone we spoke, I'll deny it. Estelle is responsible for her own life. She should've taken actions to avoid that violent person."

I died a little inside. "That's not right. Some people can't help themselves."

"The hospital isn't liable for this. Don't go getting any ideas in your sweet head. Gotta go." Herman ended the call.

"I'm sorry about Estelle," Rosemarie said.

I rubbed my eyes, surprised they were dry. "This is terrible. I should've checked on her sooner. She didn't call yesterday so I visited her first thing this morning. I found her in the kitchen and called 911. I held her hand, but it wasn't enough."

"You helped by finding her. It's a shame Chili's missing. He'll be devastated when he hears the news."

"It's stunning to know someone can be repeatedly battered and no one notices. I didn't know."

"Domestic violence happens all the time. Many attackers are savvy enough not to strike a person's face."

"Chili didn't hit his mom."

"I didn't mean to imply he did. But since it wasn't a one-time thing, she likely knew her attacker and didn't report him or her to the sheriff's office."

Her words settled over me like a rime of frost, providing crystalline clarity. Estelle was in trouble before she came to me. I didn't cause her beating by asking questions about Chili's whereabouts. Who could have done such violence to another person?

"Pete was right," I mused aloud. "People disappear for a reason. Whatever got Estelle killed is likely the reason Chili vanished. If the assailant beat Chili too, I pray he's mending. If he knew about Estelle's previous beatings, why didn't he take her with him?"

"I don't have the answer," Rosemarie said.

"Sorry. I'm frustrated at my failure to find Chili, and now Estelle's dead. She probably knew more about Chili's disappearance than she let on, so why'd she ask me to find him?"

"Playing devil's advocate here," Rosemarie said. "Perhaps she wanted to make sure no one could find him. Everyone knows you're a good finder. If you couldn't do it, he's safe wherever he is."

"Maybe, but now I'm honor-bound to find Estelle's killer and her son."

Chapter Ten

When Pete called for our nightly chat at bedtime, I braced for the retelling of my day, knowing he would be concerned.

As soon as he heard my strained hello, his face dominated the video call screen. "Something happened, didn't it?"

"Yes, it did." I exhaled a shaky breath. "Estelle Bolz died today. I was at her house."

"Your mother's friend?" Pete asked. "I'm sorry to hear that. Was she ill?"

"Someone beat her. Battery, the cops said. She was on the floor when I found her. She died in the ambulance."

"Are you all right? Why didn't you call me earlier?"

"I'm fine. My friend Rosemarie helped me decompress this afternoon. This was my day to help her clean the rental. I didn't call you because you were working and because I needed to stay busy."

I paused as Estelle's face surfaced in my thoughts. "It was awful seeing her like that. I kept thinking that someone did this to her. Then she mentioned playing bridge. Her wires must've been scrambled by the blows. All I could think to do, besides calling for help, was to sit with her and hold her hand. I thought I'd saved her, but I was too late."

"You did a good thing, a hard thing, for a friend." Pete's fierce expression softened. "You gave comfort when she needed it most."

Tears blurred my vision. "I failed her. I couldn't find Chili, and now she's dead. I owe it to her memory to find her son."

"This sounds serious, River. Let the cops handle it."

I sat up in bed, needing my wits about me. Pete couldn't help his protective instincts, but I'd made my decision. "The cops couldn't find Chili in a week, so how can they figure out what happened to Estelle?"

"That's your big heart talking, hon. In a few days, your favor for a friend escalated from a missing persons case to homicide. I'm worried about you and I don't want you caught up in this deadly rip current."

"There's no crime wave on Shell Island. No one else has been assaulted or gone missing. Only Chili and Estelle Bolz."

"Should I fly home? I can catch a red-eye to Jacksonville tonight."

At that I smiled. Pete Merrick hadn't had a home in a long time. The fact that he considered me home meant the world to me. "I'm okay. My week is full, first with tutoring and with prepping for a Chamber dinner for a hundred people on Friday night. I won't have time to ask questions or to spend every waking moment with you."

"Work is important, but you're my priority. I've got key appointments this week that need finessing, but they can wait if you need me. Either way, I'm still planning on coming next week."

"That's fine. I miss you."

"Miss you too."

Estelle's death made the obituary page of the Tuesday paper. Her brief obit read like a death notice, announcing her funeral arrangements on Saturday. She'd been so much more than a woman who died. She loved her boys and her dry-cleaning business and playing bridge. None of that was mentioned.

My hands curled in frustration. I wanted to help Estelle, but I needed to be more objective. Charging around blindly wouldn't help either of us. Maybe the cops found traceable evidence in her house. Maybe they were close to catching her killer.

A call to Lance netted a terse reply that he was busy and had nothing to share. That was disappointing, so I baked a batch of chocolate chip cookies.

At tutoring that afternoon, I enjoyed hanging out with the fourth graders and feeling like a positive role model. Later, I worked in my commercial kitchen, staging food for Friday's catering event at the Chamber by prepping baked beans, making a gallon of my barbeque sauce, and preparing more of the twelve desserts they'd ordered. I already had seven smoked Boston Butts in the freezer for the dinner, so the rest of the meal could be prepped later in the week.

Meanwhile, I inched closer to touching the black cat who now appeared on my deck for breakfast and dinner each day. His approach to eating reminded me of a SWAT maneuver. He watched me leave, swarmed down on the food, inhaled it, and bugged out. Sometimes, though, he lingered on the deck with me.

I tried out more cat names in my head but nothing felt right. I'd never had an outdoor cat before. Seemed like he should trust me by now if he wanted to be my cat. Yet he sniffed every meal like I'd poisoned him. What a major pain. Wait a minute. That was a great idea for his name.

"You like the food, Major?" I asked on Wednesday evening. "You want more?"

He gazed at me intently. Unfortunately, I didn't understand cat telepathy. "Major. That's what I'll call you. You are strategic and autocratic. You stayed put when I sat here with you, so you're brave. I'm calling you Major."

Major drowsed in a pool of sunshine, his eyelids at half-mast, and purred.

A victory! This was the first time he'd purred in my presence. The triumph made me giddy. I'd done something right. I made one kitty happy. After several days of regular meals, his coat gleamed, his tail reached higher.

Now if I could achieve the same satisfaction with the Bolz family's troubles, I'd be overjoyed. I still had no idea of Chili's whereabouts, or if he was even alive. Estelle's death felt surreal. I wanted to help them but how?

On Thursday, I tutored kids in the morning. Before I jumped

into baking again, I drove to the church where the bridge club met, bringing along a packet of my toasted almond cookies from the freezer. Mom's friends were delighted to see me and the treats. Their white heads and faces blurred as they hugged me and reminisced about the good old days.

When I got a moment to speak, I said, "I'm so sorry about Estelle's death."

"It's terrible," Lizzie Collins said, wringing her hands. "We had the same members for ten years, and within a few months two are gone. The universe has it in for bridge ladies."

"Sure does," Nance Alvarez said. Her watery violet gaze turned sharp. "We have openings and we don't want to fill them. Unless...Would you join us, River? You'd fit right in."

"Oh!" I sucked wind big time, not expecting this wrinkle. "My catering schedule is too variable, and that wouldn't be fair to you ladies. However, my brother could substitute for you when he returns from trade school. He intends to open his own handyman business and will have free time while he's getting established."

"Your Mom used to brag about how good a bridge player Doug was," Lizzie said. "Of course, he can join. It'll be like having your mom with us again."

Doug would be surprised, but everyone was smiling again. "One more thing before I go. I was with Estelle before she died, and she mentioned bridge. Specifically, she said 'check bridge.' Does that mean anything to y'all?"

A dozen ladies shook their heads.

I tried again. "Did she owe a check for bridge or is there a certain check variation of bridge y'all play?"

"Nope," Lizzie said. "We pay our dues in September, and everyone is caught up. Never heard the phrase 'check bridge.' We play duplicate here."

Having struck out with the bridge club, I visited Estelle's church, The Place for Prayer, to see if I could help with her funeral on Saturday. The doors were locked tight, the parking lot deserted, and the phone number for the office bounced straight to voicemail.

Bummer.

On my way home, I stopped by the Flower and Garden Shop and purchased a potted azalea for Estelle to be delivered to the church. Then it was on to my commercial kitchen to bake two pound cakes, two apple pies, and two peach pies. For the peach pies, I used the fresh peaches I'd canned last summer. The kitchen smelled like cake and sweet cinnamon all afternoon.

Afterward, I glanced around my home and realized I wanted to be proactive for Estelle and Chili today. With Estelle's passing so raw, my first choice was to circle back to finding her son. Lance told me earlier that he'd searched Chili's place, vehicle, and boat. Though the cops had Chili's truck, I'd found no clues to his disappearance in his place, so his boat was the only place left I could search. A check of the time showed I could squeeze in a quick trip to Bayside Marina where he kept the boat.

Mom's car hadn't been run in a while. I should drive it. But when I went to get into her old Buick, Major sat on the hood of the vehicle, unflinching.

"You are not a hood ornament, kitty," I said, shooing him with repeated flips of my wrist. "Move along."

He regarded me steadily, jumped down, and skittered behind me. When I opened the door, he rushed inside, jumped over the seat, and perched on the backseat.

Traveling with a potentially feral cat inside a vehicle struck me as a bad idea. I opened the rear door and tried my best to get him to leave. "Here, kitty, kitty, kitty." Nothing. "Major, get out of the car." More nothing. He wouldn't even look my way.

Dare I lift him out? I approached cautiously, reaching with my right hand for the kitty. I got to within a foot of him, and he hissed at me. Message received. He intended to ride in the car.

I closed the door and took a moment to regroup. I had been in and out of my van all week, and the cat had shown no interest. Now, when I was headed to the marina in Mom's Buick, the cat wanted to come? Had to be coincidence. Right?

Lordy, I'd been around this cat for almost a week and already I was thinking it knew more about Shell Island than I did. This had to be the quickest transformation to Crazy Cat Lady the world had ever seen.

So, traveling with a cat. Not knowing how this would go, it seemed prudent to lower the windows in case the cat changed his mind. Moving slowly, I got in the car, cranked it, and powered down the windows. The radio came on and the cat never flinched. It sat upright on the backseat as if it were his command post.

"Okay, here we go." And yes, I was now talking to the cat too. "We're headed to the marina to look at Chili's boat. I'm familiar with it, so I hope I'll spot something different about it. Maybe there is a clue to his disappearance."

The cat lay down until the car stopped at Bayside Marina. Then he rose, sniffed the air, and leapt out the open window. I thought about calling him back, not wanting him to get lost, but what did I know about this cat? He may know the marina better than I did.

The sun inched toward the western treetops as the time neared four o'clock. Folks with kids were meeting buses or running the kids around to activities this time of day, which is probably why the marina appeared deserted. I parked near the gangway, the only car in the lot beside the shiny truck over at the office. I grabbed my purse and walked dead center on the dock.

Having been here before, I knew where Chili docked, and I soon found his boat, *Reel Fine*. My first impression was of tidiness. The fishing poles and a net were slotted in holders around the console, and oars were lashed to the interior sides. The anchors were stowed away. No extra seat cushions or empty buckets littered the fiberglass seats or deck.

Nothing cluttered the console. The chrome gauges and rails gleamed. The white expanse of boat decking looked showroom clean.

When I'd seen Chili's boat before, it had empty soda cans in a five-gallon bucket, a map clipped to the console, a GPS on the console dash...that was missing. "Now that's interesting," I said, talking to myself. "The way those things work, you can track where the boat has been. Did someone steal the boat's GPS? Or did the cops take it into custody? Either way, it's something I should ask Deputy Hamlyn."

Major meowed loudly, then jumped into the boat. His landing thump startled me, and if not for grabbing a piling, I would've fallen overboard. "You scared me, Major. Did you know Chili?"

The cat seemed to be sniffing, so I sniffed. The odor of saltwater prevailed, but I didn't smell fish. Every other time I'd met Chili at Bayside, his boat had reeked of fish, bait, and marine fuel. Now it smelled squeaky clean.

Chili liked things tidy, but he'd never before gone to this level of OCD cleanliness. Odd. Why would the boat be so clean? To erase evidence? There was a good chance something happened on this boat, given its state of uber cleanliness and the missing GPS.

The afternoon sun beat down on me, reminding me that the mild spring-like temperatures of March would soon yield to intense summer heat. Who would I report my findings to? Estelle was dead. Deputy Lance Hamlyn told me to butt out. Even Pete wanted me to drop the case.

The cat leapt out of the boat and bounded up the gangway. Obviously, he was done here. I followed the cat off the dock, but I wasn't ready to go home.

A light inside the marina office drew my eye. Not much went on here that the dockmaster didn't know about. I hurried toward the office.

Chapter Eleven

"River Holloway, as I live and breathe," Garnet Pierce said, enveloping me in a friendly hug. "Haven't seen you in months. What brings you to the marina? Looking for some fish?"

The dockmaster's tan cargo pants and turquoise polo reeked of cigarette smoke. I held my breath during the embrace, until I couldn't any longer, then got a whiff of her cinnamon-candy breath as she disengaged. Garnet had the misfortune of having a man's rugged jaw and fierce brow, and no amount of makeup could mask those features or her masculine build. Consequently, she accepted it and dressed like a man. Even her hair was cut military short.

Garnet's only concessions to femininity were her dainty gold hoop earrings and her French-style manicure. Strangers often didn't know what to make of her, but Garnet didn't give a flip about anybody's opinion. This was her domain.

There was an earthy smell in here from the live worm bin and a fishy overture from the aerated bait shrimp in the far corner. The aisles were crammed with fishing lines, rods, nets, lures, boat supplies, clothing, and snacks.

"Don't need fish today," I said, "though I'm concerned that Chili Bolz is missing. He was supposed to hook me up with sea bass last Friday. He vanished last Tuesday. You know anything about his disappearance?"

Garnet ambled behind the sales counter, taking a moment to reposition the artificial lure rack she'd brushed up against. "I told the cops everything I knew. Chili was here in the office on Tuesday when you called about the fish you needed for Friday. After he lit out, I didn't see him again. What's the deal, gal? You turning into a private eye?"

"Chili and I have been friends since forever because our moms were friends. Estelle called me last Friday and asked me to find him. She said the cops weren't getting anywhere."

"That's true," Garnet said. "If Lance Hamlyn had half the brains he thinks he has, he would've solved this case last week. Chili couldn't have gone far. His boat's here, his truck's locked up in evidence."

"I heard the same, but there has to be more information. I'm trying to determine if there's anything that might seem normal to the cops, but a little off to people who knew Chili. Like did he have any new friends or get in arguments with anyone at the marina?"

Garnet's chair creaked as she eased into it. "That Chili. He could charm the pants off all his charter clients, especially the women. They thought he was their best friend, but most of the time, Chili came down here and kept to himself."

"Oh?"

"Yeah. I took his silence as a personal challenge. I'd get him talking when he came in to pay his fuel bill. Mostly he griped about unreliable crew on his charters. It was his favorite refrain, how nobody in this county wanted to work for a living. He viewed the influx of retirees and tourists as fodder for his business, and he held everyone else in contempt. He thought the world of you, though, and of your cooking. If you'd had sea legs, he would've asked you to crew for him."

"I don't," I said quickly. "Have sea legs. Offshore fishing is not my thing, much as I need work. I'd rather sit in meetings all day than be stuck on a boat, and I hate time-wasting meetings. I've got to stay busy to pay my bills. Getting back to Chili's charter business. Was it steady? Did he have repeat customers?"

"He did. There's folks who will only fish with Chili. He did that, made himself the gold standard for local charter captains."

"Surely his calendar didn't end the day he disappeared. Doesn't he have clients scheduled?"

"He kept his calendar on that phone of his, so I wouldn't know.

He did mention some high roller clients were coming soon. He wanted everything perfect for them."

"In what way?"

"In every way. Chili loved big tips. To make sure he got them, he expected fresh bait, blue skies, primo marine gas, gourmet lunches, coolers stocked with beer, sodas, and water, and a big haul."

I loved big tips too. Who didn't? Was Garnet being helpful or wasting my time? I tried again. "He aimed high all right. Were those expectations a problem for him?"

"All of them, though he counted on those shrimp paste wraps and chocolate chip cookies you made for those charters to seal the deal. Between you and me, he took credit for your food. Didn't you ever wonder why you never got catering requests from his customers?"

My smile tightened. "I'm happy to see him succeed, and he paid me well for the charter meals."

"Um hmm."

I blew out a huff of air. Did the cops find questioning people this difficult? So far, Garnet had tried to impress me with how on top of things she was. I had two questions for her.

"About his boat," I began. "I noticed how tidy and clean it is. I've seen the *Reel Fine* on various occasions, and it didn't meet this cleanliness standard. You know anything about that?"

"Well, sure," Garnet said, leaning back in her Boss Hog chair. "He hired me to pressure wash it for him when he was in here last Tuesday. Said the whales expected top of the line service, and he was darn well providing it."

That made sense. My hopes plunged. "What happened to his GPS?"

"Cops took it into evidence, along with all the papers on his boat."

"He have any charters this week?"

"Nope."

"I feel bad for Chili. Those clients will be disappointed when he doesn't show. They might leave bad reviews for him online. I wish we could help him somehow."

"See if Lance will let you use Chili's phone and notify his customers. I'm sure Chili would appreciate the courtesy."

"Deputy Hamlyn already told me to butt out of his case. He isn't helpful."

"It's his job to be helpful."

"Maybe." I glanced over at the T-shirt rack and beyond that to the exit before looking at Garnet again. "I should go. Thank you for answering my questions. I owe it to Estelle to keep asking questions about Chili."

"Be careful. You stick your nose in the wrong place, and you're likely to get shark-bit."

Her cautionary words sounded harsh. "Not a problem since I'm fresh out of ideas. You going to Estelle's funeral on Saturday?"

"Nope. Gotta work. Saturdays are busy around here."

"All right then. If you remember anything about Chili, please let me know." I handed her my business card. A glance out the door confirmed what I suspected. Major perched atop Mom's old Buick.

Garnet nodded toward the black cat. "Quite the statement your cat is making."

It felt good to hear someone say Major was my cat. "I'm his meal ticket. This is the first time we've gone anywhere together. He showed up on my back porch a few days ago, demanded food, and settled right in. You recognize him?"

Garnet pursed her lips for a long moment. "We had a black cat around here for a while. I haven't seen him for months."

"That cat have a name?"

"Yep. Damn Cat."

I was not calling the cat that, even if it was the same feline. "If you hear of anyone missing a cat, let me know. Meanwhile, I'll keep feeding it."

"Gotcha."

I paused next to the ball caps. "One more thing. Were you friends with Chili's brother, Kale?"

"No." Garnet's mouth closed tightly.

Interesting. I would've missed the flare of alarm in her eyes if I hadn't been looking.

Chapter Twelve

Major and I drove home, my mind roiling with new questions. Garnet gave the appearance of being friendly and affable, but she had strict barriers. Were they a result of a life hard-lived? Or did she have secrets? It bugged me that I didn't know much about her.

I caught the black cat's eye in the rearview mirror. "Did you live at the marina, Major?"

He huffed out a breath. Guess he had secrets too. I wasn't planning on using his dock name, but I needed to know if he responded to it. "Did they call you Damn Cat?"

The cat turned his back on me and lay facing the rear seat. Clearly, he didn't respond to the name, whether it had been his or not. "You'll always be Major to me, kitty. Don't you worry about that."

Five minutes later we were back at my place and Mom's old Buick docked in the carport. This time tomorrow I'd be loading my catering van with food for the Chamber event. Major scampered out the window and darted into the woods. I hurried to my commercial kitchen and donned an apron. On my timeline of prep work for today was making iced tea, sweet and unsweet. They'd specified fourteen gallons, but for this crowd, I was bringing sixteen, even though there'd be a wine bar. Southerners loved their iced tea.

Coleslaw assembly was next on my to-do list for today. My dressing has a citrus base and just enough vinegar for the expected punch of tart. From the compliments I'd received over the years, my slaw was the perfect accompaniment to the Boston Butt. Thanks to the wonder of an industrial sized food processor, making a large quantity of slaw went fast. Sure enough, I had gallons of tea made and buckets of slaw marinating two hours later.

I pulled out my cookie book and paged to my favorite butter cookie recipe. Making a triple batch, I added tear-drop chunks of dark chocolate to the center of each cookie. By dinnertime, my feet ached, so I made light of dinner with a peanut butter sandwich. My brother called, and I moved to the living room sofa, propping my feet on the coffee table.

"Guess what," I began. "I volunteered you as a sub for the duplicate bridge ladies."

"You're kidding, right?" Doug asked. "I'll be working my tail off in the daytime. I have to launch my business."

"Those ladies live in older homes. They need a handyman, especially a qualified one with a business license that they know and trust."

"Oh, didn't consider that angle. I'll find a way to make it happen," Doug said. "I like the way your mind works."

My mind was thinking that these living room walls needed a fresh coat of paint. Would Doug charge me now that he was a certified and licensed handyman?

"An entrepreneurial mindset is necessary or your business won't succeed. Why do you think I take my cookies everywhere I go?"

"Because you're a compulsive baker?"

We both laughed. "Did you hear about Estelle Bolz?" I asked.

"Yeah, saw it in the online newspaper. That isn't right."

He didn't know all of it. "I found her."

"I had no idea. Sorry. That's terrible. Are you okay?"

"I'm handling it, though the images keep popping in my head. Pete thinks I should stop looking for Chili."

Doug snorted. "I know you're in love with the guy, but separation isn't good for your relationship."

"Trust me, I feel the lack of his company. I want to marry him. He makes me happy, but every time I think about packing up and moving to California my toes dig into the sand. I want to be with Pete, but I'm afraid to leave my island comfort zone. I'm hoping time will clear my thoughts."

"Or break your heart. I can stand on my own two feet now, Sis. You don't have to worry about me."

My fingers stroked the lightly textured sofa cushions. "That's a part of my indecision, albeit a small part. I'll always be your big sister, and concern for you comes as naturally as breathing since I'm the eldest. My reservations about moving out there may seem trivial in the face of everything else, but I've worked hard to get established here. I have repeat customers, enough of them that I can pay most of my bills with Holloway Catering. I won't get rich this way, but I set my own hours and no one bosses me around. This level of job satisfaction may not happen elsewhere."

"Sounds like you love your business more than Pete."

"Why can't I have both?" I asked, noting the throbbing in my temples.

"Pete's probably saying the same thing. At this rate, you two have a low probability of living together. Someone's gotta compromise."

My lips turned down. "Traditionally, the woman gives up her life for her husband's. Marriage to a business troubleshooter would be a lot like being a military wife. Lots of relocating."

"Are you trying to convince me or yourself?" Doug asked.

"I'm being cautious," I said. "That's all. For months I thought he didn't care for me, only to have him make a grand gesture on Valentine's Day to show how much he missed me. I want him and a family, only how can I manage everything?"

"Huh." Doug paused. "Sometimes you need to jump in with both feet. It may not be what you want, but if you keep stalling, you'll never know what life with Pete will be like."

We talked a little more, but his relationship advice resonated in my thoughts long after the call ended. Did I care enough about Pete to put my business second? At bedtime, Pete didn't call and my call to him rolled to voicemail. In a jarring week, his unavailability tonight hit a sour note. Some nights he called, some nights I called, but we always called. It wasn't like I could run over to his house and check on him. California was a world away from Georgia.

I tossed and turned for most of the night and checked my phone each time I awakened. Nothing from Pete. My irritation turned to concern.

Friday dawned with clear skies and a light breeze. The first thing I did after waking up was to leave another message for Pete. I couldn't afford to dwell on him being out of touch. I had work to do.

I didn't see much of the day, except through the windows of my kitchen and when I loaded the van. I showered and changed clothes quickly, arriving on site a few minutes ahead of schedule. The Chamber president broke into a rare smile as I pulled into the loading zone.

"Thank goodness you're here," Harvey Flosky said, tugging down his sport jacket. Looked like the same one from last year, the one that kept riding up. "I was afraid something happened to you."

"I'm early, Harvey, and everything is fine, same as I told you yesterday when we spoke. The food's prepared. All I have to do is set it up."

"The buffet tables are ready for you," he said as I placed my ramp and rolled the first cart of food to ground level. "You got any of those cookies I love set aside for me?"

I handed him a bag, remembering he'd made the same request last year. "Got you covered."

He snatched the bag, whipped out a cookie. Moments later, his face wreathed in rapture. "Long as I am Chamber President, this catering job is yours. I don't know how you infuse so much flavor in these cookies. I can't get enough of them."

He was too cheap to buy them from me during the year. I managed a fleeting smile. "Good to know."

The next twenty minutes passed quickly. I checked tasks off my list as I finished them. I wished I could afford a large freestanding buffet unit. Business was good, but not that good. Instead, I owned four eight-quart stainless steel chafing dishes, though I only needed three for this job. I positioned a large clear vat of slaw atop a pre-chilled ice block, which fit into a special base. It cost a pretty penny, but I'd splurged with top of the line products, and that investment continued to pay off in terms of product performance and satisfied customers.

Harvey came over and critiqued the dessert table set-up until I handed him another cookie with a stern admonition, "This is the last one."

"Right," Harvey said with a twinkle in his eye.

"You heard Chili's missing?"

"I did. I also heard tell his Mama got dead, and you nearly saved her."

"Nearly isn't good enough. I grieve for the Bolz family. I've known Chili since elementary school, but was his family always here?"

"Nope. They moved here about twenty-five or so years ago. Estelle opened that dry-cleaning store, and the kids helped out occasionally. They never had much but always scraped by."

"She ever own another business on the island?" I asked, my curiosity ratcheting into high gear.

"Not to my recollection," he said.

Interesting. She'd always been around to do things with her sons, but Harvey said she just barely got by with her dry-cleaning income. Not once had I questioned how she paid her bills. Until now. "How'd she manage?"

Harvey shrugged. "Beyond my pay grade. You'll have to sweet talk her banker with some cookies. Though, if I knew her financial situation, I'd tell you in a heartbeat for more cookies. I'm very susceptible to cookie bribes."

Though he said this in a laughing manner and I laughed, his comment bothered me. I considered Harvey an official representative of our community. Was he admitting he took bribes?

We parted ways, and I got the "seconds" of my dishes set up in the back, the warms on warmers and the colds on chillers. The extra gallons of tea I stashed in the refrigerator.

Patsy from the wine bar station hurried over to admire the

buffet setup as soon as I returned to the banquet room. She was four years younger than me and walked like she was going to a fire. We'd been in the same Sunday school class when I'd observed firsthand her tendency to eat crayons.

Those days were long gone, and now she looked like she could play pro football. Not that her size or looks mattered to me. Patsy had grown up to be a sweet but shy woman.

"Harvey tried to mooch wine off me," Patsy said. "I said no, but then you gave him cookies. You're making me look bad."

"Harvey loves my cookies, and I love having this catering job. We understand each other." I placed the serving spoons and tongs in accompanying dishes beside the warmers.

"I'd kill for a slice of that cornbread. I still dream about your yummy cornbread from last year. That butter looks perfect for spreading. You think anyone'd notice if I had my piece right now?"

I hoped she was kidding. "Sorry, Patsy. I can't hide a missing slice from the pan. You'll have to wait like everyone else."

She nodded toward the kitchen. "No second pan that's messed up back there?"

"Sorry."

"It'll kill me to wait, but I'll do it." Patsy sighed. "My boss at the wine bar said you went out with Deputy Dawg twice last weekend. What happened to Mr. Excitement?"

"Deputy Hamlyn accompanied me while I asked if anyone knew Chili Bolz's whereabouts. I'm still dating Pete Merrick."

"Uh-huh. Does Pete know the dog's been sniffing around?"

"He does. Lance accompanied me for safety reasons. If you'll notice, I'm not carousing bars tonight, and I'm without a male escort."

Patsy burst out laughing. "Girl, you're a mess. Worse, you're single-handedly going to add five pounds to my weight with this meal. I plan to try all of your desserts, especially the cookies that Harvey raves about."

Though Patsy was a large woman, she was linebacker solid everywhere. A few desserts would quickly get burnt off a woman as active as she was. "He likes them because they remind him of the ones his grandmother used to make. Your mileage may vary."

"That's three men you've got eating out of your hands. How do you do that? What's a gal got to do to get a date in this town?"

I never thought of Patsy as dating. She didn't appear to have time for socializing. "I'm not sure. Who'd you like to date?"

"I had an itch for Mr. Missing Man himself, but Chili never once looked my way."

"His loss then," I said. "You'll find someone else."

"Tell me the truth, River. Does everyone think I'm interested in women?"

That question was emotional quicksand, and I'd rather not get sucked under. "I don't pay attention to rumors, Patsy, and you shouldn't either. Who you date is your business."

"They do think I'm a lesbian! That's not fair."

My hands shot up reflexively. "Whoa. I didn't say that. I said that gossip goes in one ear and right out the other. I'm not interested in hearing it, and I do my best not to repeat it. This is the age of being yourself. If you want to date men or women, fine. If you want to identify as a man or woman, fine. Anything goes today."

Patsy's face darkened. "I'm trying not to be offended by what you said."

"Good, because no offense was intended. Do whatever you like with whoever you like, just own it."

"How do you mean?"

"Be confident in who you are and what you like. If a man interests you or he shows interest in you, give him feedback. I'll bet you didn't talk to Chili the entire time you wanted to date him."

Her eyes rounded. "I couldn't."

"Guys have nerves too. Let 'em know you're friendly. Is there anyone else you're interested in? Anyone who's here tonight?"

"Haven't thought about it. Still daydreaming about Chili. Any chance of him coming home?"

"Your guess is as good as mine."

Chapter Thirteen

People raved about the food, and the dessert bar emptied on the first pass through the serving line. As the Chamber made their yearly award presentations, the rest of the food vanished. I held back four pieces of buttered cornbread for Patsy, and she was ecstatic about that at night's end.

Patsy and Harvey helped me haul my empty serving dishes to the van, and I drove home on a wave of joyous adrenaline.

I done good.

Ten people took business cards and said they'd call me. Two couples already asked me to reserve specific dates on my calendar for catering.

After I unloaded the van, changed into a nightgown, and settled in bed, my phone buzzed on the bedside table. I'd muted my phone during the event, so I hoped this was Pete calling for a bedside chat. In the darkness, I glanced at the lighted phone display and saw Pete's name. I also noticed several missed calls from him earlier this evening.

"I've been trying to reach you for hours," Pete said on the audio-only call. "Are you okay?"

"Hi, Pete," I said, a spurt of adrenaline surging through my exhaustion. It was great to hear his voice. I settled back into bed for our pillow talk. "My phone was muted because I had a catering job tonight."

"All night?"

"All night. The Chamber's annual awards ceremony. I've been prepping all week. It was a big job I managed by myself. Everyone raved about the food."

"I nearly hopped a plane when I couldn't reach you for four hours. I worried something happened to you."

I frowned. His strong reaction to my unavailability was unusual. "I'm fine. No need for concern. I was working. I was actually concerned for you because I couldn't reach you last night. I left you two messages. What's going on?"

"Things got crazy out here again." He paused for a shaky-sounding breath. "I've had it with these people and this company. They lied to me from the start. I was a fool to come out here, to link my name to Dalbert North's. He totally misrepresented the situation and sat back to watch the fireworks."

"That sounds awful." Would he quit North Merrick? I needed more information. "What happened?"

"Just when I had everything sorted out from the last takeover attempt, another take-down team attacked the company. The cartel thugs injured two coworkers, landing one of those men in the hospital."

My eyes opened wide. "Cartel? As in drug gangs?"

"Same outfit as before. The second takeover attempt caught me by surprise. I thought we sent them packing in January, but these people are set on acquiring North Merrick no matter what I do. They play dirty. I can't turn around this business, not in a year, not in a million years. They had an inside man in accounting that I fired three days ago, and I've hired a crack team of outside accountants to find the money he stole. I'm heartbroken over what's happened."

He had my full attention. Exhaustion fled. I sat up and clutched the phone tightly. "Pete, I'm so sorry. You had high hopes for North Merrick. But a cartel? You can't fight a criminal organization by yourself. This isn't normal."

"Agreed. This is a first for me. Nothing like this happened at any of the other companies I turned around. I didn't want to worry you with details as they unfolded, but you should know what I'm up against so that you're careful too. I received three death threats this week. I've never walked away from a fight, but this is one fight I can't win. When I couldn't reach you this evening, I thought they'd abducted you to force my hand. I've never been so scared in my life. I should've remembered your catering job tonight. That's on me. Between guns and the death threats, I'm under an incredible amount of stress."

No wonder he looked so haggard on the video calls lately. And no wonder he hadn't answered my call the night before. "No amount of money is worth this level of pressure. You're essentially working in a war zone. Run, don't walk away. Rest assured, I'm fine. I would've kept my phone on if I knew about your situation. Are you okay?"

"I just left the hospital where I was sitting with a loyal staffer who got shot. Please carry your phone tomorrow. You're more than the love of my life, you're my lifeline in a sea of corporate corruption."

"Shot? They're shooting people?" My voice broke as I talked. I took a moment to regain control. I needed to be the voice of reason. "It's not safe for you out there. I thought corporate takeovers happened via computer or through share acquisition. Your life is at risk. I'm scared for you. I'm sorry your employee got shot, but I'm happy you were spared, even if that makes me a bad person."

"You're not a bad person. You're kind and generous. I'm serious about your phone though. You'll keep it handy tomorrow?"

"Of course, but my phone will be muted again for part of the day," I said. "Estelle's funeral is tomorrow."

"Oh." He hesitated. "You still searching for her missing son?"

"Yes. Now more than ever, I owe it to her to find Chili."

"I wish you would let it go. Someone beat that woman to death."

He meant well. I said that to myself silently before I spoke. "I'm careful."

An uneasy silence settled on the line until he said, "Two guys from Shell Island called me about the deputy who accompanied you to the bars. They thought I should know about the man you were dating. Their words, not mine."

The air went out of my sails at his comment, and emotion colored my words. "It wasn't a date. I told you Deputy Hamlyn accompanied me to the bars. It wasn't a big deal to either of us, and I thought you were happy I had backup."

"I wasn't happy he was with you instead of me, but I trust you. It's just the irritating calls on top of everything else kept me running on fumes all week."

"You have nothing to worry about here. I assume you're coming home. Shall I fly out to help you pack?

"It isn't safe for you here, though that's exactly where I want you. I'll manage."

"I wish you were here already," I countered. "Come home, let's live our lives together. You need a new job without death threats."

"You're the woman I want to spend my life with. Don't give up on me, River. I'm sorting things out here, and I need to know you're safe in the meantime."

"I'm safe. The doors and windows are locked. Major is out back."

"Major?" His tone soured. "Who's he?"

"A cat. I acquired a black cat this week. Didn't I mention him already?" I yawned and sagged back into the pillows. "Sorry. I'm so tired I can barely keep my eyes open. It's been a long day and a grueling week. I miss you."

"Miss you too. I want to be with you, and I'll make it happen. Hang in there."

"Be safe tomorrow. Love you."

"Love you."

The call ended, and I stared at the shadowed bedroom ceiling. Pete's company was under siege again. Others got hurt but Pete was okay. He would fix things, but he'd sunk his life savings into North Merrick. Getting his money out and walking away from a company that had his name on it would be difficult.

But at least he was talking about it.

Progress.

Chapter Fourteen

People occupied every seat of The Place of Prayer and ringed the walls. I stared at the cavernous space, built of no-frill warehouse materials. Two big viewing screens crowned a raised platform complete with a podium, microphones, and a dozen musical instruments. The traditional padded pews surprised me, but I'd never stepped foot in here before, so I shouldn't have had any expectations one way or the other.

Local ministers had been alarmed when this windowless box of a church went up. The sheer size of it was daunting. Then they'd scoffed because the preacher, a woman named Debra Findlay, would never fill the seats. They'd been wrong about this place and Pastor Debra.

I wandered down the carpeted center aisle, looking for a place to sit, nodding at the people I recognized from last night's dinner. Lucky for me, Vivian Declan waved me up to her pew, third from the front on the left. She stepped out in a cloud of something sinfully sexy to squeeze me in between her and Ms. Milly, one of the bridge ladies, who mostly smelled like moth balls.

"Hey, Ms. Milly," I said respectfully. "Good to see you."

She gave a terse nod of her cap of tight, white curls. "Good to be sitting on this side of the stage."

At that, I glanced to a nearby table holding an urn and a photo of Estelle. The azalea I sent sat on the floor in front of the table. "Me too." I turned to Viv and spoke quietly. "Thanks for the seat. I didn't know Estelle had so many friends. Everyone in the community is here."

"Last of her line, if Chili's dead," Viv whispered back. "Most folks came for the show."

I couldn't conceive of a universe where a funeral was entertainment. The ones I'd attended were staid and proper. "Show?"

"Your first time at the POP?" she asked.

I nodded and even understood the acronym for Place of Prayer.

"Hold onto your hat." Viv chuckled. "This place is about to rock out."

A door near the platform opened and a group of musicians in dark clothing filed in and took places behind the instruments. Every microphone matched to a person.

The lights went down, the screens glowed, and a spotlight focused on a slight young woman. The music began and she belted out a melancholy tune while the screens flashed photos of nature until they stopped on Estelle's photo. Then the music intensified, the screens populated with words and half the people in the room stood and sang along for thirty minutes.

A traditionalist, I was surprised by the ebullient atmosphere. Prayerful and yet not what I expected for nondenominational worship. Because I couldn't see over the person in front of me if I remained sitting, I stood too, as did Viv. Ms. Milly staunchly sat on the pew.

A vibrant redhead in a black robe joined the group on the dais, and the music quieted. Prayers and words of comfort flowed from Pastor Debra. She commended Estelle on living a sober and upright life and for being a wonderful mother to her sons. The pastor often raised her arms to the ceiling theatrically, the flowing sleeves of her robe making her appear angelic. After the prayers, everyone was invited to the social hall for refreshments and to meet the family.

Viv and I exchanged glances. "What family?" I mouthed. "Chili's not here and Kale is dead."

"Should be fun. I'm game if you are," Viv said.

"There's no book," Ms. Milly complained as we filed out. "In all my days, I've never been to a funeral where there's no book to sign.

These newfangled churches aren't doing it right."

"Maybe it's next door," I suggested.

"If it is, write my name in it," she said, with a dismissive wave of her bony wrist. "I've had enough of this hoo-rah."

No one was quite sure of Ms. Milly's age. Somewhere between ninety and a hundred, but we wouldn't know for sure until she died, and maybe not even then. "Can I help you to your car?" I asked.

She nudged me out of the way with her cane. "I can part the crowd as good as Moses, and I don't want to give my great grandchildren any reason to put me in a home. I'll do it myself."

I stepped out of her way with a glance to Viv. "Yes, ma'am."

When she'd thumped her way down the aisle a piece, Viv and I shared a smile. "I hope I'm that agile at her age."

Viv put a hand on her hip. "Honey, they don't make 'em like that anymore. She's outlived all her children and most of her grandchildren. You and I will be lucky to have thirty more good years, but sixty more? Puh-lease. Besides, who wants to be that wrinkled?"

I thought of what a blessing it would be to be older, to have a wealth of children and grandchildren. I'd always dreamed of having a large family. It would happen, I silently promised myself.

We joined the throng edging toward the reception hall. From the outside, the two structures mirrored each other. Only as I was now seeing, the social hall was smaller than the church itself as it had rooms branching off it. Consequently, noise echoed in the packed hall. My gaze automatically drifted to the food table.

Rows of store-bought cookies in plastic trays on one table and another table with cups of pre-poured punch. No one attended either table. I opted not to eat the generic cookies, though I did take a cup of the warm punch.

"Who are the men by Pastor Debra?" I asked Viv, who clung to me like a blonde-headed burr.

"Didn't you hear about them?" she said, munching away on one of those sandwich cookies.

"No. Who are they?"

"They hung out at the Wine and Dine last night. Deputy Dawg kept his eagle eye on them."

I studied the two dark-suited and dark-haired men. They weren't handsome per se, but there was something about them that drew my eye. "So?"

"Get this. Ralph Ferarrelli and Anthony Barnegas say they're Estelle's long lost cousins. They moved into her house."

"That's gutsy." Neither name rang a bell. "Did they pay for her cremation?" I asked, craning my neck to see the men.

"No. That's even bigger news. Pastor Debra received an anonymous donation and instructions for Estelle's funeral. Whatever money was leftover could go to the church. There was enough money for a casket funeral, but Pastor Debra went the ashes route and pocketed the rest. Ms. Milly is furious that they treated her friend that way. She gave me quite an earful before you arrived."

Viv ought to be the one asking questions about Chili's disappearance. She had a much closer tie to the pulse of the community. "Did Ms. Milly spring for the expenses?"

"No one knows who did it. Pastor Debra found a big brown envelope of cash on her doorstep. She dutifully paid for Estelle's modest cremation expenses and banked the rest. Lance saw red when he heard about it, or so he said. The only item she had left to give him was the envelope and the letter, and those he had to fish out of the trash."

"How do you know all this?"

"Bar talk, gal. You want to know anything about this berg, hang with me at the bar."

"No thanks. Pete didn't like that at all."

"Deputy Dawg wishes you'd come back out to play."

"He shouldn't. He knew it wasn't a date last weekend."

"Speak of the devil." Viv nodded toward the determined man striding toward us, hands in his pants pockets. She rewarded Deputy Hamlyn with a broad smile. "Why, Lance. How good to see you again."

"Afternoon, Viv, River."

I managed a smile, wondering how many people would report to Pete that I'd had a conversation with Lance. Surely, no one could misconstrue this meeting as a date. There were easily a hundred and fifty people squeezed into this room.

"You find the guy that killed Estelle?" I asked.

My comment caused his head and neck to lift. "There are no leads."

I nodded toward the two strangers in the room. "What about the newfound relatives?"

He scowled. "I checked. They arrived after she was dead. I ran a background check too, just in case. No red flags."

"Viv says they moved into Estelle's place. Is that legal?"

"They claim to be her relatives."

"Claim is the operative word here. I don't believe their story, and I never heard of them before. Did you run a background check on them?"

"Why should I? It isn't like Estelle was worth millions."

I barely heard him over the animated conversations nearby, so I asked him to repeat it. Finally, I understood his words. Estelle had nearly nothing in her estate, so he thought there was no point in investigating her so-called relatives.

"What about life insurance?" I asked. "They may try to claim that."

"If they do, that's the insurance company's problem. I have no reason to vet them."

"Their sudden appearance seems suspect. Can't you run a background check on them as a favor for me?"

The two men in question flanked Lance. "Is there a problem here?" the tallest one asked.

He towered over me by six inches and walked with the rolling gate of a waterman. The threat in his voice made me retreat a step.

"No problem, Mr. Ferarrelli," Lance said.

He looked small next to the other two men. They easily outweighed him by fifty pounds and towered over him as well.

"Good." The two men walked out of the hall.

"Whew. That one's intense," Viv said. "Wonder if he's intense about everything?"

"Don't sleep with those men," Lance warned. "They're dangerous."

"I'm craving a little intensity," Viv said, trailing after the men.

"Vivian!" Lance called, but she didn't stop. "I'll rescue her in a minute. Listen, it's too loud in here. Can we meet outside to talk about the case?"

"I can come to your office on Monday morning."

"How about something sooner? Let's meet for breakfast tomorrow at Aunt Ida's. Seven too early for you?"

My mouth watered already. There was always a chance the gossip patrol slept in on Sundays. "I can make seven."

"Good. Excuse me while I keep Viv from making a mistake."

He hurried away and it occurred to me that I'd made a date with the man. Rats.

"Ms. Holloway?" a woman's voice said.

"It's River," I said to Pastor Debra. "You gave such a lovely tribute to Estelle. Thank you for that. What can I do for you?"

"Please follow me into the sanctuary."

I did, puzzled when she stopped beside Estelle's urn. "This is for you," she said.

The urn might as well be teeming with snakes. "I don't understand."

She gestured to the ash-filled container.

I searched deep for a voice. "You want to give me Estelle's ashes?"

"That's what my instructions said. You're to take possession of the ashes."

She sounded adamant. How could this be? "I read in the paper you were in charge of the arrangements."

"I did everything that was requested. Now, I'm finished."

My jaw dropped. My temples throbbed. "She should have a cemetery plot. A headstone."

"Those purchases weren't specified in my instructions. If you want those items, that's outta your pocket."

Chapter Fifteen

I was supposed to pay for Estelle's cemetery plot and headstone? I stared at the brass urn sitting on my kitchen table in bee-stung horror. As if I owned a spare cemetery plot or knew what Estelle Bolz should have on her tombstone. A person's remains were special, sacred. I couldn't dump her ashes in the backyard, and I darn sure couldn't buy the lot beside her son Kale's empty grave. Didn't matter anyway. That space was already occupied.

Best not to make a decision in haste.

How bizarre that I ended up with her ashes. We weren't blood kin. Oh, when I was little she used to say I was the daughter she never had. She knew my mom. I knew her kids. Chili had never been my boyfriend or even my best friend. We were friends. As adults, we'd done business together, but omigosh.

Her ashes rested in my kitchen.

"Welcome home, Estelle," I said to the urn. "Make yourself comfortable while I change into comfy clothes. I still don't know where Chili is, and I don't know who beat you to death."

To my relief, neither Estelle nor the urn replied. I texted Viv to see if she made it home okay, and she said she was fine. After I donned shorts and a sleeveless blouse, I grabbed a glass of iced tea and a book and padded to the front porch. I turned on the ceiling fans and settled in for an afternoon of relaxation. Just me and my favorite author. I deserved a vacation after the week I'd had.

Not three pages into the story, Lance's SUV rolled into my drive. So much for my time out. I sighed as he sauntered up the sidewalk, hands in his pockets, in his usual polo shirt with the sheriff's office emblem on it and black pants. His heavy aftershave preceded him up the stairs.

"Afternoon, Deputy Hamlyn." I gestured to the empty rocker near the glider I occupied. "Have a seat if you like."

"Hey, River." He eased into the rocker. "Good to see you taking it easy."

"At Estelle's funeral today, I realized life is short. I need breaks from responsibilities or I'll turn into a drone." I nodded to my glass. "Would you like water or tea?"

"I'm good. Got a question for you about the funeral and decided not to wait until morning to have this conversation. See or hear anything related to either case?"

Uh-oh. Breakfast at Aunt Ida's was definitely off. "I got nothing. You learn anything new?"

"The only new-to-you information I have is the Bolz brothers had criminal records. Each caught several speeding tickets and one DUI arrest. Both did community service after dyeing the water in the city hall fountain."

I grinned at the memory of a happier time. "I'd forgotten about that prank for Kale's graduation. Neon green as I recall."

"That's right. Glowed in the dark too, the file stated."

"How'd they pull that off?" I wondered.

"The file said Kale claimed he'd overheard someone talking about a similar prank elsewhere, so he researched it online and purchased bioluminescent sea algae to doctor the fountain. Despite their good-old-boy exteriors, both Bolz sons had decent smarts."

He was talking about them both in past tense. He believed Chili was dead? I wouldn't. I couldn't give up hope. "You weren't even here then."

Lance rocked slowly in his chair. "True. I lived in Texas. But the sheriff kept meticulous notes on everything."

"That doesn't sound like the Sheriff Vargas I know. If you've got good records, it's because of his office manager."

Lance watched a car go by before he answered. "Doesn't matter who recorded the information. The upshot is that both men have a criminal history."

The following silence was freighted with meaning. I leapt from each cookie crumb of information he'd shared with mounting concern. Speeding tickets and school pranks weren't stepping-stones to murder. "Neither of them *ever* touched their mom with intent to harm. Chili wouldn't do that. He held his mother in high esteem. He would do anything for her."

The deputy sat there, poker-faced and still, waiting for me to spill my guts. I no longer believed information sharing helped Chili, not if Lance twisted the facts to frame my friend. I let the silence build between us.

"What's the deal with Estelle's ashes?" he asked, his dark eyes laser sharp. "I saw you carrying the urn to your van."

Did he think I took them without permission? I wasn't liking this roundabout interrogation. "The request surprised me, but Pastor Debra insisted." Wait a minute. He was supposed to be information sharing with me. I could fish for information, same as he was doing. "Those two men who claim to be Estelle's relatives, you decided to research them?"

"Checking into them now. I'll let you know if anything turns up. Meanwhile, if I were you, I'd give those gentlemen a wide berth."

"Not a problem for me, unless they attend the Beville's golden wedding anniversary next week. Gloria Beville's daughter asked me to recreate their original wedding cake for the centerpiece of their Lowcountry Boil."

"Doug coming home to help you with that one?"

I wish my brother was done with his training. "Not yet. He's pretty much stuck there for the whole term until he passes all the certification testing. But I did the Chamber dinner by myself. I can do this one too."

Lance's face took on a calculating expression. "You have all the equipment you need?"

Where was he going with this? Did he think I didn't know my profession? "I've catered this meal plenty of times. All the prep work is done ahead of time. Then it's a matter of sequentially adding the food to the pot and monitoring the cook time."

"That's on Thursday, right?"

"Yeah. Were you invited?"

"Yes. I plan to attend, so I can lend you a hand."

My first impulse was to argue with him. I didn't want to spend time with him socially, but an extra set of hands would be nice. "Well, okay."

"You don't sound enthusiastic."

I scowled at him. "Extra help is often more trouble than it's worth. Say, Garnet mentioned Chili kept his charter bookings on his phone calendar. Any chance of loaning me his phone to notify his clients?"

"Not a chance," Lance said, "because I don't have it. His phone is missing."

"Didn't know that." I paused to regroup. "Did you track it?"

"I know how to do my job, River, but to answer your question, yes. His phone is out of service. I can't track it."

Sobering news. No Chili and no phone. Things didn't look good for my friend.

Later that afternoon, Dasia and Jerry Allen dropped by. I'd never seen Dasia's face so animated. It looked like she was fixing to bust from good news. Her jet black hair appeared blue in this light.

"Hey, y'all. Come on in." I waved the tall couple inside. "Would you like some tea?"

"No thanks, though we have a business proposition for you," Jerry said, waving his briefcase. "Is this a good time?"

I motioned them past the living room and into the kitchen. "Sure. Let's sit at the table if we're talking business."

They followed but stopped short of the table. "What?" I asked.

Dasia pointed to the urn. "You've got Estelle?"

Heat flushed my face as I hurried forward to move Estelle to the pantry. She just fit on the lower shelf. I slid into my seat. "Long story. What can I do for you?"

"Jer and I've been talking about the future," Dasia said, sitting beside Jerry. "We do okay with Neptune's Harvest, but we want to expand."

"Okay," I said, testing the waters.

"We have connections to nearly every commercial fisherman in the state. Further, we know which people are reliable, and which ones should be avoided, for a variety of reasons. We've fool-proofed our supplier list."

My face felt tight like a mask. Why were they talking to me about their business dealings?

"We're having a baby," Dasia burst in. "We're planning ahead, wanting to be financially secure. College may not be in our kid's future. Heck, neither of us went to college, but we want to be set so that college could be an option. Bottom line, we need to make more money."

"Don't we all." I laced my fingers atop the table.

"We got to talking these last few weeks," Jerry said, "and it would be better financially if our income didn't vary so much. We're sure you're in the same boat."

I nodded. "My income varies from week-to-week. I pay my bills and save any extra toward the next money pit disaster."

"What if we had a fool-proof idea for making consistent income?" Dasia's eyes gleamed. "Would you want in?"

"I'm a one-woman show, but I'm happy to listen to your idea."

"You're the best cook in the county, hands down," Jerry said.

"We want you to come into business with us," Dasia blurted.

"In addition to our reputable supplier base, we have contacts up and down the Eastern Seaboard, a network of retail outfits like us," Jerry said. "Don't you see? It's perfect!"

Nothing was perfect or even clear. They had seafood. They thought I was a good cook. "I don't understand."

Jerry and Dasia looked at each other and then said together, "River Cakes!"

I had no idea what River Cakes were, but they scared the pants off me.

Chapter Sixteen

Dasia clasped her hands together, her face luminous. "It's perfect. We can't charge supermarket prices for River Cakes, but with limited and consistent distribution to other wholesale outlets like ours, a boutique food product like this would flourish."

It was all I could do not to rub my temples. The Allens thought they had a winning idea to make us all rich, but I was still in the dark about the details. "You're excited about River Cakes, which I assume you want me to make. What are they?"

"Your crab cakes! *Everyone* knows they're the best in the world. People will shell out big bucks for your crab cakes."

I shook my head. "My crab cakes are too expensive for most consumers. People will pass them up for the heavily breaded and affordable ones in any supermarket's frozen food section. Besides, I don't mind cleaning a dozen crabs for a specialty seafood dinner every now and then, but this sounds like I'd be picking crabs every day. No way."

Dasia jumped up and planted her hands on the kitchen table. "What if you didn't have to pick the crabs? We're considering hiring pickers several days a week. We could make an exclusive deal with you for the meat. It would be win-win for both of us."

The idea sparked in my mind, and then the potential for failure snuffed it out. "You're saying I'd have sufficient picked crab to make into crab cakes. That product would be perishable. If the crab cakes didn't sell before their expiration date, I'd be stuck with an expensive picked crab bill, my ingredients, and the loss of my time for a day. No thanks. It isn't a good deal for me."

"I see where you are coming from," Jerry said, his face lit with enthusiasm, "but hear us out. We could offer small batches on a trial basis in our shop. You know, I'll bet a good local market would be Creekside Grill. They'd pick them up for one of their weekly lunch specials."

People had been after me for years to mass produce this or that. I'd investigated the process and it was so much more work, plus cooking for larger scale operations was often hired out or done in large scale batches. Cooking was the part of my profession I loved. I didn't want to lose that connection and become a number cruncher. I loved the status quo.

However, Jerry and Dasia were so enthused about this. Was I even giving the proposal a chance? What if the financial risk could be minimized?

"I appreciate your faith in me and my crab cakes," I stated calmly. "This idea is intriguing, but bringing a consistent product to market, creating attractive packaging, licensing, and more, well, the process takes my breath away. How could I get it all done and keep Holloway Catering afloat? I'm a one-woman show."

"And we're a two-person show," Jerry persisted as he tugged Dasia into her seat. "We can do this by providing the picked crab and serving as your wholesale vendor. Will you at least consider this idea? We could start small, with pickers working one day a week, and you whipping out a dozen River Cakes for weekend sales."

He sounded confident. I had to be the voice of reason. "Why would islanders buy expensive crab cakes when they can create their own? After all, that's the beauty of living here. You can spend the day catching crabs and then have a crab boil. There's no cost involved."

"Many people don't have time to crab," he countered. "Others don't want that crab boil smell in their yard or don't want to pick the meat. And even if they picked the meat for crab cakes, they'd lose. Their crab cakes can't hold a candle to yours. Think about summer tourists. They can't get enough fresh local seafood and they're willing to pay for it. Residents will jump at the chance to purchase your fresh crab cakes for special company. Everyone will pay a higher price for a premium product."

"I hear what you're saying." This new idea was more my speed. "The smaller-scale idea for River Cakes appeals to me, but it ties me up one day a week for crab cake production. Let's talk specifics. What would you charge me for ten pounds of picked meat?"

He named a figure and it didn't suck. For a specialty item, people expected more than a quarter pound of meat, so three crab cakes to a pound. Mental alarms blared. The margin was bad. "I'm hanging up on the accounting angle. I could bring the product to market, and even if they sell out, still be in the red."

"That's where our partnership pays off. River Cakes would bring people to our store. Once we see heavier foot traffic and collateral sales, we can absorb more of the picker labor cost, giving you a price break. Both of us would have close margins initially. That's a risk everyone takes in business."

We talked about possibilities until my head buzzed. "Let me think it over for a few days. I need to factor in the price of bulk spices, which may lower my production costs."

They left and I surveyed my house. It was serviceable, nothing fancy, and I liked it that way. Going into the River Cakes business was risky. My products would be available commercially, but would that hurt my catering business in unexpected ways? Would my customers stockpile crab cakes in their freezers and cease booking me for their special events?

To offset that eventuality, I might need to charge as much for the crab cakes as I would for catering a crab cake dinner so that there would be a tangible value added for my catering service. Only, who would pay that much for a crab cake?

If I got into financial trouble, I might not be able to pay my taxes. I could lose my home.

Aye yai yai. So much for a relaxing afternoon at home. I set aside my book and reached for the calculator.

*   *   *

That evening, Pete sounded tired on the phone. "You all right out there?" I asked, sitting up in bed.

"I'm surviving," he said. "How're things at your end?"

After spending hours thinking about River Cakes, I needed to focus on another reality, the one where Pete and I spent a few days together. "I've got a catering job this week, but I could hop a plane after that, if you want company."

"It isn't safe out here for you."

"For you either."

"I've reached out to three potential buyers for my shares of North Merrick. They've been impressed with the company's performance this year. I could have a deal in hand very soon."

"Will a buyout satisfy the terms of your original deal with Dalbert North?"

"If I make sure his employees are protected, Dal will give his blessing. He's happy not to be involved in the day-to-day operation of his firm. He doesn't want to be CEO again. Enough about me. What's happening at home?"

Every time he used the word home, I glowed inside. He would come home soon. I clung to that thought as I gave him a rundown of the funeral and the subsequent business offer to make River Cakes. "It's never a dull moment here."

"Wish I was there. It won't be much longer until I can shed this company like a bad sunburn."

"I'm sorry North Merrick didn't work out."

"Life is like that. Opportunities arise and you don't know if they're golden unless you try them. North Merrick isn't the right fit for me. It's been a struggle since day one, and it nearly ended us. Hang in there, River."

"We're in this together, but the separation is hard on me. I miss you. I want you here so we can share each sunrise together."

"I want that too. It'll happen, babe."

"I'm counting on it." My grip tightened on the phone. "I need your advice on a business matter. I'm on the fence about the specialty product called River Cakes that I would make in batches. I ran the figures several times and it could work. Of course, the more volume, the better the price point, but I'm struggling with direction. Is this something I should do? Would trying this limit us or add stress to our relationship?"

"I can't help you with direction. That's your decision. I'm happy to review your figures if you like. Have you researched start-up grants? Someone at the Chamber may have a direct line to seed money for a new start up."

"Didn't think of that. Thanks for the tip."

"About the other..."

"What other?" I asked.

"The Bolz situation. As far as I'm concerned, the farther you distance yourself from Estelle Bolz and her missing son, the better."

I thought about Estelle's ashes, no longer stuck in my pantry. "I'm committed to learning the truth. Something doesn't sit right with all of this. Nothing hangs together in regard to motive or opportunity. If the truth is out there, it darn sure found a good hiding place."

"Some truths are like that," Pete said.

Chapter Seventeen

The next few days passed in a blur as I prepped for the Gloria and Harold Beville golden wedding anniversary party on Thursday. Major the cat was noticeably absent, but I hoped he'd return.

On the day of the occasion, I arrived an hour early at the location, Marsh Hammocks. After setting up my steamer pot outside, I wheeled out the tubs of shucked corn, red potatoes, chopped sausage, peeled onions, carrots, and thirty pounds of shrimp. On the next hand truck load, I carted tubs of spices, four pounds of softened butter, a half-gallon of cocktail sauce, a dozen salt and pepper shakers, two deep tubs of coleslaw, and four pans of cornbread. The last load included my dispensers of sweet and unsweet tea, along with a water dispenser topped off with citrus slices.

My friend Patsy Wilson set up a wine bar on the opposite side of the swimming pool. We exchanged nods as we each prepared for the guests.

Red and white checkered tablecloths draped a dozen tables for eight under a pavilion. Each table held a pillar candle surrounded by seashells and sand dollars. Ceiling fans whirled overhead. Festive lights ringed the eaves and circled the palms and oaks. Stacks of dinnerware and the buffet serving tables were already set up inside the pool house where I'd be serving. I stashed my cornbread in the oven to keep warm. Coleslaw went in the fridge, condiments on the buffet table. Everything else I hauled to the prep station beside the cooker. I immediately fired the burner to heat the cook-pot water.

I wrestled with the big concave slab of oak to get it strapped to my hand truck, then I wheeled it down the ramp and wrangled it on the table. This specialty serving piece was the perfect accompaniment for a Lowcountry Boil. I'd oiled the wood grain to a sheen, and the bright colors of each ingredient would add to the eye-pleasing entrée.

Lastly, I unloaded the wedding cake to a free-standing table in the pool house. The cake tiers were perfect as were the original ceramic bride and groom figures from the cake of fifty years ago. I hoped the Bevilles loved it.

I'd just dumped in a handful of Lowcountry Boil seasoning mix into the heating water when Deputy Lance Hamlyn caught my eye. He wasn't wearing his work clothes, but with a red polo shirt and dark jeans on, he looked like he could spring into law enforcement mode in an instant.

"You got here early," Lance said, stopping close to me. As usual, his hands were in his pockets.

My eyes watered at what must be a double dose of his aftershave. The man could do with some moderation. Retreating a step, I reached for a long-handled spoon to stir my simmering pot. "Had a lot to unload."

He frowned. "You should've texted me your arrival time. I expected to do the heavy lifting."

"I got this," I said resolutely. His disapproving tone rubbed me the wrong way. In truth, he was starting to irritate me any way I looked at it. I could barely leave my house without him turning up. I didn't need a keeper.

"What's left to do?" Lance asked.

"The cooking."

"I can help with that. We dump everything in the pot, right?"

"If we were making enough for a small group, that'd be right. To make enough for a hundred people. I'd need a really big pot. So I'll cook everything sequentially in my normal-sized pot."

"I'm your guy. Tell me what goes in when."

I didn't exactly need his company, but I didn't want to antagonize him either. Getting on the wrong side of the law would truly wreck my future.

"I've got a check list. I'm adding some sausage to each pot of veggies, and then we'll boil the shrimp last. They want the meal ready at five thirty, so that's our target time."

I pointed to the veggies in turn as I scooped out the right proportion of each to add to the boiling water. "We'll repeat this five times."

"Got it." He covered the pot with the lid. "Have you thought about a larger pot?"

"Takes too long to heat more water." I gestured at a stack of pans on the nearby food cart. "The aluminum pans are to collect each batch as it comes out of the pot."

"How'll you remove the food without losing the heated water?"

With the fragrant spices perfuming the air, I no longer smelled his aftershave. Lucky me. "I've got a sieve on a stick. My brother made it for this purpose."

"You've thought of everything."

"I wish. There's always something I could've done better."

"I've never heard any complaints about Holloway Catering, so you're doing a great job of customer satisfaction."

"The biggest shortcoming looming in my face is failing Estelle. Now she's gone, and we don't have any idea who killed her or where her son is."

Lance grimaced. "I thought we'd leave the case at the office. This is a party. Would you like something from the wine bar?"

"No thanks. I don't drink when I'm working. And I hoped to mention Chili's name to people here. Take the evening off the case if you like, but I'm not."

"You're a handful, you know that?" Lance asked, moving close to crowd me again.

I didn't miss how his voice roughened and dropped to a more private volume. Retreating, I reminded him, "I have a boyfriend."

He made a show of looking around. "No boyfriend in sight."

I didn't like his attitude or his version of the truth. "Pete is coming home soon. He has a few business hiccups right now."

"He shouldn't leave you to fend for yourself."

Annoyance colored my voice. "He didn't leave me. I chose to stay here initially. Then his job became dangerous, so he asked me to stay here."

"Still, with your looks and the way you cook, he should've put a ring on your finger."

I planted my feet and barred my arms. "I don't care for your tone or your macho mindset. I'll have you know Pete asked me to marry him."

"No ring on your finger," he repeated.

The timer rang, so I started scooping veggies into the pan. "Not that it's any of your business, the lack of a ring is my fault. He proposed. I wanted to make sure of our feelings for each other."

He had the grace to look flustered. "Well, damn."

I gestured to the clusters of people arriving. "You're under no obligation to help me. Be a guest tonight. I don't need a helper. Circulate."

"I said I'd help and I meant it."

"Even if I won't date you?"

"Even so. I'd rather be over here than out there. Everyone treats me like I'm a cop. You treat me like a person."

"People here are slow to trust outsiders." I sealed the pan of cooked veggies with foil while Lance scooped the next batch of veggies into the pot. I sprinkled more spice on top.

"That's true, but you're different."

"My parents stressed treating others as you'd like to be treated, and that's what I do. If you want a friend, be a friend."

"Like my helping you?"

"Branch out to make other friends. What are your interests? Do you like hunting, fishing, sports, the arts?"

He shook his head. "No."

"What subjects interested you in school?"

"Cars. Girls. Sex."

"Sounds like you share interests with Vivian Declan."

"I'm interested in you."

"Refocus, guy. Not happening."

He grinned. "See. You make me smile."

"You're impossible."

Gloria Beville's daughter Josey joined us. She raved about the cake and asked if I could move up the dinner timeline.

I shook my head. "The meal you requested has a defined cook time, and I need every minute between now and five thirty to have all the food ready at the same time. My only option at this point is to consider making two different boils. That means some guests will have a longer wait for their food while others are eating."

"No. Mother wouldn't like that. Neither my brother nor I can get the audio-visual stuff to work and my dad is bored. He wants to go home."

I looked at Lance. He used technology in his job. "Lance can give you a hand with the AV equipment."

Lance shot me a thunderous expression. "Be a friend," I mouthed silently.

"Sure," Lance said. "I'll take a look at it."

When they went off together and the slide show began, I heaved a sigh of relief. I also got my batches cooked more efficiently. Lance didn't return, and I noticed he wandered through conversational groups. I could only imagine how those conversations were going. Most of the older crowd would want to know who his family was. From the way each group he joined dispersed, I guessed he wasn't making connections.

Soon, the meal was cooked. The buffet line started, and then I kept busy replenishing the serving table.

After the guests filled their plates, Patsy from the wine station came through the line and saw me removing an empty pan of cornbread. "No!" she cried, her hand covering her heart.

I stashed the pan on my service cart and pulled the last one from the oven. "It's okay. I have one more."

"That's good because I have been dreaming about your cornbread all evening. Think anyone would mind if I took three slices?"

"My lips are sealed."

She loaded her plate, but before she left she leaned in and asked, "You heard anything about Chili?"

"I haven't had a chance to speak to people tonight. This meal required a lot of tending and I cooked everything on site."

"It looks and smells amazing. I hope you never move away. I'm in a serious, committed relationship with your cornbread. But I'd give up cornbread if Chili came home."

"I want that too."

"Deputy Dawg hasn't found anything?"

"Not that he's shared with me."

"He's a conversational Black Hole. He inadvertently sent plenty of people over for drink refills when their glasses were nearly full. Good for the Wine and Dine's bottom line because we're paid by how many empty bottles we have, but bad for the hostess."

"Gosh, I don't understand. He's easy to talk to."

"You're easy to talk to. I've always wanted to be just like you, and not be so shy."

"You're not shy about your job."

"That's easy because it isn't personal. None of the guys around here have ever flirted with me, but Chili talked to me like I was a human being."

"He didn't talk to many people."

"That's right, he didn't, which makes me sad that he's missing. I should be doing something. I've gone out a few times in my little jon boat, checking to make sure he isn't in the marsh or on one of the marsh hamlet islands, but I don't know what else to do."

"I'm at a loss too. He's been gone for over a week now. I want to find him as much as you do."

"He better hurry home or he won't have one. Those so-called relatives of his are making a lot of noise inside Estelle's house."

If I were a dog, my ears would've pricked up. "What do you mean?"

"I heard it at the post office this morning. Ola Mae and Valerie were complaining about the racket."

Ola Mae Reed and Valerie Slade were sisters who lived next door to Estelle's house. They would certainly know what those men were doing over there. Something I needed to check out, first thing on Friday.

Chapter Eighteen

"What a treat to see you, dear, please come in." Ola Mae waved me and my plate of cookies into their dark parlor the next morning, while her sister Valerie bustled off to the kitchen. I couldn't remember the last time I'd been in their house, maybe twenty years ago when I was selling fundraiser gift wrap for elementary school. Everything looked the same. Dark wood chests topped with marble and draped with lace marched along the walls. Floral sofas squared off against each other, while gold drapes paired with lacy sheers to guard the windows.

Widowed in her forties, Valerie moved in with Ola Mae, who was also a widow. I believed Ola Mae was the oldest sister by a few years, but it was difficult to tell. These dainty, petite seniors were pushing the heck out of ninety by my estimation, and my guess was neither one of them weighed a hundred pounds soaking wet.

Valerie returned with tumblers of iced tea and small plates for the cookies. Her thin hands shook as she passed a glass to me. She bit into a cookie and hummed in delight. "You truly have a gift. Never stop cooking. I haven't tasted anything this decadent in years. Now you didn't come to hear me natter on about your cookies. To what do we owe the pleasure of your visit?"

"Thanks for the tea and the compliment, though I'm sure you know why I really dropped by." I accepted the tea and carefully set the tumbler on a coaster. Rumor had it that both ladies poisoned their husbands so I knew better than to consume anything they made. "Before she died, Estelle asked me to look into her son's disappearance. I haven't discovered anything helpful so far, but last night I heard about the commotion next door. What's happening in

Estelle's house?"

"We're concerned," Ola Mae said. "Her shade-tree relatives are tearing the place apart."

The thought of the older house next door being gutted saddened me. "Are they dismantling the interiors to sell the wood?"

"Doubt it," Ola Mae said. "Nothing is passing through those doors but those nasty men, going for pizza or carry-out. No one's emptied the garbage. That place must reek to high heaven."

"Besides the hammering and sawing," Valerie said, "we hear things breaking over there. I bet they smashed all of Estelle's good china and pawned the silver. It isn't right. Those hooligans have no respect for Estelle's property."

"Did you call the police?" I asked.

"We did. A nice young man came over, took down our complaint. Sat right where you're sitting. He drank tea and ate four cookies. Then he went next door. We opened the window to hear him. He told the men to keep the noise down, and that was it. The deputy drove away, and the noise resumed immediately. Those men are disrespectful."

The deputy must not've known not to eat here, meaning he was an outsider. Chances were Deputy Lance Hamlyn, the newcomer on the force, took the call. At least he listened to the ladies. It wasn't his fault the men next door resumed their noisy work as soon as he departed.

I thought back to my arrival and walking up Ola Mae's sidewalk a few minutes ago. "I didn't hear any banging when I came up your walk."

"They're sneaky that way," Valerie said, waggling a bony finger. "They think nobody pays attention to two doddering old fools next door, but they're wary of strangers."

"We should go to the police station right now and file a formal complaint. That would net you another cop visit next door."

"That nice young deputy said he'd take care of all that," Ola Mae said. "He's a handsome devil. If I was sixty years younger, I'd make a play for him."

Ola Mae and Lance. I couldn't imagine them together, but then I'd never known Ola Mae or her sister when they were younger. To my knowledge, they were the oldest seniors in Riceland County who still lived independently.

Even so, this destruction shouldn't be continuing. "We should request a copy of that report, to make sure he filed it."

"You youngsters aren't very trusting. The cop said he did it, and I believe him. Now if you can send him over for tea and cookies again, we'd love that."

"I think I know which deputy you mean. The new one, right?"

"They all look new and young to us," Ola Mae joked. "He said his name was Hamlet. I asked if he knew the story and he didn't. Imagine being named Hamlet and never reading that classic. So then I asked if he knew Shakespeare, and he said he'd never had the pleasure."

Hamlet, huh. Sure sounded like Hamlyn to me. "Got it. I'll ask him about the police report, just to be on the safe side. Meanwhile, do you ladies feel safe here? Have those men next door threatened you?"

Ola Mae shook her head. "No, can't say as they have. Mostly they look right through us. Valerie and I wondered if we were already invisible. We hope to be raptured up instead of going through the throes of death."

"Good luck with that." I smiled at them and rose. "I need to get going. Thank you for your hospitality and the information."

"It's great to see you," Valerie said, showing me to the door. "Please come again. And if we don't speak again before we pass, we'll tell your mama what a good job you're doing."

My eyes teared up at thought of them visiting with my mom in heaven. "Thanks."

I hadn't gone three blocks from their house before my phone rang. Technology and the car company linked my phone to the van's audio system, so the caller ID came up on the dashboard screen.

Deputy Lance Hamlyn. What did he want now? "Hello," I said.

"I kept meaning to ask you to bake cookies for the guys at the station, but I forgot. Today's the office manager's birthday, and I know it's short notice, but could you bring something over this afternoon?"

"I have emergency chocolate chip cookies on hand, or I could bake something fresh. What's your preference and how much time do I have?"

"Three o'clock would be perfect. Bring a cake with Fran's name on it and the cookies. How much for all that?"

I quoted him a price, and he agreed to it. "How many people we talking about?"

"At least a dozen, maybe more if we leave enough for second shift."

"Sounds like you need a sheet cake then. What kind?"

"Anything as long as you put the icing from last night on it."

"Gotcha. See you at three."

I turned and drove to the grocery store. I needed a lot more eggs and butter to fill this order. Belatedly, I realized I should've asked Lance about Ola Mae and Valerie's police report. Oh, well, I'd see him at three.

Chapter Nineteen

Somehow, I squeezed tutoring between baking the cake and icing it. My new kitty cat hadn't reappeared, and I was concerned for his welfare. Major needed someone who looked out for him.

I piped out "Happy Birthday Fran" in pink atop the buttercream frosting. It looked darn good, if I did say so myself. Carefully, I boxed the cake and plated the thawed cookies. It would be a shame if I got all the way to the Riceland County Sheriff's Office on the mainland and they had no plates and forks. I gathered up spare plates, napkins, and forks left over from other gigs.

The drive passed quickly, and I wheeled my cart of goodies into the lobby.

Fran Lipinksi rose from her seat and buzzed me into the administrative side of the building. Though she had an entry level job, she'd dressed as if it were Easter Sunday in her orange sherbet colored suit, dyed-to-match pumps, and perfectly bobbed chestnut hair.

"Happy Birthday," I said as I followed her down a corridor.

"I can't believe that rookie did this for me," Fran exclaimed. "He's the nicest guy. He even takes extra shifts nobody wants." She gazed longingly at the cake. "I can't wait to taste this. I've heard great things about your baking. Deputy Hamlyn came in this morning raving about that meal you cooked last night, especially the cake. I love me a good cake."

"I hope you love buttercream frosting. Lance specifically requested it for you. I put it over a butter cake."

"Sounds perfect." Fran ducked into a utilitarian breakroom that had a kitchenette on one side and a narrow table for eight on the other. Two industrial-looking coffee machines hogged the counter, so I placed the cake on the table with the cookies. It hardly took another few seconds to put out the forks and plates.

I glanced over at Fran. "Do you have a large knife? Otherwise, I can grab my cake knife from the van and cut the cake before I leave."

"I've got a knife right here," the woman said, pulling a serrated knife from a drawer. "Go ahead and slice half of it. I want a big piece. It is my birthday after all."

"Not waiting for the singing of Happy Birthday before you try it?" She gave me a do-it look. "Got it. This knife will do fine." I had noticed on the way in that this place looked deserted. "Where is everyone?"

"Briefing room. Big news today, didn't you hear?"

"No. I've been too busy to turn on the radio or TV. What happened?"

"Since the story is already splashed on the news, I can share what I know. Remember that dead man? The one that died at sea six months ago?"

Wow! A chill slid down my spine. She was talking about Kale Bolz. "I remember."

"He rose from the dead. Literally. Turns out, he was hiding in Florida all this time. He faked his death, so now we charge him for it and for all the wasted rescue effort. He'll go to jail for a long time."

To say I was stunned was an understatement. How could he do this to his mother? To Chili? To his friends? "Unbelievable. Where is he?"

"In transit. A few deputies went to meet the Florida officials at the Georgia-Florida line. Since the offense happened in our jurisdiction, we get first crack at him."

"Why'd he do it?" I asked.

"Don't know." Fran paused to sample her cake. A blissful expression spread over her face. "Oh my gosh. This is the best dessert I've ever tasted. I wish I didn't have to share this cake with another soul, but eating this whole thing would make me fat. Girl, you have ruined me for any other cake!"

"Glad you like it." Energized by the news of Kale being alive and hopeful the brothers might somehow be reunited, I made quick work of slicing half the cake. "Any chance of seeing Deputy Hamlyn before I go?"

"You could ordinarily, but he rode shotgun on the pick-up route. Said to tell you he'd get with you later to pay his bill."

Usually I got a hefty deposit for any catering job. This request happened on the fly today, so Lance hadn't paid me a dime. Would I ever see that money? He'd better pay me.

I handed Fran the sealed invoice. "Make sure he gets this."

"Will do."

Nothing more I could do about getting paid right now, so my thoughts slid to another matter. "This morning I visited Ola Mae Reed and Valerie Slade. They're upset about the noise coming from Estelle Bolz's house. Although I guess its Kale's house now. Anyway, the sisters told me Deputy Hamlyn responded to their noise complaint. They'd like a copy of his report."

Fran's eyebrows furrowed. "I don't remember seeing a noise complaint pass through our report pipeline. All of them cross my desk. You sure he wrote it up?"

"The ladies said he did, and then they said he stopped next door to speak to the two loud men."

She tossed her empty plate and plastic fork in the trash. "Don't tell anyone I'm doing this, but I'll show you the log."

I followed her to her desk and then stood behind her as she pulled up Deputy Hamlyn's online report folder. She typed in Ola Mae Reed's name and hit search. Nothing. Valerie Slade's name. Nothing.

I didn't doubt Ola Mae and Valerie's word for a heartbeat. Why didn't Lance write up that call? "That's odd. Men who claim to be Estelle's cousins are destroying her house. I'm making a formal request for another patrol officer visit to their home. Those men are disturbing the peace and more."

Fran pursed her lips. "You have to fill out a form as a walk-in."

"All right." I sat down at a chair by her desk and wrote out my complaint.

She scanned it into the system. "The deputy on patrol in this sector will get the notification. Someone will check within the hour, depending on where they are on their patrol route."

"Thanks. Maybe this deputy will make a record of his visit."

The next morning Ola Mae phoned me first thing. "You've got to come over here. You won't believe this."

"Believe what?" I asked, setting my coffee mug on the counter and sliding onto a kitchen stool.

"Those horrible goons," Ola Mae said. "They ruined everything. Please come see. The sooner the better."

"All right." I could've pumped her for more information, but I wanted to view the damage.

Ten minutes later, I parked in Ola Mae's driveway. One police car with flashing lights sat on Estelle's lawn. I hurried up the steps to join Ola Mae and Valerie on their porch.

"What's going on?" I asked.

"This neighborhood's gone to hell," Ola Mae said. "Not much left of Estelle's beautiful home."

I glanced at Valerie. From her glassy expression and tear-stained cheeks, the destruction upset her. "It looks the same on the outside," Valerie said, "but the inside is ruint."

"The built-in bookcases look like kindling," Ola Mae recited as she drew numbers in the air. "The drywall is all punched out. Garbage and thick dust are everywhere. Smells like the toilet overflowed. Deputy Hamlet cracked the windows over there and nearly stank us out. It's better now, but if you really breathe deep you'll smell it."

I inhaled and sure enough there it was, the foul taint of sewage. "Catch me up."

"Yesterday afternoon, a very polite youngster dropped by,

Deputy Gil Franklin. He's so handsome with those blue eyes and graying temples. Reminded me of my husband when he was that age. Anyway, he listened to our story and took notes. While he was here, the guys at Estelle's place turned on some noisy machine, and we couldn't even carry on a proper conversation over here."

"What'd he do?" I prompted when Ola Mae stopped.

Her eyes glowed with excitement. "He charged over there, knocked on the front door. One guy answered, tried to close the door on young Franklin, but the deputy wasn't having it. He hollered for the men to stop, a shot was fired, and Franklin returned fire. One guy's hurt bad, the other just winged. Before the ambulances came, Franklin cuffed the men together and to the porch. Then he asked us to watch them while he cleared the house. The guys kept groaning, but who cares? Our troubles are over now. The louts are gone, baby, gone."

I laughed at her tone and the dismissive motions she made with her hand. "That sounds good. Now you'll have peace and quiet."

"You stopped them by making another police report. Thank you." Her gleeful expression clouded. "It's such a mess over there. Nobody can live in that place now. It's a tear-down. When you find Chili, he'll be heartbroken."

"I've had no luck finding Chili." I eyed the house expectantly. The cop car had gone, though crime scene tape crisscrossed the doorway. "Excuse me, I'd like to peek in the windows next door."

"Suit yourself. Every cop in the county and most of the neighbors did the same thing."

I hurried over and peered through the windows on this side of the house. Sure enough, in most places, the walls were bare to the two-by-four studs. What on earth were those men looking for? Why would anyone think Estelle stashed something inside her walls, air ducts, or floors?

I rejoined the petite seniors on the porch. "That was historic property those men destroyed. I hope Kale Bolz sues them for damages."

"He's dead," Ola Mae said, giving me a stern look. "Pretty sure he can't sue from Davy Jones locker."

"Not dead anymore," I added, pleased to be the bearer of good news. "Yesterday, he got caught in Florida trying to renew his driver's license. Dead men don't need a license, but living ones do. He's in our jail. Because he faked his death and ran off for months, the judge said he was a flight risk and denied his bail."

"Land sakes," Ola Mae said. "Never heard tell of such a thing before."

A cop SUV cruised slowly on the street. It signaled and slowed like it was going to Estelle's house. Then the driver veered into Ola Mae's driveway and parked behind my catering van.

To my surprise, Deputy Lance Hamlyn emerged from the vehicle and joined us. I rose from my chair, but Ola Mae and Valerie sat tight. "What brings you here, Deputy Hamlyn?" I asked.

"You." He handed me a folded piece of paper and then shoved his hands in his pockets.

I opened it and saw a check for the birthday cake and cookies. "Thanks." I would deposit this payment on the way home. I gestured toward Estelle's house. "It's a shame what happened next door."

He shrugged. "We'll get to the bottom of why those men went on the offensive and tore up the house, but I gotta tell ya, I've seen a lot in this job. People do strange things."

I shook my head at his comment, eyes watering a bit from his strong aftershave. "The house wouldn't be in such dire straits if you'd filed your report and followed up. Why didn't you?"

His expression hardened. "I spoke to the men, wrote the report, and filed it. If the official paper copy is missing, that's not my fault. Our records person often misfiles records in the wrong month. How'd you even know about that?"

"A little birdy told me."

"That little birdy better watch her step or she'll be looking for a new job. It's against department policy to talk about internal procedures with civilians."

That sobered me. Fran could lose her job from me shooting my mouth off.

I must've looked stricken. Lance's lips curved momentarily. "Don't worry. It's the sweetness effect again. I swear River, you could feed the President your cake and he'd tell you state secrets. I won't say anything against Fran. I know you were trying to look after these fine ladies."

"Thank you. I didn't mean to get her in trouble. What about next door? It appears the men were searching for something. You know what's missing?"

"Sure don't. Look, I had another reason for stopping. We need you at the station. Can I give you a lift?"

Then I'd have to hitch a ride back to Ola Mae's and pick up my van before I could go home. I didn't like that scenario. "I'll follow you there. What's this about?"

"The case."

Chapter Twenty

Intending to give Kale a piece of my mind, I signed into the jail's visitation center. Thanks to technology, no prisoners were in the room, and luckily for me, no other visitors either. I sat before a computer screen and followed the directions I'd been given to contact Kale, noting the sign that stated all conversations were taped.

Kale Bolz appeared on the monitor before me. "Hey, River. Thanks for coming."

I'd known Kale Bolz for over twenty years. He looked like a paler, leaner version of himself. His blond hair, usually cut short, now brushed his shoulders in lank wisps. Wherever he'd been hiding, it hadn't agreed with him.

Revulsion and disgust at his selfish behavior rose in me. I couldn't hold my emotions inside any longer. "Shame on you, Kale. You put your family through hell. Your mother cried and cried. We thought you were dead."

"I'm sorry. I had to do it." He hung his head. "Bad people were after me. Still are, and they have a long reach."

"I don't believe you, and I can't stomach your excuses. Your mother raised you better than that."

He timidly met my heated glare. Tears filled his eyes. "She did, and if I could tell her I was sorry, I would. It was run or die. I couldn't risk her knowing I was alive. I left to protect her, but my leaving made everything worse."

His earnest words settled around me like a scratchy blanket. I didn't want to feel any sympathy for him, but I did. Kale had always been straightforward. I could see him making that choice to protect his mother. Darn it. I would not feel sorry for him. He broke the law.

"Why did you ask to see me?" I asked.

"You're my friend. I need your help. I need you to—"

"Wait." I raised a hand. "Don't put either of us in harm's way. This conversation is recorded."

"I can't help that. Please. Just listen. Someone beat Mama to death, and according to the local paper which I've been reading online, Chili's missing. He could be dead in the woods, and I'd never know. He wouldn't abandon Mama unless he had no other choice."

Rats. I believed him. I'd come in here ant-stomping mad and now I believed Kale's story. "The cops searched for him, but no luck so far."

"He knows how to live off the land and stay out of sight. I gotta believe he's out there. If not, this was all for nothing."

"What'd you get into?" I asked.

"I don't want you involved in our mess. Let's change subjects. Rumor is you have Mama's ashes."

"Pastor Debra gave them to me, saying she anonymously received the money for the cremation and instructions for the memorial service. I don't know what to do with Estelle's remains. There's your empty grave in the cemetery. Your mother gave you her spot. There isn't an empty spot adjacent to it. Should I put her ashes in your plot, since you clearly aren't dead?"

"I don't know what to do. My life isn't worth a sack of dried beans. I might be the last of my line."

"What about those cousins of yours?"

His gaze narrowed. "What cousins?"

"Two burly men at the funeral claimed they were Estelle's cousins and moved into her house. Then they took the inside apart. What were they looking for, Kale?"

Kale shook his head. His color paled even more.

"Is this why you disappeared?" I asked, needing answers.

He chewed his lip and said nothing.

"If that's all you have to say, I've got food to prepare."

"Don't go. Please find my brother."

"Your mother asked me to do that. I looked and I can't find Chili. I don't have the skills to search all the forests and swamps around here."

He took his time responding. "I heard you found Mama, that you called the ambulance."

My eyes moistened. "I wish I could've saved her, but she was too far gone."

"Was she conscious?" he asked.

"She'd been beaten pretty bad, but yeah, she roused when I spoke to her."

"Whatever she said, it means something."

"Estelle mentioned the bridge club and a chess move. I went over and talked to the bridge ladies. We don't know what she meant."

"You're our only chance, River. Keep doing what you're doing. Chili needs your help now. I'm beyond anyone's help."

"What about a lawyer?"

"That's why I asked for you. I need you to contact Jude Ernest for me."

My brows shot up. "The retired ambulance-chasing lawyer?"

"Jude Ernest is the man I want."

"Can't you call him? I don't have his number."

"Nobody has his number. You gotta go out to his place."

Word around the island was that the former Savannah shyster bought the old Ferguson place, but Ernest had been seen wandering around the county in a daze. Half the islanders thought he was a drunk, and the other half thought he had dementia. Either way, folks steered clear of him.

Maybe I could convince Patsy or Vivian to go with me, and it wouldn't be too bad. "I can't believe I'm saying this. I'll do it, but I wish you'd pick someone with good hygiene and mental acuity for your lawyer."

"He's the one I want. Promise me you'll go see Jude." His eyes drilled into me. "Alone. That's really important."

Air strained in through my clenched teeth. Kale's request boxed me in. "From his former TV commercials, he's an odd duck, and that's the most flattering thing I can say about him."

"You'll be safe with him. Please. You're like a sister to me. I wouldn't put you in danger. I need this. You're my only lifeline."

The sister card. How many times had Kale and Chili called me L'il Sis? More than I could count. They'd looked out for me in school too. I couldn't deny him this request.

"Okay," I said slowly. "I'll find the lawyer."

"And look for Chili. We can't give up on him."

"You don't ask much, do you?"

A buzzer sounded. According to the posted rules, that signaled the end of the visit. The screen would go dark regardless. "All right," I said. "I'll do it."

He nodded and faded from sight.

Chapter Twenty-One

"He tell you anything?" Lance asked when I reached the jail lobby.

After connecting with Kale and agreeing to help him, I felt the weight of every cop's censure as I exited the secure area. I shrugged and continued toward daylight. I'd never been a fan of fluorescent lightning, and today the artificial light made me feel like I'd been inside for years. "Listen to our recorded conversation."

Undeterred by my reply, Lance opened the lobby door and ushered me toward my van. I thrust on my sunglasses against the glaring sunshine. We were still in spring, so at least it wasn't blisteringly hot yet. A few more steps and I could get away from this place of locked doors, guards, buzzers, and bells.

"Why'd he fake his death?" Lance prowled along beside me, hands in his pockets. "The only thing he said when we questioned him was he wanted his one phone call. Imagine my surprise when you were his call, but you didn't answer your phone, so I went looking for you."

"Must've left my phone on silent mode this morning. Sorry to have missed that call and put you to the trouble of finding me. As for why Kale chose me, I've known the Bolz family for twenty years. Our mothers were good friends. Kale requested me because I am his friend, even though we'd lost touch in recent years."

"You don't know what he was up to?" Lance asked.

"Should I?"

He gazed at some distant point before he turned to me. "We believe Kale is connected."

My speedy pace slowed. "Connected to what?"

"Underworld figures. That explains the two goons who tore up the Bolz family home."

I watched enough police dramas on television to know where this conversation was headed. "Guns, drugs, or prostitution?"

Lance broke stride and grabbed my arm. "He tell you that?"

I wrenched free of his grip and sailed on to my vehicle. "He did not. I made a wild guess based on every cop show I've ever watched. These days there are also thieves who ply the internet stealing secrets, but I don't see Kale tapped into anything high tech."

Lance scowled. "Me neither. He mention his brother?"

"Only that he's upset by his mother's death and Chili's disappearance."

"That's it?" His neck reddened, and his face clouded. "I thought we were sharing information, partner. Aren't we on the same team anymore?"

"Listen to the tape. That's why conversations in jail aren't private, so you'll know everything." I unlocked the van and opened the door. "Kale's afraid for his life. He believes he'll die in your jail. If that happens, I won't rest until I know the truth. I'll go to every newspaper and TV show that'll have me until I get to the bottom of what happened to him."

Lance held the open door and watched me buckle my seat belt, his dark gaze unreadable. "Are you threatening me, ma'am?"

I shot him a killer smile. "Why deputy, don't you know the difference between a threat and a promise?"

If you hadn't lived on Shell Island forever or weren't an unabashed explorer, you'd never find Jude Ernest's place. Old man Ferguson hadn't added anything to make the entrance to his place stand out, and Jude must've adopted the same low-key philosophy. There were no mailboxes, street signs, or paved roads jutting off Island Road to indicate the driveway was anything more than a logging trail.

A rutted, overgrown lane through acres upon acres of pine

timber was the only access point, unless you came up the tidal creek, and good luck with that, there were no docks, no obvious access points to the property on the bluff.

Ferguson had reclusive ways and spouted conspiracy theories amidst warning of the rise of the machines. He'd died a few years back. Nobody missed him for a few months, so once his place went on the market it stayed there for years. Nobody wanted to buy the house where a crazy man had lived and died.

Then Jude Ernest arrived and the real estate sign at Ferguson's place vanished. Most people connected the dots. Since the lawyer was a bit different, no one thought anything of his presence there.

I missed the overgrown turn-off on the first pass, so I circled and eased back until I found it. Knee-deep brush obscured the lane completely. No one had been in or out of here in at least a month, maybe more. I crept slowly down the rough track until I came to a cable stretched tight across the road, about thigh-high. Stout posts in the tree line supported the cable, so there was no way I could drive around it.

This barrier hadn't been there when I was a kid. The cable looked shiny new. Jude Ernest must've installed it.

If the cable was padlocked to the post, my only option was to hike the couple of miles down to the house. I didn't want to do that. Jude Ernest didn't know me from a hole in the ground, and he had every right to protect his property. He probably shot trespassers.

Weapons. He might be armed. I didn't own a gun.

Omigosh. What if he took a shot at me? I glanced around my van for something to use for self-defense. There was my purse, my wadded up rain jacket, a few sales coupons I kept hoping to use, a pink sun hat, three empty water bottles, and two heat screens to block sunlight through the windshield on summer days. In the back I had several cases of water bottles and my service carts. That was it because I'd taken my knife roll inside for sharpening.

My gaze settled on the glove box and a memory surfaced. Before Christmas, Chili took a pocket knife out of his pocket and gave it to me. Said I needed to keep it. That the knife would protect me.

I clicked the compartment open and fumbled through the junk I kept in there, including my bugspray, until I found the knife. My fingers closed around it and I sighed in relief. The knife had a nice heft to it. Solid and yet it had many blades and whatnot that opened. I struggled with the main blade, chipping a nail, but I got it open. Then I flipped out all the other parts. Looked like I could turn regular screws, open a bottle of wine, and much more. I had no idea what to do with the hex-head thingy.

I folded everything back inside the handle except the sharp main blade. Then I exited the van and doused my clothing and shoes with high-test insect repellant. Carrying the knife, I waded through the sedge grass to the cable barrier. I followed it to a rock-solid post, where the cable spliced together. That wasn't coming apart with a knife. I traced it to the other end. Padlock.

Crap.

Tears threatened.

No. I'm stronger than this. I promised Kale I'd deliver this message. I already failed Estelle. I couldn't fail her son. Could I jimmy the lock with my knife? I yanked on the lock and the u-shaped shackle didn't budge. The tip of the knife didn't fit in the keyhole.

A duo of horse flies dive-bombed my head. Rowdy insects in the woods were making fun of me. How could I do this? Failure was not an option.

I could load my purse with water bottles and hike to the house. I knew the way. But Kale wouldn't have sent me here if I couldn't get through. *Think, River.* I studied the stout lock again, turning it over in my hands and running my fingers over its surface. There. Near the keyhole in the bottom. A small circular disc the same color as the lock. What was that about? I opened a smaller knife blade and a few minutes later, pried off the disc. Beneath it lay an irregular opening. Six-sided.

Like the hex blade on the knife Chili gave me. Coincidence? I didn't think so. I was supposed to open this lock and go down this road. I wrangled the tool in the opening until it clicked. Exulting silently, I drove my van over the dropped cable, then locked the cable again, in case anyone followed me. No point in making it easy for anyone else to get down the lane.

What had the Bolz family gotten into, I wondered as I bumped down the grassy tract, hoping I didn't bust an axle on my van. Mobile phone coverage was spotty in this area of Riceland County. If I broke down or got a snake bite, I was on my own.

So I'd do my best to make sure that didn't happen. I'd stay on the road, creep along, and when I walked in the tall grass, I'd stomp my feet like the Bolz boys taught me all those years ago. I wasn't a true outdoorsman, but it amazed me that a city lawyer would suddenly go off the grid like this.

One thing for sure, Jude Ernest would have an interesting story to tell.

Chapter Twenty-Two

The ramshackle house looked forlorn. Paint had long since been a wistful memory for the cottage. The metal roof wore a beyond-chic rusted patina. The windows glinted darkly in the clear light of day, and tall grass ringed the porch steps. If Jude Ernest lived here, he didn't use the front door.

I shut off the motor and got out of the van, Chili's knife palmed in hand. "Mr. Ernest? Kale Bolz sent me out here."

No answer. I repeated what I just said, louder.

Nothing.

I trudged through the grass, mounted the three wooden steps, and knocked on the front door. "Hello?" I called loudly. "Anybody home?"

I tried the knob. Locked. I tromped down the creaky stairs. What now? My mission had been clear. Come here and tell this lawyer that Kale needed legal representation.

Had this wilderness trek been for nothing? Did Jude Ernest even live here anymore? If I left him a note, would he see it? Kale needed a lawyer today.

I'd come so far. Might as well circle the house and try the back door. If it was open, I could leave a note in the kitchen.

Heart in my throat, I waded through the knee-high grass, promising myself a shower and tick check as soon as I got home. I called out again. "Hello, anybody here? This is River Holloway. Kale Bolz sent me."

I rounded the house and a shambling hulk of a man sat on the back steps smoking a cigar. My feet stopped moving. Several facts registered at once. The birds were still chirping, the grass was trampled back here though not a manicured lawn by any means, and an old Jeep slumbered nearby.

The knife felt uncomfortably hot in my hand. I held it out of sight. "Mr. Ernest, I'm here on behalf of Kale Bolz. He needs your help."

"Heard you the first coupla times, cutie."

The gravel-laden voice and the nickname sounded familiar. A name from my childhood surfaced. "Uncle Jay?"

"Yep. In the flesh, though I've gone to seed."

Gone to seed fit the matted gray hair, tangled beard, darkened skin, camo clothing, and stout boots. When I knew him, he'd been one of a succession of Estelle's citified beaus, each of whom we'd been instructed to call uncle this or uncle that. Uncle Jay hung around longer than most. I hadn't seen him in ten years, hadn't known he was a shyster lawyer in Savannah.

He drove a nice car back then and flashed cash around, taking Estelle and the boys out to dine at nice places. He'd always had a kind word for me too.

"Wow. I didn't recognize you. What happened to you?"

"Life happened. It knocks you down enough times, you take the hint to do something else."

"Where's the big car?"

"Repo man snatched it. Lost a few cases in a row, made bad investments, that sort of thing."

The pungent scent of the cigar didn't cover the acrid smell of his unwashed body or dirty clothes. "You got running water out here?"

He gave a slight head shake. "Haul it in."

"Electricity?"

"You ask a lot of questions, Miss Nosy Parker. My turn. How'd you get through my gate?"

Keeping my distance, I showed him the knife. "I used this."

He sat up straighter, his eyes alight with interest. "Where'd you get it?"

"Chili gave it to me before Christmas, told me to keep it in my van."

"You know where he is?"

"He's missing. I'm looking for him. Have you heard the other big news?"

"Guessing Kale turned up if you're here. Didn't know Chili was missing. That's huge news in my world."

How did I tell him Estelle was gone? "There's more news, and it isn't good. You kept company with Estelle at one time, so it may be hard to hear this."

"Something happened to Buttercup?"

I nodded.

"Spit it out girl. She in the hospital?"

"No. She died. I found her on the kitchen floor. She'd been severely beaten. I called an ambulance, but she died on the way to the hospital."

Jude Ernest let out a string of cuss words that blistered the air. "Who did it?"

"The sheriff's office investigated, but there are no leads."

His chin quivered. "She still at the morgue?"

"No. Someone paid for the cremation and arranged her funeral, which was a few days ago. The anonymous requester specified I take the ashes."

He pondered that while drawing on the cigar. "She always thought of you as her daughter."

"Estelle and her sons were my friends. After my father died, Estelle and the bridge club were the only friends Mama had. Estelle was a good friend."

"What is this world coming to?" he asked.

Like I knew. I had an even better question. "Why has so much happened to the Bolz family in the last six months? Kale faked his death, Estelle died from a beating, and Chili is missing. Two alleged cousins trashed her house. Those can't be coincidences. What were they into? Did Kale bring this tragedy on their heads?"

"Kale is a good boy. Not too deep, but he always minded his

manners."

"When's the last time you saw Chili?"

"I haven't seen him in nearly a month. He visits regularly on high tide, bringing me supplies from town on his launch."

"Didn't you wonder why he didn't show?"

"I figured something important came up."

"It did, and he's gone to ground. Are you afraid for your life too? Is that why you hide in the woods?"

"Nobody is after me. Got tired of people criticizing my every move. Except for the Bolz family and now you, no one knows where I am."

"People know. Rumor around the island is you bought this place."

"I did no such thing. I'm squatting. Chili said the man that lived here died. Figured no one would mind if I laid my head out here in the midst of such natural splendor. I never want to see a stoplight again."

Squatting? "What's wrong with you? Why don't you rent or buy a normal place and live like the rest of us?"

"Can't do it. Burnt the hell out. I need to process all that I saw and did in Savannah."

"You've been here for months, so you should be better by now. In any event, Kale expects you to be his lawyer. He's in big trouble."

"Gotcha. I'll do my best to help him. I'll swing by Estelle's place and take a shower before I head to the jail."

"Weren't you listening? Two men tore up Estelle's house. Knocked out the walls, drilled through the ductwork, and poked holes in the floors. Crime scene tape is on all the doors."

"You mentioned that before, but I didn't realize the property damage was so extensive. Damn. Who did it?"

"Ralph Ferarrelli and Anthony Barnegas."

The color drained from his face. "I recognize those names. They're dangerous men. We gotta get Kale in federal custody as soon as possible."

We'd get back to the two scary men in a minute. "Don't take

this the wrong way, Mr. Ernest, but are you a real lawyer? You didn't get disbarred?"

"I'm as real as they get. Just got tired of chasing ambulances. I found out the hard way that clients who file claims lie, and that crooks aren't the only ones who get pissed at being ripped off."

"People are looking for you?"

"No one's looking for me. I dropped out of society. My mailing address has been Estelle's business for the last two years. I'm not a complete vagrant. The IRS can find me, if they want me."

"Shower at my place, if you like. Do you have lawyer clothes?"

"Estelle stored my stuff in her attic. I didn't want it anymore, but she said she'd hang onto my clothes. Not like those suits would fit now anyway. I've dropped thirty pounds living off the land and eating Chili's spare fish."

"You can try my brother's clothes. Or we can visit the thrift shop for something quick. Kale needs an advocate who can work the system."

"A fed owes me a favor. Soon as we hit civilization, I'll ring her."

"Sounds like a plan." I used my knife as a pointer. "What do you know about Ferarrelli and Barnegas?"

"I know we don't want anything to do with their kind. Not sure who they're working for now, but they're fixers."

"You think they killed Estelle?"

"Evidence will prove who killed Estelle, but if I were a betting man, I'd lay odds they had a hand in it."

"I wish I could prove it."

He stood, stretched, and pointed to my hand. "You gonna stab me?"

"Nope. Just being cautious." I folded the knife blade into the hilt. "I didn't realize I knew you when Kale asked me to contact you. The Uncle Jay I once knew was kind. I hope that's still true."

He shot me a fierce grin. "Kind to the ones I love, a shark to my opponents."

"Even better. Kale needs a shark in these treacherous waters.

Maybe he'll open up to you, and we can find out where Chili is."

"You think he's alive?"

I nodded, feeling sure. "Somebody sent the money and arranged for Estelle's funeral. It wasn't Kale, and it wasn't you. That leaves Chili. He must've had cash reserves hidden somewhere and then made that anonymous donation. That's the only thing that makes any sense. He must've gone to ground and is following your example of living off the land."

"Hard to believe I'm a role model for anyone, but that's neither here nor there." He gestured to his Jeep. "Drive around the house on the same path you walked just now. We'll exit the back way."

"There's another way in here?"

"Yeah. That's why I like this place. The boys hunt in these woods. They helped me hack out a path to an old fire trail in the woods. We don't use it often, so it looks as overgrown as the front entrance."

I glanced at the tall grass with growing uncertainty. "Your vehicle has a high clearance. My van doesn't. I need it for my catering business. I won't get stuck, will I?"

He grinned, showing straight white teeth. "If you do, I'll pull you out. No worries, cutie."

Chapter Twenty-Three

True to his word, Jude Ernest pulled me out of a hole in the nonexistent road. When we arrived at my place, I checked the van for damage and was relieved to see it was in good working order. I also noted several missed calls on my phone.

They had to wait. Jude took scissors to his beard and shaved his face in the guest bathroom while I stripped. Three ticks were crawling on my clothes, but none were attached to my skin. After a brisk shower, I dressed and started the washing machine. Meanwhile, Jude bathed.

I searched my brother's closet for clothing options for Jude. The suit from Mom's funeral was the only one Doug had. For an agonized moment I stood there holding the hanger, realizing I had no right to give his suit away but also realizing he didn't need it today. Jude would return the suit when he was done with it. A suit had no place in his reclusive lifestyle.

I laid out the suit and other clothing selections on the bed and hurried to the kitchen to fix Jude something to eat. He would be hungry enough to eat anything, but I wanted to make a good impression. I thawed out a container of shrimp gumbo and another of steamed rice. I'd recently learned how to make quick breads in coffee cups in the microwave. Not the same as pan-baked cornbread, but it worked in a pinch.

It looked so sunny outside, I opened the back door, leaving the screen door latched and allowing spring-fresh air to fill the room. As I warmed the food and poured glasses of iced tea, I heard drawers opening and closing upstairs. The lawyer came down in a pair of Doug's workout shorts and a T-shirt. "Smells amazing down here."

I frowned at his attire. No way could he wear that to court. "Suit didn't fit?"

"Nope. Thanks for trying. The sleeves and the pants legs were too short. Looked like I jumped into them too far. Let's catch a bite and then visit the men's shop in the plaza. I can afford to buy a suit."

"Okay. You look better without the beard. Want me to trim your hair? I do my brother's all the time."

Unconsciously, he smoothed his hair away from his leathery face. "No thanks, I'm used to it being long. I dug through the bathroom drawers and found an elastic band to secure it. Hope you don't mind."

My turn to blush. I didn't mean to criticize his choice of hair style. "We're good as long as you help Kale."

"My federal contact is already looking into his charges. I'll meet her at the station in an hour."

"That's cutting it close," I said, thinking of how long a suit fitting might take.

"You're right. It's a damn shame to inhale food that tastes this good, but I can't let Estelle's son down." He glanced at the urn nestled amongst my kitchen cannisters. "That her?"

"Yes."

While we ate, I perused my call log. Three calls and voicemails from Lance, one from Pete with no message, one from tomorrow evening's client. I listened to the client's voicemail quickly. He wanted a change of dessert from key lime pie to lemon meringue. I texted back that I would make the change. The guys would have to wait for return calls until I had a moment to myself. Kale was my top priority right now.

A familiar kitty mewed in my back yard.

"You have a cat?" Jude asked, turning at the sound.

"Kind of. A black cat visits here occasionally. I hoped he might become a permanent resident, seeing as how he once decided to take a ride with me out to Bayside Marina. But he goes where he likes. I'll set food out for him before we go."

"You don't have to go with me to get a suit."

I ran water over the dishes in the sink and opened a can of cat food. "I have a responsibility to get you to the jail. If you can't help Kale, whatever this mess is, it will swallow him whole."

"He's lucky you're his friend. Some wouldn't be so diligent."

"Some don't know him like I do. Some didn't promise his mother to find his brother."

"All righty." He rose and patted his flat belly. "First rate meal. Never tasted better. You making a go of Holloway Catering?"

I shot him a smile over my shoulder as I headed to the door. "Doing okay. Not setting the world on fire income-wise, but my clientele is growing."

"Let me get that screen door."

I paused so he could open it. Major watched from farther away than usual. Guess Jude's presence freaked him out. I cooed to the cat that it was nice to see him again then went back inside, securing the doors.

"That cat looks familiar." Jude turned away from the porch as I hustled the dishes into the dishwasher.

"He's a black cat and he knows his way around the island. Maybe you have seen him before."

"Perhaps. Getting back to Holloway Catering. You could hire an assistant and charge more. No reason people wouldn't pay more for good eating like that."

I did not like people telling me what to do, and the thought of being responsible for someone else's livelihood scared the willies out of me. "Let's leave fixing my life to another day, okay?"

"Message received." He raised his hands in surrender mode. "For a little thing, you sure pack a punch."

My height wasn't short. He was very tall, somewhere north of six feet, but I didn't want to argue. "Keep that in mind." I swept past him to gather my purse and keys.

Major may have meowed, but when I glanced at him, darn if

he didn't look cherubic.

Good grief.

The men's shop had exactly one suit in Jude's size and it was light blue. He walked out wearing the suit and new shoes, carrying a shopping bag with new jeans and a ventilated fishing shirt, looking like he would burst into an oldies dance routine at any minute or start quoting Ernest Hemmingway. Maybe the pastel-colored suit would fool his opponents into lowering their guard. I hoped so, for Kale's sake.

While Jude met with the lawyers, cops, and the judge, I slipped over to the minute market to buy the disposable phone Jude had requested. He also asked that I put my number in his phone. It took a bit to get it sorted out, but I entered my number and name in his phone, then sent myself a text from his message center so I had his number.

I drove to tutoring and an hour later I returned to the courthouse parking lot. While I waited for Jude to emerge, I listed a mental inventory of what I needed for the surf and turf meal for two tomorrow evening. Best if I made the pie tonight. Lemon meringues tasted better the second day anyway.

A crisp rap on the locked van window startled me out of my reverie. I glanced up, feeling anxious and vulnerable. Deputy Lance Hamlyn. Oh. Shoot. I forgot to call him.

I lowered the window and nodded. "Good afternoon."

His face and neck were red and this time of year it wasn't from sunburn. "You didn't return my calls," he gritted.

"Had a busy day," I said, flashing my the-customer-is-always-right smile. "What can I do for you?"

"You didn't tell me Kale requested a lawyer."

"Kale is my friend, and I contacted his lawyer. He needs a professional advocate."

"Jude Ernest?" Lance sputtered. "You think that ambulance chaser is a pro? You should've called me for a recommendation."

"Kale is my friend, regardless of what he's done. As a deputy, you uphold the law. Kale broke the law by faking his death, so we are on opposite sides in regard to Kale's fate."

"You should've told me. I thought..."

"You thought what?"

"I thought things were different. That we were friends."

"Friends," I repeated, knowing that my interest in him was platonic. He'd hoped to date me. Time to draw the relationship line more firmly in the ground. "We are acquaintances who share a mutual interest in finding Chili. I've said this before. Regarding friendship, I have a boyfriend, we're practically engaged."

He made another show of glancing at my hand. "There's still no ring on your finger."

"Get this through that thick head of yours. I'd never cheat on Pete. Besides, I'm not interested in dating you. Do you understand?"

"This isn't right."

"I'm sorry if you read anything into our collaboration. I'm sure there's a nice woman out there for you."

The courthouse doors opened and Jude Ernest walked out hand-in-hand with a stunning redhead, almost as tall as he was. Kale was nowhere in sight, but he'd already proved to be a flight risk.

Jude and his lady friend headed for my van. Lance tapped his fingers restlessly on the outside of the door. "This is out of control. Too many people are involved now. You could get hurt."

His comment struck me as odd. "You know something I don't?"

"Be very careful who you trust is all I can say."

"Good advice," I said to his retreating back. Why did Lance fix on me as a dating prospect? Why was he warning me?

"A friend of yours?" Jude asked, chinning toward the retreating deputy.

"No. What's the news?"

He introduced his companion as Agent Samantha Kress.

"Good thing we got here when we did," Jude said. "Deputies locked Kale in an interrogation room. They were badgering him to admit all kinds of crimes. Kale nearly broke. This has been hard on him."

"Does he have a deal?" I asked. "Is he safe?"

"Yes. Look, Sammy and I have catching up to do. She'll make sure I get home. All right if I touch base with you later?"

"Sure."

He leaned in closer. "Did you get the burner?"

I slipped him the phone in the guise of a handshake, and he nodded. "See you later." With a jaunty wave, he walked away with his lady friend.

Huh. His new everyday clothes were still in the back of my van, his other clothes in my washer. He'd turn up sooner or later. The good news was that Kale was safe.

One Bolz brother accounted for, one to go.

Chapter Twenty-Four

I waited to call Pete until the meringue finished baking. I didn't want to chance under or over cooking this pie. I rechecked my food inventory list to make sure I had remembered everything for tomorrow's customer. I'd purchased fresh produce for an awesome salad. Tomorrow I'd pick up filet mignon from the butcher shop, fresh mahi from my favorite seafood market, and fresh Brussels sprouts from the farmer's market.

Twilight had settled on my yard when I cozied up to the phone in my living room. It felt good to put my feet up on the coffee table. Pete answered on the first ring. He looked harried and a bit drawn on the video call. "Where have you been?" he asked, his emerald eyes blazing with emotion. "I needed to talk to you."

Not the loving greeting I'd hoped for, but he didn't know the crazy day I'd had. "It's been hectic here, and I didn't want our conversation to feel rushed. Are you okay?"

"Hectic day here too," he said. "The good news is I'm coming home tomorrow."

I sat up straight and replayed his last sentence in my thoughts. It took everything I had not to jump up and down and shout hallelujah. I'd see Pete tomorrow. He'd be here. Holy cow.

I tried to figure out what changed to allow him to leave. "You found a buyer?"

"I wish. Every deal I attempted failed. The board froze my company stock. I'll take a big financial hit, but I've got to move on. North Merrick is a hostile work environment, and I've served the board with legal papers." He winced as if in pain. "They didn't take it well. Dalbert North is threatening to sue me for breach of contract."

While I was sorry about the business failure, I wasn't sorry Pete was coming home. Having to walk away from a firm he'd put his name on must be eating him up inside.

Studying his image more closely, he seemed pale. "You look exhausted. I know you had high hopes for this company, but it's been trouble since you went out there. If you think it's the right thing to do, I'm glad you're walking away."

"It isn't easy for me to pull out, or I would've done it months ago. I'm no quitter, but I've made enough noise that if something happened to me, the right people will investigate."

Took me a moment to digest his words. Something had happened. Something bad. "More death threats?"

"These people do not play nice." He panned the phone's camera down to his arm in a sling. "They nearly got me today, River. I'm not just walking away. I'm hightailing it. I have a ticket to fly home tomorrow. Because of the time difference and a layover in Atlanta, it'll be late before I land in Brunswick."

They hurt him. Sympathy caused me to curl inward at his pain, clutching my belly. "Omigosh. Someone shot you?"

"A man stabbed me. Really jacked up my arm. I pressed charges, and I don't want to talk about it right now. I've been living it all day. I'll be fine, so don't worry."

"I am worried. You got stabbed. Someone hurt you. This is terrible."

"It's been a losing battle the whole time. I thought I could turn this place around, but the problems run too deep. I'd hoped to save the world and be your knight in shining armor. Not this time. I'm not the guy."

"You are that guy, but those people don't deserve you. Come home, rest up, and you'll be ready to fight a new battle."

"Maybe." He glanced away for a few seconds. "I'm just so tired."

"I understand, hon. Can you get some rest tonight?"

"Yeah. I hired a security company to watch over me and make sure I catch my plane. I don't have to worry about another attack tonight."

Guards? He must be worried. "I'll pick you up in Brunswick. What time?"

"My plane arrives at eight forty-five. Last flight of the day."

A smile filled my face. "The timing is perfect. I'll be done with my catering job by then, but I'll have a van full of pots and pans. No telling what I'll smell like."

His lips quirked up. "You'll smell like home. I can't wait to see you and be with you."

We ended the call and I looked around my house. I'd always loved living here. It had been my grandmother's and my mom's place. I knew every inch of these walls, from the windowsill my brother cut his teeth on to the toilet handle that needed an extra jiggle after every flush.

Pete had never lived here, though he'd spent the occasional night. Most of our together time on the island had been at his place, a custom-built beach house he'd sold prior to his move to California.

Consolidation he'd called it when I protested the sale, thinking he might want that beautiful house again someday. Now he'd move in here. He was right. We both wanted togetherness, but this place wasn't up to his usual luxury standards.

Would he see my gracefully aged home as coming down in the world?

For that matter, where would I put his stuff? I could easily donate excess clothes to the thrift shop tomorrow to make room in my closet and dresser, but he'd still be camping out in my space. The rooms and closets in this sixty-year-old house were tiny. I'd used up most of the bedroom floor space when I upgraded to a king-sized bed. No way would two dressers fit in the bedroom.

To the best of my recollection, Pete had at least six power suits and an entire closet for dress slacks, shirts, and ties. One entire rack for his fancy shoes.

He thought he'd had challenges in California. Living here would be a lifestyle change for him.

But at least he'd be alive.

And mine.

I clung to that thought.

Chapter Twenty-Five

First thing in the morning, I went on a culling-out and sprucing-up spree in preparation for Pete's arrival. Old clothes were bagged, junk moved to the attic, and a flurry of housecleaning ensued. Jude texted he'd pick up his Jeep later and instructed me to leave his clothes in the vehicle, which I did right away.

After donating my clothes to the thrift shop, I headed to the butcher shop, the farmer's co-op, and the seafood market in preparation for tonight's client. Each item checked off my day's list filled me with a sense of accomplishment. Holloway Catering might be small potatoes, but we offered top quality.

At Neptune's Harvest, Dasia Allen pushed her long, jet black hair over her shoulder. "Have you decided about River Cakes?"

I'd thought about it so much I couldn't reach a decision. It would be a headache gearing up to commercial production mode. At any one time, a lot of resources would be tied up in product, and if the marketing didn't pan out, I'd be at risk, not the Allens.

Still, who turned down a business opportunity like this? Pete would probably tell me to go for it. *I'm not Pete*, I told myself. There must be a reason I can't decide.

"Sorry," I began slowly, feeling my way through this commercial quicksand. The storefront room smelled faintly of seafood and bleach. "I've been so busy, I haven't had time to draft a business plan to study the cost of scaling up for a venture of that magnitude. One thing I know for sure, it represents a change of customer focus for me. As a small business owner, I enjoy seeing the smiles on customer's faces from a delicious meal. The thought of going into larger production mode and having more financial risk scares me."

"Thinking small will keep your profits small," Dasia said as she weighed out the amount of mahi I'd requested. "We want you as our business partner, but if you don't want the opportunity, say the word and we'll ask someone else."

Pete shared her entrepreneurial mindset, but I loved being small. I didn't have to worry about other people being out of work if I didn't have enough bookings. I didn't appreciate Dasia pressuring me to decide.

Suddenly, my answer crystallized. I enjoyed working for myself. I didn't want anyone looking over my shoulder, guilting me into doing something that didn't feel right, and criticizing my decisions.

"Thanks, but no thanks." I reached for my business check book. "You helped clarify my thoughts. This is a good business opportunity for you and Jerry to explore, but it isn't the direction for Holloway Catering right now. I'm officially out."

Her eyes opened wide. Clearly, she'd expected me to throw in with them. "We want to move on this right away. We won't wait until you're ready."

More pressure from her. Already I was super happy with my decision to pass. "I don't expect you to. As you said, there are other caterers in town."

Dasia's face fell as she rang up the sale. "We really wanted your crab cakes. They're Jerry's favorites."

"Sorry. They will remain exclusive products for my catering customers."

Driving home, I felt carefree, as if a load had been lifted off my shoulders. Now if I could manage to find Chili Bolz, I'd be home free. But that had to wait. The house was ready for Pete's homecoming, and I had a catering job tonight.

Some hinted wedding bells were in the offing for widowed bank president Gary Browning and Alberta Kimball. Gary had been with the bank as long as I could remember. Alberta retired here from Chicago about a year ago. She'd made a big splash on the dating scene upon arrival and caught Gary's eye. They'd been an item ever since.

I hoped it worked out for them. If I catered their wedding, that exposure would be good for future business. So getting tonight's dinner perfect carried double weight. Sometimes I was tempted to prep a few dishes in my home kitchen, but by law my business cooking had to be done in my commercial kitchen. The entire outbuilding in my backyard was modular, which meant that if I ever moved, I could take the kitchen with me, though it would be costly to do so.

Major zipped through the yard, which prompted me to refill his cat food and water bowls. He didn't show himself again, so I put him out of my mind. You could lead a cat to canned tuna, but you couldn't make him eat.

First on my to-do list was making a lime marinade for the mahi I'd purchased at Neptune's Harvest. The longer the fish marinated, the more succulent it would be. People loved my crab cakes, but they raved about my fish. I'd cook both the mahi and the steak on a charcoal grill tonight. My mouth watered thinking about the blend of surf and turf.

I had, of course, purchased extra mahi and filet mignon for a late dinner with Pete. His return was a special occasion for us.

I heard a noise, so I opened the door and listened. The cat. It was yowling. I called him, but he wouldn't come out of the pine forest. There was nothing back there for him to get caught on. Maybe a lady cat was in the neighborhood and they were courting. I trusted he was all right and returned to work.

Next, I blended a delicate marinade for the steaks. Not too much extra flavor, but just the right amount. Too soon to apply it to the steak, but it was ready for application when I fired up the grill.

The cat yowled a bit more and then quieted. Thank goodness for that mercy.

I prewashed my lettuce and chopped salad veggies, setting aside what I'd hold in reserve for Pete and me. Those salads went in the fridge with the marinades. It was too soon to fool with the bread, so I roasted the Brussels sprouts. While they cooked, I worked on a balsamic reduction and toasted almond slivers.

Suddenly, an object pressed into my back. "Stick your hands up," a mechanical-sounding voice ordered.

I started to turn around, sure my brother was pranking me, but the pressure in my back intensified. More, it felt like a cylinder. A gun? Oh, dear heaven.

"I'll shoot if you turn around," the intruder said. "Do as I say and you won't get hurt."

Fear bolted through me, quick as lightning. My eyes watered, my knees wobbled. I cried out but no sound came from my too-tight throat.

I squeezed in a breath a million moments later and fought for composure. Surely I could talk my way out of this. What did I have to lose?

I gulped more air and tried to sound normal. "I'm cooking. Let me turn everything off. Please."

The cylinder jabbed me again. "Do it."

I cut off the gas burner and the oven, a big hole forming in the pit of my stomach. From the reflection on the glass-fronted microwave, a mask covered my intruder's head and neck. The bloody-mouthed zombie mask terrified me. A shudder tripped down my spine. *Stay calm. Do what he says and you'll live.*

Calm. How could I identify this person later? From the deep mechanical voice, I presumed my intruder was male. He appeared taller than me but not by much. I couldn't tell his skin color, age, or anything else.

Fury clouded my thoughts. Who would threaten a caterer? I had thirty-five dollars in my wallet and enough money in the bank to cover three months of bills. That was it.

"What do you want?" I asked, a tremor in my voice.

"Tell me everything about the Bolz family."

He most likely didn't want me to start in elementary school. "Estelle died last week. Kale's in jail. Chili is missing."

"No. Their family business."

"Which one? Estelle owned a dry-cleaning business. Chili has a fishing charter boat, and his brother ran a shrimp trawler."

The cylinder ground into me again. I cried out in pain. "The other business," the intruder insisted.

"I don't understand."

Quiet followed. Each second ticked in my ear like an old-timey wind-up clock. I could barely hear myself think. Would he kill me now?

"Two men tore up their house," the masked man stated.

Not a question, but at least I knew something about this. "They claimed to be cousins."

"Mob."

"This is a quiet place, for families. We don't have the mob on Shell Island."

"Things change."

I tried to parse information with my lizard brain. A man in a zombie mask held a gun to my spine. He claimed the mob had a foothold on my island. Estelle's alleged cousins were rumored to be connected, but this was the first I'd heard of a consistent mob presence. The normalcy of thought caused me to lower my hands and begin to turn around to talk to this person. "What do they want on Shell Island?"

"Hands up. Don't move. I ask the questions here."

Heat flushed my face. How could I forget he held my life in his hands? "Sorry."

"Where's the money?"

My jaw dropped. "What money? They had enough to get by, they weren't rich. They were nice people."

The man-made unintelligible sounds. "They weren't nice people."

His statement rankled. Anger mixed with fear had me steaming. "I've known that family for nearly twenty years. If they were bad people, I'd know."

"People wear two faces."

Or zombie masks. I must've snorted because the intruder asked, "What's so funny?"

Fear made me bold...or stupid. "You don't even have a face, Mr. Zombie Mask."

"Better that way." He poked me in the back again. "Who was Estelle's business partner?"

"She didn't have one. She cleaned people's clothes and played bridge. No way was she criminal of the month."

The urgency in his voice heightened. "Tell me who it is."

My throat closed again and I whispered a response. "I don't know."

He swore loudly and I very much understood the foul words despite the mechanical distortion. "How can you be so stupid?" he asked.

I bit off every smart-mouth response that sprang into my head and said nothing. I heard something being moved behind me.

"You own a fire extinguisher?" he asked.

Fire? This wasn't good. Dread added to the emotional cocktail in my bloodstream. "Mounted on the wall by the door. Why?"

He smacked the back of my head, and I stumbled into the counter. My hip hit the countertop hard. I cried out. The cold barrel pressing into my back moved with me. "Because you'll need it in about two minutes. Your cat will be fine once the sedative wears off, but you might want to find him before then. Count to twenty before you move, or I swear I'll shoot you where you stand. If you tell the cops I was here, I'll return. Start counting."

"One, two, three, four," I began, feeling the pressure leave my back as soon as I said two. "Five, six, seven." I smelled smoke. "Eight, nine, ten," I said in a rush.

Forget twenty. I turned to find him gone and a roll of paper towels ablaze on my center island.

I swore, dashed for the extinguisher, and doused the flames. Using my big tongs, I hefted the smoldering mass to the sink. Crisis averted. Tears flowed down my cheeks, my legs barely supported my weight. I held out a hand and it trembled. I gripped both hands together and took stock.

I didn't get shot.

I was alive.

My commercial kitchen survived a fire, and fortunately most of my client's dinner for tonight was marinating, refrigerated, or in the oven. The balsamic reduction and almond slivers had to go. They would've picked up aerosols from the fire and the extinguisher, but I could easily replace them.

The cat.

He did something to the cat.

I raced outside, mute with fear. I wanted to call the cat's name, but I didn't want to give the intruder any reason to return. When Major cried out before, the sound came from the pines on the south side of the property. I checked there first.

Nothing.

Teary-eyed, I dashed through the woods and nearly stepped on him. The cat didn't protest when I touched him, but his chest slowly rose and fell.

I scooped him up and carried him inside my house. After laying him on an old blanket on the washing machine, I considered my options. If I called 911, the intruder would hear the sirens. He would not be pleased.

Not doing that.

Wait. I had a cop's private number on my phone. I called Lance. "Someone broke into my kitchen and drugged the cat."

"You okay?" he asked.

"Shaky, but I'm alive."

"I'll tell dispatch to send a unit out there right now. Lock the doors."

"Too late. The guy is gone. He set a fire in my commercial kitchen. I put that out first and rescued the cat. Now I'm next door in my house. I think I should take the cat to a vet."

"Most likely the intruder gave your cat a tranquilizer. If he's breathing easily, he'll wake up naturally. No need to spend money on a vet."

I stroked the cat's head. "I don't feel right about not taking him, but he is breathing, and in fact his breaths aren't as slow as before."

"Right. He'll wake up soon and be good as new."

"You know a lot about cats."

"Seen a few in this job." He cleared his throat. "Your safety is more important than the cat's. Lock the door. Stay inside."

"The door is locked. Lance, the intruder said if I called the cops, he'd return. I don't know what to do. I'm calling you as a cop, but if cruisers tear out here with sirens blazing, I could be in trouble. I need you to come, discretely."

"Told you that lifting those rocks to look for Chili was dangerous. Heavy hitters are involved in this case. I can't break free right now. Can you shelter in place until I can get out there in, say, an hour?"

Sunlight slanted in the laundry room window, warming my skin. "I'm rattled to the bone, but I can't sit tight in my house. I've got a catering job tonight. A VIP client. If I blow off this customer, I might as well hang up my spatulas. Getting the dinner to come together on time is a carefully orchestrated event. I need to be over in my commercial kitchen right now, prepping the ingredients and staging the production."

"Can you secure the other kitchen? If so, go ahead. Keep the phone close at hand until I arrive, which should be within the hour. I'll take your statement then for the police report."

Police report. Ugh.

Was I doing the right thing?

Would my actions prompt the masked man to kill me?

I couldn't give in to a bully. I was scared, but fear was a normal response. I was normal, my intruder wasn't. With a last look at the sleeping cat, I charged out the door. "I gave you my incident statement orally a minute ago."

"You have to file a written statement. Are you outside now?"

I loped down my back steps. "Yes. I'm on my way to the commercial kitchen."

"Walk at a normal pace."

"Forget that. I'm running." I dashed inside and locked the door behind me. "I'm in."

"No intruders?"

I turned in a circle, surveying the room. "Not that I can see, and unless he's a contortionist or hiding in the walk-in fridge, I'm alone here."

"Good. I'll be there soon."

Chapter Twenty-Six

Deputy Lance Hamlyn strolled into my commercial kitchen forty minutes later, wearing sneakers, jeans, a fishing shirt, his usual heavy-handed aftershave, and police gloves. His cop eyes checked every corner before pinning me. "You okay in here?"

"I'm good for now," I said, locking the door behind him. I zipped back to the stove, turned off the gas burner, and covered the pan. "You're early."

"I cleared my schedule to keep you company this afternoon and help you with this VIP client tonight. Figured you'd feel safer if you weren't alone. I gather that black garbage bag outside is the paper towels?"

"This really spooked me. Thanks for the company and the offer of help. I'll take you up on both, if you don't mind. I won't be alone later because Pete's flying home tonight. As for the paper towels, I couldn't leave them inside. I aired this place out by opening the windows and then I sanitized every surface before I started making the balsamic reduction again."

I drew a deep breath. "I wish I'd brought the cat over here. Can we go check on him?"

"The cat will keep a few more minutes," Lance said. "We'll check on him after I search the area for signs of your intruder. Meanwhile, are you hurt?"

"Physically, I'm fine."

"I hope you don't mind. I brought a supply of my black police gloves for policing and catering. My hands are much bigger than yours and I wanted to make sure we kept things sanitary." Lance took a moment, glanced around my kitchen again. "Everything seems in order. Where's your fire extinguisher?"

"Good thinking. I don't think your hands would fit in my smaller gloves." I pointed to the wall mount. "Where it belongs."

"You used it so you have to refill or replace it. If it has a metal valve, take it to the fire station. They refill them for a minimum charge. It's cheaper than buying a new one."

I walked over and studied the fire extinguisher. "Metal. Guess I'll be making a trip to the fire station soon."

He withdrew a folded sheet of paper from his pocket and placed it on the counter. "Start on your police statement while I snap pictures of the paper towels and clear the woods. How'd the guy get in?"

My face heated. "I opened the door because the cat made a ruckus outside. Guess I forgot to lock it when I got back to work."

"Not a good plan to leave your door unlocked, but at least your lock isn't busted." He opened the door, locked and unlocked it a few times. "Any serious burglar could pick this cheap lock in less than ten seconds."

"I've never worried about people breaking into my kitchen before. The lock works fine for nonserious burglars. What would anyone want from my kitchen? Pots and pans?"

He made a small laugh before he asked, "Was anything stolen?"

"Yeah. My pride. My innocence too. Armed intruders aren't commonplace on Shell Island or in my kitchen."

Lance shrugged. "We're seeing big city crimes on the island. It isn't a sleepy little summer tourist spot anymore."

The memory of that creepy voice came roaring back in my head. "You don't have to tell me."

"What did the intruder look like? Can you describe him or her?"

"I think it was a guy even though the voice was distorted."

"Distorted?"

"Something mechanically altered the sound. Like you see on

TV shows when someone wants anonymity. The voice was gorped up, but it sounded deep."

"You can do anything with those phone apps. It might be a woman even if the voice sounded deep."

"Good to know, but I don't think it was an app. We had an interactive conversation. There wasn't time for him, or her, to speak privately into his phone, change how it sounded, and then play it back for me to hear."

"They make devices you can wear for that, but you would've seen it over his or her mouth."

"I wasn't allowed to turn around and see the guy. For convenience sake, I'm calling the intruder a man. I saw a quick reflection in the microwave door. He wore a zombie mask, and I can't tell you his race. No skin showed in the reflection, though that's all of him I ever saw. One hand held a piece of cold metal on my spine. He said it was a gun."

"They sell voice changing boxes at most party stores. He could've worn a mouthpiece under his mask."

"That's creepy." I never wanted to hear one of those voices again. "The ordeal scared me more than any Halloween fright I ever had."

"You've got nothing else on his appearance? What about height and weight?"

"Didn't see his body. His reflection made him appear taller than me, but not by much."

"How tall are you? About five-six, five-seven?"

"Five-six. He might be five-eight. That's my best estimate."

"Not much to go on, unless we find that mask. I'll see if our local party store carries those masks and voice devices, but it's likely a criminal purchased the mask elsewhere to avoid detection. I'll dust for prints, but if he wore a mask and disguised his voice, not much chance of fingerprints."

"How do we catch him?"

"We don't. Quit playing amateur detective and let me find Chili. If you aren't involved, no one will bother you."

I wasn't keen on having another intruder visit me, but I wanted to find Chili. I'd have to investigate without Lance knowing. "The intruder said Estelle, Chili, and Kale had a family business. I listed their businesses, and he said that wasn't right. Then he asked me about the money. I had no idea what he was talking about and he got mad. What money? What were the Bolzes doing?"

"Leave the investigation to the pros, River. That's the only way you'll be safe. Estelle is dead. Chili may be dead. You wanna be next?"

"Of course not. None of this makes sense."

"From what I've pieced together after those men trashed Estelle's house, the Bolz family operated under false pretenses."

My lips pressed tightly together. I didn't believe him. I'd known these people all my life. If there were big secrets in their lives, how did they stay hidden in such a small town? Everyone knew everyone else's business on Shell Island.

Once again, Lance and I were uneasy allies, though he didn't know it. I planned to keep it that way.

I grabbed a pen and silently filled in the statement form. Lance went outside, took pictures, then ducked in and out of the trees.

"Don't see any indication of someone standing out there and watching your place," he said when he returned. "This must've been a desperation move. The intruder knows of your connection to the Bolz family."

"When you say family like that, it makes me feel like I'm part of the mob. I'm not, in case you're wondering."

"No wondering about that. You're the town's beloved baker, the woman who shattered Jerry and Dasia's get-rich-quick dream."

My head reared back. "You know about that?"

"Everyone knows about that. Jerry's been over at the American Legion all morning drowning his sorrows in beer. He already picked three fights with the staff. I took the disturbance call because I'm a member and they want to avoid bad publicity. I drove Jerry home and put him to bed."

"Good grief. I'm even happier I decided against their crab cake mass production scheme."

"Probably a good move on several fronts. Jerry has an anger management problem. You didn't hear it from me, but he's smacked Dasia around a few times."

The news upset me. "I hope you arrested him for that."

"She didn't press charges. Oh, the things I could tell you about people in this town."

Almost as if islanders were wearing two faces.

Suddenly, I felt more alone than ever. My good friends the Bolzes had likely been operating under a false flag. The mob infested our fair shores. An armed intruder threatened me.

Not a good week or a good day, but help was on the way.

I just had to hold it together until Pete arrived tonight.

Chapter Twenty-Seven

When we unlocked my house to check on the cat, Major streaked past us into the woods. "What'd I tell you?" Lance said. "He's fine."

"He's alive, but he won't forget the incident," I said, rubbing the lingering chill from my arms. "I know I won't forget it."

"Remembering will keep you safe," Lance said. "I'm sorry this happened to you."

"Me too. I don't want to seem uninterested in finding the intruder, but I've got work to do and my timeline is already compressed."

"I'll be there after I scan my report and your statement form into the system."

A few hours later, we packed the van and made the trek to my client's house. Despite the lingering fright from the intruder, my planning and organization skills paid off big time. Widowed banker Tucker Browning beamed from the moment we arrived. His housekeeper had dressed a table for two with a pristine white tablecloth, a low slung bouquet of roses, and elegant china. The silver service gleamed, while the crystal glasses mirrored the strong colors of the late afternoon sun.

Additional vases of roses accented the sitting room, the foyer, and the living room. Soft jazz filled every corner of the house, adding an easy, feel-good vibe to the already romantic atmosphere. If this wasn't the night Tucker was proposing, I'd been dating the wrong men all my life. With so much effort focused on the perfect dinner and ambiance, Alberta Kimball would be swept off her feet.

Lucky woman.

Lance and I unloaded the van in record time. He seemed to anticipate my every move, which made everything go smoother. "You sure you haven't done this before?" I asked. "I've had other assistants, and we always end up tripping over each other."

"This is a first for me," Lance said as he fired up the charcoal grill and I brushed the steaks with marinade. "However, in all fairness I excel at spatial awareness. It comes in handy for detective work."

"Good thing you're in that field then," I said, laying out the covered glass baking container holding the marinated steak on the adjacent work bench. I flipped the container over a few times to even out the marinating sides. Satisfied, I pulled my checklist from my chef coat pocket.

We were on schedule. Time to pop the mini bread loaves in the oven. They would add that heavenly aroma of baking bread to the house. The marinated mahi stayed in the cooler a while longer, too soon to grill the fish. Those pre-cooked Brussels sprouts would only need reheating, and I had time for that after the bread finished. The salad and dressing were chilling, and lemon meringue pie was perfect sitting out on the counter. If the ambiance, food, and flowers didn't seal the deal, that pie certainly would.

A masterpiece, if I did say so myself.

I glanced at the sideboard, which featured wines Tucker had selected. They were the most expensive brands of red and white the wine shop carried. I was impressed.

"Should I fill the water glasses?" Lance asked.

"Too soon," I said. "Condensate will ruin the timeless appeal of that flawless table. After Alberta sees the picture-perfect setting, we'll remove the china and fill the water glasses."

"They don't eat on these dishes?"

"We'll plate their meals in the kitchen, and I'll carry the filled plates out."

He nodded toward the tray of blue corn chips and guacamole I placed beside the wines. "Not something high-powered and fancy for the appetizer?"

"Tucker said these were Alberta's favorites. The client is always right in the catering business."

"A lot goes into this. I never knew caterers were so scripted and choreographed. You're good at this, River, and you're an excellent cook. Not everyone in your niche has both skill sets."

I silently basked in his praise. "I'm interested in retaining my clients. That's why I do my best to ensure there are no surprises."

"But if you have surprises, you can roll with them," he said. "Few women could have rebounded the way you did today. You've got game."

"I got something," I said, hearing the crunch of tires on the crushed shell driveway. I waved Lance toward the kitchen. "Alberta's here. Time for us to vanish."

His eyes twinkled. "Are we hiding?"

"No, but we stay out of sight until needed. Tonight is about Tucker and Alberta. Like kitchen elves, our goal is to be invisible."

"Not quite what I pictured when I agreed to help, but I can try channeling my inner kitchen elf," Lance said as we hurried out of the way. "I'd rather be in the dining room, watching the Big Moment transpire."

"Forget it," I said. Then I looked at the goofy grin on his face. "You think he's proposing tonight?"

"That's the rumor," Lance said. "Heard it at the American Legion earlier today. Three times, so it must be true."

I didn't agree with his interpretation of that rumor, but we had a few minutes to ourselves for quiet conversation. I eased a back hip against the counter. "Any promising leads on finding Chili? What about the fake cousins? What happened to them?"

"Kale is the best lead we've had so far, and he's not talking, thanks to you and his low-rent lawyer."

"Hey, don't shoot the facilitator. Kale may reveal something yet. If Chili had a serious wound when he went missing, he'd have turned up at a hospital by now. I'm hoping he's okay and he's hiding out there, somewhere. What about Barnegas and Ferarrelli?"

Lance frowned at me. "Barnegas is still in intensive care with a collapsed lung. He's not talking to anyone. Ferarrelli's in our custody and lawyered up. Some high-powered Savannah firm represents them. Made it clear that both men had plenty of rights. They're an official dead end."

Thanks to my brother's brush with the law, I knew about jail and penalties for people who'd been in jail. "They weren't already in the system for something else or out on parole?"

"Clean hands, both of them, though both are rumored to be mob enforcers."

"Yikes. I thought you told me before they were fixers. Guess it doesn't matter. Both labels sound terrible." Mob enforcers destroyed Estelle's house. Far as I knew, that had never happened on Shell Island before. Whoever Estelle got tangled up with had killed her.

"A new source confirmed their organized crime association. I gave you the best information I had at the time."

"Which mob?" I asked.

Lance shook his head. "Better that you don't know. These people play for keeps. Don't stick your nose into anything having to do with Estelle. It could turn out badly for you."

I'd had my fill of bullies for the day. "Sounds like a threat."

"It's a common-sense warning. Look, most everyday lawbreakers get caught, go to jail, and get released. Some do better afterward, like your brother; others bounce back to jail until they get killed or land in prison. Ferarrelli and Barnegas are professional criminals. They are wicked smart and don't get caught."

I didn't appreciate the reminder my brother had spent time in jail. I soldiered past my bruised feelings. "Except Deputy Franklin caught them. You've got them in your jail."

"Their lawyers will beat the vandalism charges. Money will appear to compensate the family for the loss of property. I don't know how or when it will come down, but these two will skate. I guarantee it."

It wasn't fair. My mood plummeted. "Doesn't say much for our justice system."

"Justice is blind to those with the right connections. Trust me, these people are highly connected. I saw something similar in Texas."

"You've opened my mind to a reality I didn't know existed. It makes me want to barricade myself in my home."

"At its heart, the mob is a business, pure and simple. Beat the competition any way you can. If you get caught, minimize the bleeding and try a different strategy. Everyone can be bought."

"You sound remarkably calm about illegal activity for a man who's in law enforcement."

"There's no point viewing the world through rose-colored glasses. It is starkly black and white, with splashes of blood, and I'm not talking about racial anything. Black and white being the legal establishment versus the people who operate outside the law."

"Huh." I rubbed my folded arms for a moment, digesting the conversation. "You know, one thing stood out when I was searching for Chili."

Lance came to attention. "Oh?"

"Yeah. It may be nothing, but I noticed this when I went to Bayside Marina. Chili's boat looked pristine."

"I don't follow you."

"I've done business with Chili for years. His boat usually had a lived-in appearance, with personal items here and there. I've never seen it like this. It looks like someone power washed his boat and then waxed it."

His brow furrowed. "That's odd. I didn't realize his vessel was unnaturally clean."

"Again, I don't know if it means anything, but if something happened on his boat, the evidence is long gone. Though on some of the crime scene shows, they can detect blood that's been bleached. Is that true? Can you do that?"

"We have the standard blood detection kits. I could try going down there at night and spraying his boat with an indicator chemical, but if the physical evidence is gone, all we'll learn is that Chili's blood is in his boat. It won't take us anywhere."

"Unless someone else bled in the boat. Chili is a tough guy. He wouldn't have been easy to take down. If someone attacked him, he fought back."

Lance nodded. "Good point."

The oven timer dinged. I grabbed a mitt, removed the bread, and placed the Brussels sprout dish in the toasty oven. "And we're back on duty. As fascinating as this discussion of the case is, we have a job to do." I caught his gaze and nodded toward the back stoop where I'd set up my grill. "Both steaks are to be cooked medium rare. Can you handle that?"

He reached for the grill spatula and twirled it. "I've been grilling meat all my life. Of course, I can."

"Great. We'll start the fish once I've served the salad course. That way the fish and steak will be done near the same time."

The rest of the meal went like clockwork. When Tucker proposed after pie and coffee, Alberta danced a jig of acceptance. Lance and I admired the flashy diamond ring before we packed up, then I dropped him off at his car.

"Thanks for the help," I said. "You ever want to be my assistant again, I'll put a good word in with the owner."

"Sure." Lance's expression tightened. "You headed to the airport now?"

"Yeah. Pete's plane lands in twelve minutes. I want to be in the terminal before nine."

"Drive safely."

"Thanks for helping tonight feel more normal. I appreciate your kindness."

"No problem."

I drove to the airport, tired and exhilarated. After such a successful meal, Alberta would surely invite me to cater her wedding, which had been my secondary goal of the evening. With that giddy sensation of success and the rising anticipation of seeing Pete, I had to keep checking my speed. I didn't want a ticket or the delay a traffic stop would cause.

A car swerved in front of me and I hit the brakes. It was a near thing, but I avoided a collision. Then the driver maintained a speed below the speed limit, amping up my agitation.

My fingers tightened on the steering wheel. *Get a grip, River. Your emotions are bouncing all over the place.* A few minutes either way won't matter, unless Pete took that as a sign I didn't care enough to greet him the second he breezed through the security checkpoint.

Now that was nerves talking. Pete would be so happy to see me, so happy to be off airplanes and to finally be among friends and loved ones.

This is what Pete and I wanted: being together, living together, sharing breakfasts, and making a family. With each mile that rolled by my happiness intensified.

This was happening.

The man I loved was coming home.

Chapter Twenty-Eight

I parked and dashed inside the airport as the plane taxied our way. Made it! Should I have remembered flowers or made a welcome home banner? Maybe, but Pete wouldn't miss them.

My emotions still bounced all over the map. This was a big deal in my life, a new chapter. I'd be part of a live-together couple. From our dating history before he moved to California, I knew Pete's likes and dislikes. He was driven to succeed and gave two hundred percent to everything, including me.

God, I couldn't wait to see him.

A few people hurried off the plane, then a few more. I strained my neck and squinted to get the very first glimpse of him. People streamed by in a colorful throng. No Pete.

My heart thudded as the passengers thinned to nothing. Did he miss the plane? No, he would've contacted me. I checked my phone again in case I missed a message. Nothing there. He was on that plane, but he wasn't bounding off to see me.

Were his injuries worse than he'd mentioned?

On the video phone call last night, he'd shown me his hurt arm. I should've thought of how difficult it would be to manage baggage with one hand. I should have flown out to help him wrangle the flight change in Atlanta.

"River!" he called.

I glanced up, saw him alone in the arrival corridor, one hand on a cane, the other arm wrapped in a sling. My gosh. His face was so pale. I needed to get him home right away. "Pete!"

I raced to his side, brushing a kiss on his lips, gingerly

wrapping my arms around him. He'd lost weight too. The poor guy. "I've missed you so much," I breathed into his chest.

"You look and smell good enough to eat. We're not doing this again," he said as his good arm hugged me close. "I love you, and I want you beside me for the rest of my life."

"I want that too," I said into his shirt, my voice muffled because he held me so tight. "How bad are you hurt?"

"Banged up a bit, but nothing broken, or permanently damaged. Just need your tender loving care."

"You came to the right place for TLC. Do you have bags?"

He managed a wry grin. "Checked everything. Couldn't wrangle a bag with the cane and the arm in a sling."

"Let's grab them and go home."

"I've been waiting all day to hear those words."

We spent the night in each other's arms, and I'd awakened at the normal time, despite having much less sleep. I didn't want to disturb Pete's rest, so I rose quietly and dressed in the bathroom. With a steaming cup of coffee in hand, I sat on my back porch as day dawned. So far so good on the grand reunion. It didn't feel awkward having Pete here at all.

I had one of those kitchen-sink-style breakfast casseroles baking in the oven. That would give Pete a hearty meal to start putting the meat back on his bones.

Major must be recovered from his drugging incident because the cat bowls were empty. I'd filled them last night before I left for the catering job. I refilled them and waited in my chair for Pete to awaken.

I listened with my eyes closed as a black-capped chickadee chirped "fee bee." A few minutes later a northern cardinal called out, "cheer, cheer, cheer." Normal sounds for a normal day. My property wasn't on the marsh or the beach, but I could get to either one in less than five minutes. I had the best of both worlds, island living at a fraction of the cost.

Last night, Pete hadn't mentioned Estelle's ashes in the kitchen. There was a chance he didn't recognize the brass container as a funerary urn, but he'd been so weary during dinner and all he'd wanted to do was go to bed.

Would he understand that I needed to hang onto Estelle?

Every time I saw her urn, I remembered Estelle asked me to find her son, except Chili was hidden so well no one could find him. Far as I could tell, no one knew where he was either.

I sipped more coffee. Maybe Pete would have a fresh insight into the case. That would be nice. Would we be "that" couple who did everything together? If it went well, we could open up our own investigation agency, H and M for Holloway and Merrick. Or if we married, it could be M and M Investigations. While it sounded great, both of us were used to doing things our own way and in our own time. How would we feel about moving in tandem?

At a noise inside the house, I turned to see Pete coming my way. He'd pulled on a black T-shirt and jeans and already the color in his face looked better.

"Good morning," I said, rising to greet him with a kiss. "Please join me for a cup of coffee."

"Sure. Something smells great."

"Made your favorite breakfast casserole. It needs a few more minutes in the oven."

"It's worth the wait."

I got him settled, topped off my coffee, and fetched him a mug. He took the mug in his good hand and sipped the coffee. "Gosh, it's so easy to be here. Why didn't I do this months ago?"

Even his voice sounded invigorated. "Because you aren't a quitter, that's why."

"I learned a valuable lesson. Double and triple check the numbers, but also run criminal background checks on the people you plan to do business with. Even that may not have picked up the dangerous and unstable element pervasive in North Merrick. North let things get rundown too far before he sought help. I shouldn't have let his sentiment play into my judgment." He shook his head.

"Never again."

"You're done with those people now?"

"We've filed papers against each other for breach of contract. My lawyer will work it without me. If it goes to trial, I'll have to appear, but I believe they'll settle."

"I hope so. How'd you get hurt? You didn't tell me."

"Three guys jumped me in the building's parking garage. I got in some good licks, but three against one weren't good odds. The bruises will fade, my ankle's better each day, and the arm, well the arm might need more mending time, but it should heal."

"Was the attack captured on security cameras?"

"They took them out while they waited for me. But they didn't get all the cameras. I had some minis installed between my car and the elevator. The cops have those images now. Two of the three matched on facial recognition software, and they've been picked up already. The third is an outlier. The cops are looking for him. He's the one that messed up my arm."

"Can they cut a deal with the other two to get his name?"

"Doesn't work that way in the bad guy club. Thugs who rat each other out get dead right away."

"Still, he shouldn't get away with hurting you like that."

"We'll get him." Pete sipped his coffee. "Enough about me. Catch me up on what happened here yesterday. Did the romantic dinner end in a proposal?"

"It did. I'm hoping to get the nod for their wedding. Lance assisted me."

"Lance." Pete set his mug down abruptly. "The cop that keeps sniffing around? I don't like him bothering you."

"You don't know this yet, but yesterday, a masked intruder barged into my commercial kitchen and held a gun to my back. They drugged the cat too. Lance took my statement and then volunteered to keep me company until it was time to drive to the airport."

"River!" He reached for my hand and gripped it. "You should've mentioned this earlier. I didn't know you'd had trouble.

Did he hurt you?"

I gave him a reassuring squeeze in reply. "I'm fine, though the incident rattled my nerves. I didn't want to burden you with the details on your travel day. I handled it."

"You can and should burden me with details anytime. You're amazing and resilient, and I'm proud of you for persevering, but your safety and well-being are my top priority."

"Thank you, and that goes both ways. No more holing up across the country with your worst enemy. I'm thankful your injuries are healing."

"Yesterday must've been difficult with that intruder, a catering job, and a reunion with me." He released my hand to take another sip of coffee. "What did the intruder want?"

"For me to stop searching for Chili."

"Why?"

He wouldn't like this part. "Well...It seems...The cops believe..."

"Spit it out."

I stared at him unblinkingly for a long moment. "The mob is involved."

"You're kidding. Why didn't you tell me?"

"Not kidding. It's for real, and I didn't want to worry you, especially when I knew you were injured." I gave him the rundown of the two mobsters who destroyed Estelle's house and of Kale returning from the dead.

He met my steady gaze with steel. "What is the mob doing on Shell Island? It would be hard to be invisible here. What am I missing?"

"My masked intruder claimed the Bolz's had a secret family business, and I realized Chili's boat is too clean. Pairing those data points just now gave me an idea. What if our island location and the too-clean boat indicate someone was moving a product on or off the island in Chili's boat?"

"If that's the case, stay far away from whatever madness the Bolz family brought down on their heads. From personal experience, crime syndicates don't stop. People who stand in their way get beaten, broken, and dead. I'm lucky to be alive. Promise me you'll be careful."

"I will."

The stove timer rang. I rose to pull the casserole out, but Pete caught my arm. "And promise that you won't go to the marina or Estelle's house without me."

I hesitated, not wanting my wings clipped but realizing he spoke the truth. If I needed to go to those places, we could go together. Judging from the energy of this conversation, two heads were way better than one.

"Deal," I said.

Chapter Twenty-Nine

We each went for seconds of the egg casserole, and while we ate, the cat appeared on the deck and cleaned out his food bowl. I pointed Major out to Pete, but the cat scampered away before they could be properly introduced.

With full bellies, we lounged together on the sofa, not a whisper of space between us. "I barely remember the Bolz brothers or Estelle from the years I lived here," Pete said, stroking my hair. "I recognized Chili's name because you've mentioned he's your fish supplier. Did the family keep a low profile?"

His caress felt just right. Oh, how I'd missed this. "Chili and Kale stayed busy making their living. It isn't easy here. If you aren't working at a hotel or restaurant, there's not much for unskilled laborers to do. The brothers love being on the water, so they parlayed that passion into paying careers. Chili took the route of a recreational fisherman, while Kale became a commercial fisherman."

"Fishing is seasonal and dependent on skill for bountiful harvests." Pete said after a long moment. "In down-times, it's easy to see why they might've made a bad financial choice or two."

"I hate this for them. We had such fun running and playing as kids. I still can't see them as criminals. It can't be true."

"Go through it all for me again. I have a feeling we're missing something."

I started with Estelle's request to find Chili, worked my way through visiting all the local watering holes asking for Chili, then I ended with finding Estelle near death and her odd last words.

"Bridge and bridge check," Pete repeated. "You didn't mention those terms to me before."

"Sorry. Thought I did," I said. "It doesn't matter. The ladies she played bridge with don't know what that means so it's a dead end."

"Possibly. Let's try another angle. Did the brothers play sports or hunt when they were younger?"

"No sports teams, but they favored camo pants. I believe they learned how to hunt from one of Estelle's boyfriends."

"Hunters often return to the same grounds. They build blinds in trees at their favorite haunts. If not for this cane, I'd search for Chili in the woods. That seems the most likely scenario to me. Now that I think about it, a survivalist on the lam in the North Carolina woods hid out for a few years, eating acorns and salamanders. Authorities think friends helped him. What about Chili's hunting friends?"

"I don't know them, but my brother might." I texted Doug to ask if he could take a call now about Chili's hunting buddies. He texted he was too busy, but he remembered three guys who hunted with Chili and Kale. One guy died in a car wreck, one was in prison, and the other, Justin Adler, moved away a few months ago. I texted him my thanks.

"One name. Not much to go on," I said to Pete. "I have no idea where they hunted."

He smiled. "I can figure out some of that. But first, I'd like to see Estelle's house and Bayside Marina."

I sat up and stared down at him. "Really?"

"Yeah. Fresh eyes often bring new insights."

"You've made my day. It would mean so much to me if I found Chili. I wish I could've done more for Estelle. Truth is, I could never figure out if Chili hid because someone wanted to harm him, or if he's dead and someone hid the body."

"Is that why Estelle's ashes are in your kitchen?"

"Oh." I cleared my throat. "I wasn't sure how to broach that topic. I'm her temporary custodian. Now that Kale's alive, and I hope with all my heart Chili's alive, they'll decide what to do with her ashes. Meanwhile, they serve as a tangible reminder that I promised to help her son."

"We'll do what we can for Estelle and Chili, but we do it together."

"All right, partner. Let's get going."

We drove to Bayside Marina first since it was closer. I parked in front of the office, and Garnet Pierce, the dockmaster, sped outside to join us. "Howdy," she said. "Y'all looking for a charter or some fish?"

"Just looking," I said, introducing Pete to Garnet.

"You the boyfriend?" Garnet said, sizing him up from head to toe. "I heard you lived here before, but our paths never crossed until now."

"I'm the boyfriend," Pete said, giving her an appraising gaze as well. "We'd like to walk down to the dock and see Chili's boat."

"That's gonna be a problem," Garnet said. "Deputy Dawg sent someone at first light to haul that boat out of the water. Said it's evidence."

I leaned into Pete and whispered, "That's Lance's nickname."

Pete nodded his understanding, then gestured to the moored boats. "Which boat is closest in size to the one that was removed today?"

"Shoot, Jamie Vassar's boat is darn close. His motor's smaller but the boat is the same make and model. See it over there, the *Salty Lady*?"

"Okay if we walk down on the dock to look at it?" Pete asked.

"You can't be getting on that boat. That'd be trespassing."

"Just want to take a look, that's all," Pete said amicably.

Garnet looked like she wanted to say no, but another car pulled up with two elderly gentlemen I didn't recognize. With reluctance, Garnet waved us toward the vessel.

I followed Pete to the boat, careful to step over lines

crisscrossing the dock. The vessel was far from pristine, with mud stains here and there, bird droppings, a pungent fishy odor, and five-gallon buckets of empty beer cans. Muddy paw prints tracked all over the boat from stem to stern, suggesting this guy had a dog or hunting dogs. The seat cushion in the captain's chair was ripped, and sea spray obscured the windshield.

"How much room below?" Pete asked.

"Never been on this boat or Chili's, but once I heard him say he had two bunks down there and a gas stove."

"They fish offshore in this size craft?"

"Chili did. Looks like this guy's been fishing in the tidal creeks from all the mud tracked in the boat."

"Interesting."

We took our time walking back to the van, with Pete stopping for frequent rests. "Are you okay?" I asked after he stopped twice. He nodded.

We got back in the van. I searched his face to see if it'd gone pale. Nope. He looked hale and hearty, though his face was a bit drawn. I pulled away from the marina and turned to Pete. "What was that about?"

"This is the older marina, right? There's a new facility closer to the golf course?"

"Yes. What of it?"

"Bayside has a rundown look, but the dockmaster seemed eager to hustle us out of there. If those fishermen hadn't shown up when they did, I'm certain she would've sent us on our way."

I hadn't considered Garnet's action in that light, but it made sense. "I agree, but why would she do that?"

"Assuming the vehicle closest to the shop is hers, I'd say she's protecting something."

"The red truck? That's hers. Garnet, like her name. Why's the truck important?"

"It's pricey. That style costs more than some people's houses."

"You're kidding."

"I know trucks. Not only that, I know about security measures after having to implement them in North Merrick. Bayside has cameras around the marina and on the pilings near the shore side of each pier. Somebody is closely monitoring the dock traffic. Additionally, most marinas are bustling places, with cars and people and boats moving around. This one looks dead. Garnet's got money, and she's not making it there. My spidey senses kicked in."

"Spidey senses? You a superhero now?"

He patted my leg. "Only if you think I am."

I gave him a long look that ended with him grinning and me blushing. "Definitely."

"On to Estelle's house, then."

Traffic was light as we motored to the historic district. Crime scene tape still stretched across Estelle's driveway. I pulled into Ola Mae Reed and Valerie Slade's driveway next door.

"That it?" Pete asked, pointing to the aging Victorian, a sister construction to Ola Mae's place.

"What's left of it. We have to say hello to the sisters who live here first. If anyone moved a muscle on this street they'd know about it."

"Gotcha."

Ola Mae came to the door saying Valerie was under the weather.

We chatted for a few minutes, and she flirted outrageously with Pete while holding onto the doorknob. Then she turned and winked at me. "Don't let this one get away. He's a better catch than Deputy Hamlet. And if you don't want this one, I'll take him."

"Don't you worry," I reassured her, "I'm taking this one. He's a keeper."

A wistful look passed in her violet eyes. "He puts me in mind of my Denny. Young man, if this lady doesn't treat you right, you have carte blanche to move in here, no questions asked."

"Thank you, ma'am," Pete answered with a polite grin. "I might take you up on that generous offer."

"Not if River's got half the sense we credit her with," Ola Mae said. "Y'all take your time next door. I've already made our morning run to the Post Office and grocery store, so we've got everything we need."

"Before you go," I said, "has anyone else been nosing around next door?"

"Hamlet's been back a few times, but that's about it. Have a blessed day." Ola Mae closed the door in our faces.

"That was interesting," Pete said as we cut across the driveway and walked into Estelle's yard. "I have another place to stay."

"You wouldn't last long over there. Nobody with a lick of sense eats anything those women cook. Haven't for forty years, not since they each allegedly poisoned their husbands. Because they lived in different states at the time, the law didn't catch on, but those of us here made the connection. Their backyard is full of poisonous plants, in case you're wondering."

"Nope. Not wondering at all. I will avoid that house at all costs." He slowed and turned to me, leaning heavily on the cane. "Who's Hamlet?"

"She means Hamlyn. Somehow she got it wrong in the first place, and no one's corrected her, not even Lance."

"Interesting."

Already this morning I was learning new things about Pete. When he said interesting, for instance, it had a deeper meaning. "You know something?"

He tipped his head toward the neighbor's house. "Ms. Ola Mae knows more than she's telling."

Chapter Thirty

Unlike me, Pete was tall enough that he didn't need to stand on his tiptoes to peer in the windows. He shook his head after he saw the extreme damage inside, then circled the house, peering in every window.

"What does this look like to you?" I asked.

"That deliberate destruction took time and effort. Whatever these mobsters are looking for, it's important to them. Appearances suggest they think Estelle hid something inside her walls and air vents."

"I thought it might be guns or drugs, but neither of those particularly lends itself to a secret wall stash."

"It's hard to know. I was surprised at Estelle's commercial washer-dryer set, but maybe she does some of her dry-cleaning business's wash at her place."

"I wonder if the goons destroyed the appliances. If they are still operational, I bet the boys could sell that pair for at least eight hundred dollars. I'd buy the set. Imagine how wonderful it would be not to take spreads and throw rugs to the laundry mat."

"I need to take a minute," Pete said after we'd completed the lap. "Mind if we sit on the steps?"

Oh dear. His limp seemed more pronounced than before. I gestured to the wooden steps. "Please, sit. I apologize. I didn't consider walking would aggravate your injuries. I should've just done a drive-by at the marina and here."

"I'll be fine," Pete said. Then, once we were sitting on the front porch steps and facing the street, he lowered his voice. "I exaggerated my limp to justify sitting down. Cameras here too,

River. Let's wait a bit and see who shows up."

My eyebrows arched. "Where?"

"Around and about. Don't look for them. Keep your gaze on me. If you start looking for cameras, you'll give our innocence advantage away."

"You're sneaky and dangerously good at investigation strategy," I said. "I'm glad you're here to help me."

Pete reached down and massaged his calf on his hurt leg.

"I can do that." I knelt at his feet and began kneading his leg muscles. Pete groaned, and my hands stilled. "Is that too hard? I don't want to hurt you."

He grimaced, and my heart went out to him, then he tilted his head and spoke very softly. "Nothing's wrong with the leg. My ankle has a slight sprain, but your touch feels so good. I'm trying not to reach for you and kiss you right here."

"Oh. Well. I'm glad I didn't hurt you." His comment revved my libido too. I sat back on my haunches and grinned. "Impulse control is character-building they say. How much longer shall we wait? Nothing stopping us from going home right this second."

"Hold that thought," Pete said. "A cop SUV just turned onto this street. Now that's downright interesting. No lights or sirens, so he's gonna play this as a casual what-are-you-doing-here meet-up."

"And?" I asked.

"It means a cop is watching this house. He wants to know if anyone comes here so he can question them."

Lance stopped in the street, exited his SUV, and ducked under the crime scene tape. With long strides he quickly closed the gap between us. "River, this house is off-limits. You and your friend can't be here."

"Good morning, Lance." I introduced Pete and Lance, Pete not bothering to rise. "I was telling Pete about what happened to Estelle's house and he wanted to see it. We walked around the yard just now. We didn't touch anything."

"You're touching the steps," Lance said wryly, looking at Pete's cane.

"Pete injured his ankle in California before he flew home."

"I see he's banged up. What happened?"

"Workplace injury," Pete said. "Sorry to have caused any trouble. The ladies next door said all the neighbors had been looking in the windows, so I thought it wouldn't matter if we did the same."

With that, Pete rolled to his good arm side and pushed up onto his good leg, a difficult task with one arm. I handed him the cane and stood beside him. My arm wrapped around his waist.

"We haven't finished our investigation yet," Lance said, visibly relaxing. "That's why the tape's up, for all the good it's doing. Everyone's a looky-loo."

"We'll be on our way then," I said, encouraging Pete to step forward. It was like trying to move a loaded semi. He didn't budge. I struggled for something to say. "Thanks again for your help yesterday with the Tucker-Browning engagement dinner."

Lance tipped his head momentarily. "Glad to help out. Call me anytime."

"I appreciate you looking out for River until I could get here, Deputy, but I'll be helping River from now on," Pete said.

Lance gave him a dismissive glare. "If you say so." He walked away, hands clenched at his sides.

Pete headed to my van. We were most of the way there when Lance pulled away. "What was that about?" I asked.

"Staking my claim," Pete said. "Lance doesn't like the competition."

"There is no competition," I assured him.

Pete stopped, his gaze searching my face. "You've made up your mind to marry me?"

"I've made up my mind to live with you. That goes well, we'll make it legally binding. How's that sound?"

"Sounds like I'm your future fiancé. I'll take it."

"Great."

Pete took his time getting in his seat, and I could see that he had done more walking on his ankle than was good for it. "Some rest, ice, compression, and elevation are in order. Let's get you home."

His eyes brightened. "Taking me to bed already?"

"Icing the ankle."

"Oh. Not as exciting, and the TLC can wait. Let's stop at the pier. I'd love to see the ocean and hang out in our place."

"If you're sure you're up for it."

"My ankle's seen worse. I want everyone to see us, so nobody else thinks they have a claim on you."

"Pete Merrick, you're barking like a territorial dog. Next thing you'll be peeing on trees in our yard."

"Whatever it takes, hon."

Chapter Thirty-One

While Pete rested after our afternoon delight, I rose from our bed and got to work. The Ladies of Distinction luncheon on Friday would be easy. I had the menu down pat for that, having catered for them recently. However, I'd contracted to cater a baby shower on Sunday afternoon. This client, the great grandmother, left all the deciding to me, for the eats and the decorations. "Make a lot of food," she'd said in her wavering voice, "and make it good."

The only thing she'd specified were mimosas for the guests and sparkling cider for the mom-to-be, Cherie Ryland. So I went through my notes on the last baby shower I did and made a potential list in the price range we'd agreed upon. To my staples of a fruit tray, a veggie tray, and deviled eggs, I suggested chicken waffle sliders, cheesy bacon and spinach dip, blueberry tarts, cheesecake stuffed strawberries, and unicorn pretzels. I texted Cherie a copy of the food suggestions list and less than a minute later, she texted back the word "Awesome."

Good to have that settled.

I started a pot of vegetable soup for lunch, and the chopping and dicing settled me. I owned three food processors, but when I made soup, there was nothing like taking my time with the vegetables. The scent of celery, for instance, took me to a special place. Garden fresh goodness soon filled the air.

While the soup simmered, I grabbed the phone book to see if I could find Justin Adler. Not listed. I checked the internet to see if he popped up anywhere. Nothing, not even on social media. That was weird.

I needed another resource, someone who knew lots of people locally and their phone numbers. Viv Declan sprang to mind. Luckily, I now had her number in my contact list. She'd be at work at the mill, but I could leave her a message.

Viv answered on the first ring. "If it isn't my Nancy Drew friend. Find Chili yet?"

I smiled to myself. "You would've heard if I had. That's why I'm calling. My brother suggested Justin Adler might know places where Chili hunted. I don't have Justin's number. Do you have a way to contact him?"

"You still think Chili is alive? It's been a week, nearly two. Anything's possible, I suppose. Let's see, I went on a few dates with Justin but there were no sparks, no nothing, but the act. Wasn't working for either of us, so we moved on. I might've dumped his number. Nope. Lucky you. Here it is."

I jotted down the number, thanked her, and then called Justin. He didn't answer. I left a voicemail message explaining why I called and asked him to return the call.

For a few minutes, I lingered, enjoying the nourishing aromas of my soup. I had the luncheon on Friday, the baby shower Sunday afternoon, and an anniversary dinner for two on Wednesday. Then there was a big gap until the spring festival. Jobs always cropped up, but it would be nice if I had more bookings. Looked like a lot more Mondays of cleaning houses with my friend in my near future.

Wait. What about the Walker girl? She asked me to cater her wedding, and I never heard from her. I didn't have her number, but her mother owned and managed the largest hotel on the island. I called the Ocean Crest Plaza and asked for Geneva Walker.

She came on right away. "I'm so glad you called, River. We were flat out panicked last weekend when the fancy Savannah caterer that Malcom insisted upon cancelled. She said it was too far, and it was too difficult to work with my beautiful Melanie. The wedding's in five weeks."

"Five weeks? Melanie didn't mention the date when she asked

me to do it. That's very short notice."

"Yes, and I apologize that we haven't followed up. Mel came down with the flu after the bridal shower and hasn't been the same since. I'll fax you the menu."

I'd learned the hard way that people would walk all over me if I didn't protect myself. "Tell me the exact date, time, and number of people who RSVPed."

She told me. "Two thirty is an odd time. Will it be a late lunch or an early dinner? And am I to do the wedding cake?"

"A specialty baker is making the cake, and the time is at high tide since the wedding will be at Creekside Lodge. What's your fax number?"

"No need for a fax. I'll bring over my standard contract, we'll review the menu together, then I'll need a substantial deposit. For weddings, my standard policy is a $1000 deposit, of which $500 is nonrefundable. Once we sign the contract, and I have your check in hand, then I'll ink in the date. The rest of my fee will be due two days before the event."

"Yes, yes, then, please come over at once. I'll cancel my next two appointments."

"I'll be there in thirty minutes."

Much to my surprise, the menu looked doable. I'd hire my regular helpers for table service but that was easy. The other caterer must've not been as fancy as Ms. Geneva thought. Normally, I'd be racing back to my calculator at home, making sure that my numbers were fair. Instead, I asked pointblank what the other caterer had charged. The amount astounded me.

"Her fee seems high," I said. "Was she also providing the tables, chairs, linens, table décor, and place settings?"

"No. I booked those through the Lodge. She also charged me a hefty mileage fee."

"No mileage fee with me. I'll do it for half of her rate." We settled on a price, and I made sure she understood my change-order fee. Any add-ons to the contract would incur a $100 change fee, plus the supply and labor fee.

Change orders were another lesson I'd learned the hard way. Ms. Geneva initialed that specification on the contract, she signed, and I signed. I scanned the signed documents into my phone and emailed one set to her and the other to her daughter. Minutes later, I walked out of there with a check for a grand.

Next stop the bank, where I deposited the check.

No message from Pete on my phone, so I assumed he still was sleeping. I made a few turns into an older neighborhood and rode past Justin Adler's old house. The low slung brick-faced home looked as I remembered it. The graceful oak still dominated the front yard.

However, the tidy lawn was a thing of the past. A fleet of plastic trikes, trucks, scooters, and more spilled out of the open garage. Must be a young family living here now.

Mustering my courage, I stopped and knocked on the door. A harried bleached blonde I didn't recognize answered the door, baby on one hip, toddler clinging to her leg.

I handed her my business card. "Hello, I'm River Holloway. I'm trying to locate Justin Adler. His family used to live here. Do you know how to contact them?"

"You're the caterer," the woman said, pocketing the card. "I'm Anita Declan. Viv told me about you. I married her brother."

Darry Declan. Chili's friend who moved to Alaska. "Oh. Small world."

"Yes, indeed." One of her kids began crying. "Wanna come in?"

"Thanks, but no. I really can't stay. I was in the area and stopped on a whim. Is there a chance you have Justin's forwarding address?"

"I don't. Sorry. We signed a lease for the house through a property management company."

I thanked her for her time and drove away wishing I had a way to find Chili. I took a few detours on the way home, going through neighborhoods and enjoying the island's beautiful oaks. Lance phoned when I pulled into my driveway. I answered on my hands-free system.

"Heard you were asking questions again," Lance began.

I checked my mirrors. He wasn't following me. How did he know what I was doing? "I was."

"You're looking for Justin Adler? Why?"

"You're freaking me out. Did you tap my phone?"

"Can't do that without probable cause, and you wouldn't be trying to find Chili so hard if you were involved in his disappearance. I know you visited Anita Declan. The neighbor across the street calls me all the time to complain about the noise from the Declan kids. She phoned when she saw you at Anita's door. Far as I can tell, Anita has no involvement in the case, but she's renting her house from a man who used to work for Chili. I made a leap of faith and called you to ask about it. That's all."

"Oh. That makes sense. Thought you'd gone all psycho-stalker on me."

"I'm a cop, and I want to clear this case as much as you do. Did you locate Adler?"

"I don't know where he is. Pete reasoned that if Chili had gone to ground that Justin might recall some of the places he and Chili used to hunt. Maybe he's hiding at one of those hunting blinds or deer stands."

"It's been days since he disappeared. He could be halfway across the country by now."

"Perhaps, but I believe he's closer to home. Did you question Justin?"

"I followed the same dead-end trail you did. I was hoping you had better luck."

How depressing. Now there were two men in the wind. "Can you find Justin? I have limited resources, and I just landed a wedding contract that I need to plan."

"The bank president's wedding?"

"I wish. That one would be easy. This one's for Melanie Walker."

He didn't respond.

I turned on Ocean Crest Drive. "You know something about Melanie?"

"Her fiancé."

"Is he a bad guy?"

"I don't care for him. He thinks the world revolves around him."

"Oh. Melanie's that way too. Should be interesting to see what happens to them. I can't afford to get hung up on personal differences. I'm hoping they get married. I need the money."

"Pete isn't paying your bills?"

My hands jerked on the wheel. "That's none of your business."

"Sorry. I know how hard you work. I don't want him taking advantage of you."

"Thanks, but I can take care of myself."

"My offer stands. If you need me, say the word."

The call ended, and I was once again left to reflect on Lance knowing my every move. It was creepy, but he was a cop. One of the good guys. I'd had dinner with him and worked with him, but we'd never be more than friends. Heck, I didn't even consider him a friend, really, he was more of a business associate.

Lance Hamlyn's personal life wasn't my concern. Another man filled my life, a man I loved. About time I got some food into him.

Chapter Thirty-Two

Lance called two hours later, waking me from the light nap following another sexy romp. With Pete living here, we were getting a lot of exercise in bed and not so much sleep.

"Meet me at the Christmas Tree Farm," Lance said. "I have a surprise. Don't tell anyone where you're headed."

The full relaxation vibe I felt faded in a heartbeat. Pete and I were sprawled together in bed. His hurt arm was cushioned by a pillow. Aside from sleeping beside Pete, cuddling with him was my new favorite thing.

This interruption irritated me. "First, I'm not going anywhere without Pete. Second, we have plans for this afternoon," I hedged and immediately felt a wave of remorse. Lance had been kind enough to help me with that catering job. I could at least hear him out. "Is this about the case?"

"It's a matter of importance to both of us," Lance said curtly. "Twenty minutes. Bring the boyfriend if you must."

The call ended abruptly.

"What's this about?" Pete asked as I tossed the phone on the bed.

"I'm not sure. Lance said it was important. You heard the rest."

Pete nodded, his expression grim. "The tree farm, where's that?"

"North end of the island. It's been there for years, but the Bromfields don't advertise."

"You want to take this meeting?"

"I want to find Chili."

"I hear you, but from all the effort you've already put into finding him, he doesn't want to be found. He's beginning to sound like an urban legend."

I punched him playfully on his good shoulder. "Chili is as real as you and me. He's my friend and he's in trouble. We're sitting here all comfy-cozy and he's out in the woods eating bugs for all I know."

"If he's alive."

Pete's words galvanized me. I scrambled to my feet. "He is alive. I can't give up hope. If you don't want to come, I'll go by myself."

Pete sat up straighter, alarm flaring in his eyes. "Hold on. I never said I didn't want to go. We'll do this together, partner."

Twenty minutes later found us in the tree farm parking lot, and I use the term parking lot loosely because people parked near the shed-sized office when they came here in December. We'd had a lot of warm weather already in March, so grassy weeds ringed the area. The little hut that usually glowed with cheerful Christmas lights looked forlorn and empty.

Evergreen trees stretched as far as I could see in every direction, and the fragrance reminded me of happier, less stressful times.

"Where's Lance?" I wondered aloud, since we were the only vehicle here, the only people for apparently miles around. The owners of the farm spent the spring months helping raise their grandkids in Atlanta, so they weren't in residence now, another reason they didn't advertise their wares.

As if on cue, a police SUV motored up and slotted in beside me. Pete and I exited the van. Lance joined us in front of the vehicles. "Glad you could make it," Lance said, glaring at Pete. "Sorry to interrupt your other plans."

I could feel Pete bristling, so I stepped between the two men.

"What's so important you dragged us all the way out here?"

Lance glared at Pete over my head. "Found somebody."

"You did?" I searched his face, hoping against hope. "Is Chili okay?"

Lance puffed out his chest and fisted his hands on his hips. "Chili's still missing. Justin Adler was hiding at his girlfriend's house. He agreed to meet me here, but only if you were present."

I didn't understand why he spoke in a snarky tone, nor why he radiated disapproval. "Did you question him yet?"

"He wouldn't give me the time of day. Said he'd meet us here at three o'clock. We're here and on time, but I don't see him. I wonder if he played me."

My phone rang. I recognized the name on the caller ID display. It was a new name I'd entered yesterday. I selected the speaker phone option. "Justin? Where are you?"

"Can't tell you, River. Stop looking for me. I don't know where Chili is."

Behind me, I heard Pete doing something with his phone. Really? He was taking a call now?

Lance crowded closer to my phone. "This is Deputy Lance Hamlyn. We need you to come in and talk with us at the station."

"No way, Deputy. I changed my mind. I like walking around on this green earth. I haven't done anything wrong. I trust River, but I don't know you."

"Justin, I want to know where Chili used to hunt," I piped in, anxious to get results. "Did he have any favorite places?"

"He could be anywhere." Justin listed a couple of properties. "Take those with a grain of salt. We haven't hunted together in years."

"Thanks," I said, as if he'd given me vital information. He hadn't. The places he'd mentioned were large tracts of land that even I, a nonhunter, knew were common hunting grounds. We had so many hunting seasons down here, that it always seemed to be hunting season. My gut told me Chili wouldn't hide in a place with frequent traffic. He'd find someplace away from the public eye and wait out the trouble, whatever it was.

"Keep your head down, River," Justin said. "The people after the Bolz family are mean as timber rattlers."

"What's this all about?" I asked.

"Can't talk anymore. Gotta go."

The phone clicked off. Pete gazed around at me with a sheepish expression, phone to his ear. "Yeah, I can't talk right now. Handle it. Gotta go."

"Really, Pete?" I asked, my irritation focused on him. "You took a call just now?"

He shrugged. "Something came up. I dealt with it."

I heard the whine of an engine in the distance. "What's that sound?" I asked.

The men stilled as we strained to listen. Pete spoke up. "Outboard motor."

I leapt at that possibility. "Could've been Justin. Maybe he's headed somewhere in a boat. Is there a marina near here?"

"No," Lance said. "I checked the county maps before I drove out here. There's a tidal creek behind the main house on this property. The Bromfields have a dock. Even if that is a boat, and even if it is Justin, there are too many marsh islands and hammocks where he could hole up with a minimum of supplies. Too many private fish camps out there. We'd never find him."

"Is he going wherever Chili is?" I asked.

"Doubt it," Lance said. "The sheep are fleeing the big bad wolf, whoever that is. Typically, when that happens, they hide out alone. They think they're invisible that way."

I dismissed his puzzling remark and mentioned the crux of the matter. "So far we have Chili missing, his mother dead, and two mobsters with Italian sounding last names. Since our leads are few and far between, I'm inclined to believe you that this is linked to organized crime."

"Seems pretty disorganized to me," Lance said. "All we've got are Ferarrelli and Barnegas and they aren't talking. Their fancy lawyers got their cases moved up the court docket. Both made bail and are wearing electronic monitoring devices at Ocean Crest Plaza. The Ocean Crest, of all places. I can't even afford to eat lunch there."

"Maybe crime does pay after all," I said flippantly, knowing full well that all of us could afford a lunch that cost twice the usual rate, but who would do that unless they had money to burn?

Lance growled and Pete looked thoughtful.

"What a waste of time," Lance said, glancing at his watch. "Quitting time coming up soon. Meet you guys for a beer somewhere?"

"We have other plans," Pete said.

Chapter Thirty-Three

"I appreciate you saying we have other plans," I said as we retreated to the comfy sectional in my living room. "I only wish I knew what they were."

Pete pulled out his phone. "Our plans are to get to the bottom of this case. You can't stop thinking about it, and the deputy keeps dogging you. We need to solve this case and get our privacy back."

"Are you making another call?" I asked in a pointed tone.

"Nope. We're going to listen to Justin again. I faked the phone call and used my phone as a recording device."

"Oh! And there I was getting testy with you for not paying attention. That's a great move."

"I have some other moves you may like," he said with a sly grin.

My face heated. "Oh, you! Later, definitely, but for now I want to hear that recording."

"May not get us anywhere. I planned to listen for background noises."

He played the recording a few times. There was a distant sound I thought was a bird call, but what if it was a child? "Can you go back to the part just before he hangs up? I can't tell if that's the shrill of a bird or a kid."

We listened a few more times. "Could be a kid," Pete said.

"In that case, his girlfriend and her kid went with him. I don't know who he's seeing. Lance didn't mention her name. We could ask him."

"Information is power," Pete said. "We keep the power

centered between the two of us. If we start asking about the girlfriend, we may trigger the wrong kind of attention on her family. Unless we need Justin again, we'll keep this audio file to ourselves."

"Lance doesn't want me on the case unless he needs me to grill people, and if he found out about the recording, he'd be upset. He may even think we're taping him. That wouldn't be good." It was hard to put a positive spin on our actions today because we struck out. "Okay, so recapping, the whole trip to the tree farm was a bust."

"I wouldn't say that. Your cop buddy is frustrated. He wants this resolved too. Must be up for a promotion."

"Nailed it. He's angling for the chief deputy slot. I didn't care for him when Doug got arrested. He was so hard on my brother, but Doug turned his life around after his arrest. I've worked with Lance a few times now and he seems fair and decent, so I've changed my opinion of him. He wasn't responsible for Doug's troubles. Doug was."

"He wants me out of the way. He wants you."

"Just so you know, I did nothing to encourage him."

"You're a walking, breathing woman who crossed his path. For some guys, that's all it takes." An odd look crossed his face. "But you're so much more than that."

I batted my eyelashes at him. "You don't think he admires my brain?"

He folded me close with his good arm. "We're together. Whatever he's admiring, he'd better get used to doing it from a distance."

A while later, I stirred, thoughts about Chili Bolz pinwheeling in my head. Chili was out there, alone in the woods. That was what I hoped. I couldn't consider the alternative. There was a fifty-fifty chance he'd been hurt. He was afraid to come out of hiding. Also true or we'd have found him by now, but why go to ground? Was the mob gunning for his family? What business did the Bolz family have with criminals? Why did my intruder ask about money?

My disconnected thoughts chased each other round and about until the endless looping caused me to rub my aching temples.

"What's wrong?" Pete said, his voice husky with rest and relaxation.

"The case. We know some of the pieces, but the missing pieces are the crucial ones. You were right earlier. We've missed something."

"You have good intuition and judgment. Let's review what we know, focusing on the people involved. Who gives you a bad feeling?"

"Aside from the two mob associates, I'd say Garnet Pierce, the marina master. She tried to hustle us away from the docks the other day. I've been at Bayside numerous times before to pick up fish from Chili and she never budged from behind the shop counter."

"Good enough for me. Let's run over to Bayside again."

We drove to the marina and found the shop locked up tight with a closed sign prominently displayed. I searched for an hours-of-operation posting, but it wasn't there. Garnet's big red truck was gone. Granted it was late afternoon, but shouldn't someone be at the dock on a sunny afternoon like this?

"Look for Chili's boat again. Maybe Garnet lied to us before, and it was here all along," Pete suggested. "What was the vessel's name?"

"The *Reel Fine*." I shaded my eyes and scanned the dozen boats, yachts, pontoon boats, and sailboats moored at the dock. "It's not here."

"Neither is the dockmaster. Is she usually here this time of day?"

"I don't come here enough to know." I shrugged. "We're the only car in the parking lot. That's odd for a sunny afternoon in warm weather."

"It makes sense if this whole place is a front," Pete said.

I remembered about the cameras, shielded my mouth, and

spoke softly. "Let's discuss this on the road."

We pulled away, and Pete turned to me. "The dock must be a sham. We should assume organized crime owns the dock and all the boats moored there. The fishing charters Chili pulled in were icing on the fake window dressing."

"Islanders would say your statement is too incredible to be true, but nothing in this Bolz case has been as I assumed it was all along. I agree, the marina should be busier. It used to be busier. Even though I occasionally went out there to see Chili, I didn't notice the level of dock activity. The concept of the dock being a front feels right, but at the same time, how'd I miss that?"

"Why would you have reason to look beyond a dock of moored boats? That's the benefit of me coming in cold."

"I need to think." Grim reality driving my thoughts, I made random turns on familiar roads, circling a large residential neighborhood. "Okay. If we assume the mob owns or controls the dock, it follows that Garnet works for the mob, which explains how she affords that expensive truck. That also means Chili worked for the mob, and not only him, his entire family, since they were all threatened or hurt. Plus, Estelle's house was nearly dismantled."

"That fits the facts we know," Pete said.

I thought it through some more and shook my head. "That's where the scenario falls apart. Mobs typically move guns or drugs, but we have a low crime rate here and no major problems with drugs. What's the point of owning a marina?"

Pete didn't answer for a long moment. "This island could be a way station. The deserted marina is fifteen miles from an interstate highway. They could transport drugs or guns anywhere from here, and no one would know. Or they could be laundering money. If that's the case, it's likely they ran the money through the marina office."

"Maybe that sufficed until they had too much money for the marina to absorb without detection. They had the marina do double duty at first, both a controlled entry point and a laundering facility," I said, warming to the new theme as I returned to the main road. "Estelle had a dry-cleaning business. I've heard criminals target small operations like car washes and dry cleaners to funnel money into banks."

"Could be," Pete said, "but I keep coming back to the destruction of Estelle's house. That is a fact and the men who did it are likely mob-connected. Makes me think it wasn't guns or drugs. Money stacks easily in the dead zone between walls. If a money shipment went missing, and the mob thought Estelle took it, how'd it get into her house? The ladies next door would notice strangers coming and going from Estelle's house."

"If money flowed through her business the sisters next door wouldn't have seen anything at the house," I countered. "For all we know, Chili and Kale moved the physical money around. They would have good reason for going in and out of her home or business."

"If she was laundering money, it wouldn't have to physically enter her business, only her business's financial records." Pete sighed. "It's too easy to stray from the facts. We're guessing."

I maneuvered through a traffic circle and heavier traffic as I drove south. "Maybe, but laundering money fits. The cops searched her house. A drug dog would've found traces of illegal substances if vast quantities of drugs moved through that house. Guns take up a lot of space. How would those have gone in and out of the house or her tiny dry cleaners without notice?"

"Hmm. Good point. Did the cops search her dry cleaners?"

I shrugged. "If they thought her death was a home invasion, why would they? Besides, her shop has plaster walls. That's not easily accessed or repaired. It would make no sense to hide money in a plaster wall, and I know for a fact that neither Chili nor Kale ever tried to plaster a wall."

"We need a fresh angle, something to help us nail her killer."

"We could visit her shop." I hadn't connected the shop to Estelle's death before now. As a kid, I often went to work with Estelle and her sons at the dry cleaners. An idea sparked. "I remember a deer trail through the woods behind that shop. Kale,

Chili, and I played there all the time."

"Thatta girl." Pete patted my leg. "Tell me about the trail. Is it wide enough for a car?"

Could we have solved this case by driving around and brainstorming? My pulse quickened. "Used to be a narrow path. We need to see it."

"Where does the trail lead?" Pete asked.

"It runs adjacent to an old drainage swale. We never went to the end because it cut behind a parking lot for a spooky abandoned building. That place has since been torn down, and the Beach Supplies shop is there now."

"Let's check it out."

I drove behind the beach novelty store and a rusted dumpster sat where the trail used to end. Thick brush ringed the dumpster, suggesting it hadn't moved in years. "Rats," I said. "No one's used this access point lately. So much for the secret passageway theory. Let's visit the dry-cleaning shop."

"You're welcome to look at anything you like," Kendra Gillies said when I explained why we wanted to look around. "We keep thinking someone will shut us down any minute now."

"How is everyone getting paid?" I asked as I looked around the customer side of the business. It used to seem twice as large.

"One of the employees knows someone at probate. They said to petition the court to get our wages when Estelle's estate is settled. So we're keeping track of everything. I hope it gets resolved soon. I can't go more than a couple of weeks without a paycheck."

"I hope it's settled soon too. If you don't mind, I hope it'd be all right if we look and see if there's any place Estelle could've stored valuables here. I'm hoping to figure out why someone killed her."

Kendra shrugged. "Suit yourself. That island cop already came around asking questions and rapping on the plaster walls. Couldn't help him either. Estelle didn't have an office here. She did all the bookwork at home."

Pete and I lapped the inside of the building in a few minutes. "Nothing extra here," I said confidentially to Pete. "I hope they keep this place open. It's the only dry cleaners on the island."

I thanked Kendra for allowing us to look. Back in the van, I rolled my stiff neck. "That was disappointing. I was hoping to find a bright neon clue."

Pete reached over and rubbed my neck. "No such thing. But I know how to fix this."

"You do?"

"Ice cream time," Pete said. "I think better with ice cream."

I brightened. "Me too."

Chapter Thirty-Four

We waited our turn at the bustling Island Creamery. All around us, people chatted happily, kids dashed in and out of the café style table and chair sets. Outside, two dogs were tied to trees, and the bicycle rack was jammed with bikes.

"You could make a killing in a sweet setup like this," Pete said. "The location and vibe are perfect."

The sun no longer seemed quite so bright. "I'm not interested in running a storefront. Too many details would keep me from cooking. I am a caterer."

"Got it."

His curt answer surprised me. "I didn't mean to sound critical, but I like what I'm doing now. I don't want to change careers."

"I'm used to fixing things, hon. Didn't mean to imply you weren't perfect as you are. I did say the words 'you could make a killing' but I meant the universal you. Perhaps I should become a shop owner as I favor regular income."

"Ah. I get it. You're trying to fix yourself."

"I need a new direction, but I'm in no hurry to decide anything. I'm right where I want to be. With you."

"Aww. Don't make me get all weepy in public. I'm where I want to be too."

We ordered and sat with our choices. Mocha caramel cone for me, mint chocolate chip for him. A family with a toddler and an infant sat nearby and my gaze kept going to the sweet baby the mom held in her arms.

Pete reached for my hand and squeezed it. "I know," he said

softly.

Recent months kept me off-balance emotionally. I'd buried my mother, dealt with a brother getting arrested, reunited with Pete, and now I was helping the Bolz family. I shouldn't be thinking about starting a family, but that was all I could think about. My biological clock wasn't just ticking, it was going super nova.

Pete polished off his ice cream quickly while I savored mine, licking off small bits at a time to make it last.

"Keep doing that and we're not going to make it back to your place," Pete warned. "Watching you with that ice cream makes me hot."

Nothing wrong with this man's libido. "This is a family place. Rein it in. We're trying to solve this case, remember? You said ice cream would clear your head."

"I did experience clarity." He lifted my hand to his lips and kissed it. "Something Estelle said about bridge. What if she wasn't talking about her bridge group? What if she meant a physical bridge?"

"Which one? There are five river bridges on the causeway, and numerous culvert style bridges over ditches and such on the island."

"Any of them strike you as relevant? Any place that has a connection to Chili and Kale?"

"No-o-o." I answered automatically but something glimmered on the edge of my thoughts. Took me a moment but I dredged it up. A couple of times, Estelle brought us out to the old drawbridge to crab in the creek. The bridge remnant lurked in the footprint of the new tall bridge that didn't need to stop traffic to let a boat pass. "Maybe."

I explained about the games we used to play at the old bridge. Pete nodded. "Let's go there."

As the crow flew, the old bridge was midway between the bustling new marina and the old one, between prosperity and people scratching out a living. To drive from one marina to another took about fifteen minutes due to how the roads were laid out and the traffic circles. From the ice cream shop, I took King's Way as if leaving the island, then veered off to the right at the last possible moment, taking the ramp down to the old bridge.

We had the place to ourselves. The metal signs about the swift-current dangers and being kind to manatees were faded nearly to white. The recycle box for old fishing line overflowed as did the fifty-five-gallon drum that served as a trash can. Bird droppings lined the concrete siderails and the big concrete barricades where the old bridge had been lopped off.

"Didn't know this was here," Pete said, looking around. "It's like a moment out of time."

Except for the constant swoosh of cars overhead on the elevated causeway. "It's early in the year for crabbing, but this bridge is used heavily in the summer. We used to come out here about twilight. It is truly a kids' paradise. Chili loved playing the troll under the bridge and scaring me and Kale."

"Sounds like we should look under the bridge." Pete pointed to the path with his cane.

"Not much space under there. I should go."

"I'm coming too. I don't want you down there alone."

My self-reliance bristled. I wasn't used to having someone watching out for my safety so closely. It cramped my style. He meant well, I told myself as I headed under the bridge. To my delight, there was still a narrow, worn path. Kids today must still do as we had done.

I got down on all fours to crawl under the structure. Pete stood watch on the path. Underneath the bridge was tidy, no garbage here. Nothing with flashy neon lights that screamed clue either.

"See anything?" Pete asked.

"If there's a clue about Chili's whereabouts, it's hiding in plain sight."

"This feels right. The message was one only you would understand," Pete said. "Tell me everything you see."

"Dirt. Grass. Weeds. A spider web on the far side. Some spray paint that was painted over poorly."

"Can you make out what it says?"

I studied the paint along one of the girders, sussing out red letters bleeding through white paint. "Maybe 'girls rule, boys drool.' Again, not helpful."

"Any place where someone might put a note?"

"Like the secret stash?" I answered glibly.

"What's that?"

"Chili called the dirt hole up near the bank his secret stash. I haven't thought about that in fifteen years."

"If this is the right bridge, something will be there."

"Okay, but I'll need a shower afterward. I have to inch up the bank on my back to reach the secret stash."

"Sounds more and more like the right place. A little dirt never hurt anyone."

Easy for him to say. He wasn't wearing a yellow blouse. River mud ruined light colored fabric. But this was for Chili.

I inched up the incline on my back, reaching the top and hoping I'd made enough noise to scare away any snakes that lived down here. I reached into the alcove and felt the palm-sized metal box. "Got something."

"Come out of there," Pete said. "Let's examine it together."

"On my way." I scooted down the bank with the box in one palm. Delight at finding something mingled with regret. I should've thought of this sooner. Had Chili been stuck in the woods all this time expecting me to find him? Would there be anything inside this box?

Pete followed me back up to the old bridge, brushing the dirt out of my hair and off my back when we stopped. "What is it?" he asked.

"The box of secrets," I said, then burst out laughing. "This little mint tin was the Holy Grail for Chili. He loved leaving coded messages inside. I never understood them, so even if we find something, it may not make any sense."

"Open it," Pete said.

I pried the box open, hinges creaking, and there was a tiny slip of dirty paper inside. Two strings of numbers were penciled on it. "What do we do with this?" I asked. "What does it mean?"

Pete took one look at it and his face lit up. "It means we know where to find Chili."

Chapter Thirty-Five

Pete hustled me in the van. "They're GPS coordinates," he said once we were buckled in and on the road. "Drive around in a neighborhood and park. I need to check if anyone is following us."

"How do you know they're a GPS location?" I asked, following his suggestion. "They look like two strings of numbers with decimal points."

"Trust me. They're GPS coordinates."

I pulled out and motored over to King's Terrace, looping around on different residential streets before parking at Mallery Park. Kids played on the multiplex climbing set, adults swatted tennis balls beside us. "What do we do with GPS coordinates? How do we even know if Chili left them?"

"We don't, which makes me think I should take you back to your place while I check it out."

"No way. First, with your hurt ankle you're in no condition to be tromping through wilderness, and even if you went alone, the chance Chili would come out of hiding for you are zero."

Pete hesitated. "I don't like the thought of you being in danger."

"We're in danger sitting in the car. One of those big oak limbs overhead could shear off and fall on us before we could react. Someone could careen into us on the road."

"We need each other," he said.

"Yes, we do and we're making relationship progress." I turned my thoughts to Chili. "How do we follow the numbers?"

"Our smart phones can do it." He plugged the numbers into

his phone. "Head north."

"Roger that." I made my way to Frederica Road and sped past a gamut of offices and shops. "This is so cool. We'll find Chili and our lives will go back to normal. I'm looking forward to taking a shower."

"You'll get that shower tonight, that much I can promise. As for the rest, there's so much we still don't know. It's been over a week since you received the bridge clue. Chili might have moved on to a new place."

I didn't like the sound of that. I wanted Chili to be safe and alive, but Pete was right. Even if we found Chili, whatever caused him to go into hiding most likely hadn't changed.

The miles rolled by. We passed the turnoff to Sea Island and came to the fork to go toward the fort or toward the point. "Which way?" I asked.

Pete checked his phone. "Go right."

I hung a right, and a memory surfaced. "Estelle's great uncle had a fish camp on the north end twenty years ago. He didn't have any kids and the land passed out of the family. If Estelle inherited it, she sold the property."

"We're on the right track then."

My foot eased off the accelerator. "No, we're not. The fish camp became a destination site for special occasions. I've catered a few weddings there in recent years. We already passed the turn-off for it."

"It's less developed out this way. Let's try the GPS location first," Pete said, glancing over his shoulder. "Keep going."

We drove two miles. "Hold up," Pete said. "We're close."

"How close?"

"Very. See any opening to turn left?"

To my right and left were well-ordered rows of pines as far as I could see. I scanned the left looking for an access road. "No turn-ins, but the shoulder is wide enough we can pull over."

"Everybody and their brother recognizes your van. We'll bring more trouble Chili's way if we do that."

I passed a spot that looked like we could nose into it. "I'm gonna try that place," I said, turning around and heading toward the gap in the trees. I took it slow on the shoulder, inching my way into the tree line. I got us all the way in, turned to Pete, and said, "How's that?"

"Not bad. Someone would have to be looking to spot our vehicle. When I'm on this stretch, I usually push my speed a bit to quicken the trip. We've got no one behind us, no one coming our way. We should be perfect nestled in here." He jerked his thumb toward the rear. "What do you have back there in the realm of food?"

"Not much. Some water bottles and a stash of energy bars. If he's out here, Chili might enjoy fresh water and the bars."

"Great idea. Let's grab as much as we can carry and then head north, northwest."

At first it seemed like a grand adventure, following the compass on his phone. Then it became a slog. Despite his injuries, Pete soldiered on without complaint, but I couldn't hold my frustration inside any longer. "This is ridiculous. I can't see the van, and I have no idea how to get back to the van before dark."

"Let's take a break for a few minutes on that fallen tree over there."

I followed him step for step until we sat down. "Drink your water, River," Pete said.

"Saving it for Chili," I replied.

"He wouldn't want you dehydrated."

"How is he surviving out here?" I asked.

"Not very well," a male voice rumbled behind me.

Chapter Thirty-Six

My tiredness fled in a heartbeat and I jumped up. "Chili! Oh my gosh, we found you."

A wreck of a man shambled out of the trees. I wouldn't have recognized my friend without hearing his voice. Like Pete, he walked with a limp. Fading bruises camouflaged his dirty, bearded face. Leaves dotted his tangled hair.

I moved to hug him but Chili waved me off, then he sat beside me on the log. "Anybody follow you?" Chili asked.

"Nope." I thrust the bag of goodies his way. "We brought you water and energy bars."

Chili took the bag, opened a water bottle, and gulped its contents.

"I'm Pete Merrick," Pete said, extending a hand around me. "Not sure if you remember me, Chili. River and I dated before I moved to California."

"Yeah. I heard about you," Chili said, looking Pete dead in the eye. "You're the guy who broke her heart."

"Working on that," Pete said, retracting his hand. "What's your story?"

"What's going on in the outside world?" Chili countered after he drained the water and started on the energy bars.

I brought him up to speed about his mother's death. "I'm really sorry about your Mom."

"It liketa broke me. I'm gonna kill the man that did this."

"You know who killed Estelle?"

"Got a passing-good idea it was the same guy who nearly beat me to death."

"Who?" I asked. "Tell me, and I'll have him arrested so fast your head will spin."

"No names, jails, or cops," Chili said. "I can't go home yet. Besides, it's too dangerous for you."

Air hissed through my clenched teeth. "I don't know about your place, but not much is left of your Mom's house. Two guys took it apart."

"Names?"

"Ferarrelli and Barnegas. Mob enforcers, so we've been told. What did you get into?"

"Figured there'd be a Ferarrelli involved. They're behind the money laundering. It was supposed to be easy money for Mama. Everything was going great until a shipment vanished. Kale was so scared. They confronted him first when our lives went to hell. They threatened to hack off all his fingers and toes, one by one."

I shuddered. "About your brother. There's good news. He's alive and in federal custody."

Tears filled Chili's eyes. "Kale's alive and safe? Fingers and toes?"

I nodded. "He asked for me, and I visited him in jail. I saw his fingers and assume his toes are still attached too. He asked me to do something for him."

Chili tugged my sleeve. "What? Please tell me he found out where the missing shipment is. This is a matter of life and death."

"He didn't mention any missing money. He wanted me to ask Jude Ernest to be his lawyer. The ambulance-chasing guy from TV."

Chili's head popped up, and a calculating look filled his eyes. "Uncle Jay is helping Kale?"

"Yep. I didn't recognize him at first. Looks like he ceased personal hygiene two years ago."

"Take it from me, when your belly's empty for days, cleanliness pales in significance."

"No judgements from us. We're here to help."

Chili jerked a thumb toward Pete. "You trust this guy?

"Yep. He's the one."

"Day-am. He don't look like much. You two get into a fight?"

Pete cleared his throat. "I just pissed off the wrong people. Anyway, I left that life behind. I'm with River now."

"You better not hurt her," Chili said. "I may not look like much, but River's always been L'il Sis to me. You hurt her again, and I'll make your life a living hell. You'll wish you were dead. That's a promise."

"Tough words for someone in your position," Pete said.

"Pete won't hurt me," I said and changed the subject. "What can we do to get you home?"

"Not going home. Look, I sent the money for Mama's funeral to Pastor Debra. Kale and I kept emergency cash in the woods, in the event something happened. I used every last cent on Mama's funeral. Please keep her ashes until I can figure this out."

"Her ashes are safe. You haven't said what 'this' is yet. What happened? I'm not leaving here until you tell me the whole story."

"I've been broke all my life, but truly I never struggled to survive like this before. I appreciate how Mama scrimped and saved to keep a roof over our heads and clothes on our backs. She did what she had to do, and I don't want you to judge her poorly."

"I would never do that. Tell me how y'all got in this mess."

"After years of trying to make the dry-cleaning business efficient and profitable, Mama heard about this easy money job. All she had to do was make her business look more profitable on paper and bank the exterior cash flow in certain designated accounts across the region. Did it for a couple of years with no problem whatsoever. Then a shipment went missing. A million dollars. The Ferarrelli's demanded their money, but we didn't have it. I thought my brother committed suicide over this, but I'm glad he faked his death and hid out in Florida. I tried to keep watch over Mama, but the bastards jumped me and beat me within an inch of my life. I couldn't protect her in this shape, so I hid in the woods. I couldn't go to the cops because the money laundering operation was illegal, and I couldn't risk Mama going to prison. I spent a couple of nights in the woods by her house, and I left my hat upside down in the chair at my place so she'd know I was alive. When they didn't go after her right away, I thought she was safe, so I ranged further from the house. I should've stayed close to her. I screwed up. Not sure what I could've done to help her in this shape, but at least it would've felt like I did something more than look out for my own sorry hide. It pains me with every breath I take that I let her down." He glanced at me. "Did the missing money surface?"

"No. Who took it?"

"If I knew I'd get it back. You sure Kale's safe?"

"As sure as I can be. He wanted out of our county jail, so he's cutting a deal with the feds. They've agreed to move him to a federal facility. Jesup is the nearest one, and I hope that's where he goes."

"He doesn't have much to bargain with. Someone stole the money from the new drop site."

"Where's that?" Pete asked.

"Nope. Not getting you in any deeper." Chili nodded to the woods around us. "After Mama died, I've been hanging close to this place, in case you found the message. Now that you know I'm alive, stop looking for me."

"I don't understand why your mom asked me to look for you if you two had a prearranged signal you were okay. What did she hope to gain?"

"Sorry for everything, River. I don't know why she dragged you into it, but this trouble is more than any of us could handle. It wasn't my choice for her to get involved with money laundering. She did that on her own without telling Kale or me. Maybe she involved you to make sure someone kept asking questions."

"I would've asked questions no matter what. I've heard nothing about missing money, except from some crazy person who invaded my commercial kitchen. Look, this isn't your fault, Chili. Your mother got the family into this without considering the downside. You and Kale paid a stiff price already, Estelle paid with her life, and the money is still missing."

"If I knew where that million dollars was, I'd give it back. But I don't know who ripped it off. I wish Mama had never agreed to wash that money."

"We can't change the past. We have to figure out how to proceed. With a Ferarrelli still on the island, it isn't safe for you to come out of hiding. What are you doing for food, water, and shelter?"

"I've found all three from time to time. I'm getting along fine."

He didn't look fine to me, but he was mobile and his mind sounded clear. "How can I reach you again?"

He thought for a long moment. "Use Uncle Jay for now. Kale trusts him and so do I."

"Is he really your uncle?"

"Not blood kin, but he woulda married Mama if she'd said yes. Our natural father is mean as a cottonmouth, and she spent her adult life hiding from him. Couldn't get divorced or he'd find out where we were."

"With the internet, couldn't he search for your names?"

"She changed our names, but it was so long ago they feel like ours now."

If this was my only chance to ask for information, I had to be proactive. "Something's fishy about the dockmaster and Justin, your hunting buddy. Garnet is encouraging us to steer clear of the marina, and Justin Adler is downright spooked by everything. He's gone to ground too. We almost didn't find him to ask about your hunting blinds. That was before we found the GPS numbers under the bridge. How'd you come up with that clue?"

"It's an old clue. A long time ago, Uncle Jay used to leave them for Kale and me to figure out. He showed us how to get the coordinates on our phones."

Made sense. I dug in my pocket and handed him the rusted mint tin. "Here's a treasure for you. The box of secrets."

Chili pushed it back. "Keep it. Gotta be light on my feet these days."

"It's for luck, and it barely weighs anything."

Emotions flickered over his face until he reached for it. "All right, L'il Sis. I'll take it. I guess you're entitled to answers. What do you want to know?"

"Are Garnet and Justin dirty?"

He tucked the tin in his shirt pocket and shrugged. "Don't know. Sealed five-gallon buckets of money would appear overnight in my boat. I hauled the buckets to Mama's back door. Kale deposited the money in regional banks. Everything worked fine until it didn't."

"Garnet has cameras all over that dock," Pete said. "You ever break in the office to watch the video feed or spy on your boat to see who left the money?"

"Didn't want to know. I tried to make a decent living for me and Mama with my charter business. I did okay, but it was never enough to pay the bills. We needed the extra income from Mama's laundry business, which is what she called the money laundering for the Ferarrelli cartel."

"What about Justin?" I asked, needing more answers, regardless of the risk.

"Kale told him about the threat to cut off all his digits. Spooked the hell out of Justin. He didn't come around after that. A real fair-weather friend. Haven't spoken to him in six months. Not since before Kale died at sea, or I should say, faked his death at sea. Took you a while to walk all this way. You should head back now."

"It feels wrong to leave you alone out here. Though I am very thankful you're alive."

"I'm alive and now that I can range farther, I'll solve my problem. Thanks for the energy bars and the water. I won't have to hunt for tonight's supper."

"Someone took your boat," I said. "Garnet said Deputy Hamlyn towed it away as evidence."

"Trust no one," Chili said, rising and shuffling away.

Chapter Thirty-Seven

Finding Chili and then watching him melt into the woods hurt my heart. I wanted him to get his life back, but it wasn't that simple. A stolen million dollars had cost his mother's life.

"Penny for your thoughts," Pete said as I drove home.

"Not sure they're worth even a cent," I grumbled. "We did what we set out to do, find Chili, but it changed nothing. Now I feel worse because I can't help him."

"You aren't responsible for fixing Chili's problems. He's a grown man, a man that had a choice to say no to money laundering."

"I'm not sure about that. Chili would do anything for his mom. Once she was involved, he would've helped her, no questions asked."

"They worked for the mob," Pete reminded. "Let's not forget that key point."

I negotiated the last traffic circle. "I get that, I do, but—"

"But nothing. A lot of money is missing. One person is dead, two more fear for their lives. This isn't your problem. Promise me you'll let it go."

My grip on the wheel tightened until my knuckles stood out in stark relief. "I can't do that. Chili's in big trouble. I have to help him."

"Bad idea. The people who are after Chili and Kale don't value human life. People are objects to them, tools to achieve an end. Killing is their way of life because if they aren't useful to their bosses they get killed."

"People matter. My friends matter."

"Think about what you're doing. You're drawing attention to yourself from the wrong element." Pete shifted in his seat to face me. "These people, they'll twist your loyalty and use it against you. They'll come after your business and destroy your reputation. I experienced that firsthand in California. Ultimately, I walked away. Our future mattered more than my principles or my net worth. I have to know, given your intense loyalty to your friend Chili, does my walking away from the California bad guys make me a coward in your eyes?"

"It makes you smart," I said. "You didn't have a chance. The deck was stacked against you from the beginning. This situation with the Bolz family is different. I know how Chili and Kale think, and why they broke the law. With their mother gone, they'll have a chance to make their own way, without being encumbered by Estelle's poor choices."

Pete shook his head, his lips curved into a wry smile. "You could sell ice to Eskimos. You sugar coated my situation and Chili's so that we were victimized by others."

I shot him a cool look. "Weren't you?"

Pete gazed out the window at the golf course we were passing. "I wanted to hang the moon for you. Yet, I crawled home, wounded in body and spirit, and you welcomed me with open arms. I'm not that rising superstar any longer. I'm broken and poor."

"You'll make your mark on the world again. It's in your nature, Pete."

"Darn right I'll get it back."

We rode the rest of the way in silence, each ruminating on our own thoughts. Another woman might reconsider engagement to a man who'd lost everything, but Pete was the man for me. I'd learned that truth this year. I wanted to bear his children. Hearing him say he would start over proved his spirit was healing.

Now, if I could just figure out who stole that missing money. I hadn't seen anyone flashing cash at the bars the other night, no pricey cars that someone suddenly acquired, no mysterious relative that bequeathed someone a fortune. However, I wasn't tuned into the local scene enough to have a long-term appreciation of people's financial situation, but I knew who was.

Vivian Declan.

I'd call her right after I got an ice pack on Pete's ankle. It must be throbbing after hiking through the woods. And then I'd take a shower. Couldn't forget that.

The black cat sat on my front steps when I pulled into the drive. He yowled and paced when he saw me, his tail held high. "What's up with Major?" I wondered aloud.

"Who?" Pete glanced at the steps. "Oh, the cat. He's wound up and not scampering off. Odd. I didn't think he liked me."

"He doesn't know you yet. He barely knows me. But he has an agenda, though I have no idea what it is."

Pete watched the cat for a few more seconds, then he focused on me. "You carry any weapons in the van?"

"Weapons? What on earth for?"

"The cat is agitated enough to overcome his sense of self-preservation. He isn't running away. He recognizes your van, and he's letting you know he's upset. Given what we know about the dangerous people after the Bolz family, we should heed the warning."

"You got all that from the cat pacing on the front steps?"

"He ever done that before?"

"Well, no."

Realization dawned like a rogue beach wave. Something was wrong here. Pete and the cat warned of danger. I could argue that my locked house was secure, or I could pay attention.

I trusted Pete and the cat.

I needed to heed the warning. "Okay, I believe you."

"Good. Back to my question," Pete said. "What kind of weapons you got in here?"

"There's a pocketknife in the glove box and my roll of chef knives in the back. That's it. I have guns in the house that I inherited from my parents, but I don't keep them in the van."

"If you're hellbent on finding stolen money, carry a handgun. Your opponents have guns."

"I haven't shot the pistol or the rifle since I was a kid."

"We'll fix that. Meanwhile, you mentioned chef knives. I need one."

"How will you manage a knife with an arm in a sling and the cane?"

"Screw the cane. If someone's in your place, we need to defend ourselves."

The blood drained from my face. "I can't stab someone."

"You could if he's trying to kill you."

"All right. I'll get my knife set." I clambered over the seat and brought the roll of knives forward. "Which one do you want?"

"They're all sharp?"

"Absolutely."

He pointed to the eight-inch chef's knife, the longest blade. "Then I want that one."

I gave it to him and selected the meat cleaver for myself.

He shook his head. "Better if you take a smaller knife you can palm. If bad guys are inside waiting to get the drop on us, the element of surprise will help you survive."

I exchanged my choice for a paring knife. "I should go first."

"Think again. I'm not a hundred percent, but I'm highly motivated to protect my future fiancée."

"Okay, but only if you use the cane to mount the steps. I'll unlock the door and you can enter first with your big knife."

"Sounds like a plan."

The cat vaulted off the steps when we emerged from the van, yowling from the azaleas. If bad guys were inside, they had plenty of notice we were coming. I walked beside Pete, carrying both knives and my keys, my pulse skittering like water beads in a hot skillet.

We made it up the steps, trying to be as quiet as possible, but every footfall thundered in my ears. Pete propped his cane against the house, palmed the knife in his good hand, and nodded.

I went to unlock the door, but it swung open as I pushed the key in the lock. Pete brushed me aside and entered, a fierce expression on his face. I followed and stopped immediately.

The lamp lay on the floor, sofa cushions were upended, throw pillows slashed. Books littered the floor along with my unpaid bills. Every cabinet door gaped wide. What few paintings I'd inherited with the house lay akimbo on the floor.

The cat darted past me, straight through the living room to the kitchen and out the open back door. "Major!" I yelped, following the cat. "Come back."

"Dammit, River," Pete said. "Let me go first."

Recklessly, I ran ahead and halted on the back porch. Pete limped up beside me. Through the woods, I heard a motor crank. "The intruder is getting away," I said. "I'm calling the cops. Maybe they can catch 'em."

After I dialed the emergency number and Pete verified the house was indeed empty, we sat on the reassembled sectional sofa, Pete's ankle propped up and iced. Quickly, I returned the knives to my van and changed out of my muddy shirt, hiding it in the other dirty clothes in the washer.

Two patrol cars showed up. I recognized both deputies, Gil Franklin and Lance Hamlyn. "Y'all can't be in here," Lance said, shaking his gloved finger at us. "We have to process the house."

"Go right ahead." I gestured broadly. "We live here and you can exclude us from any samples you take. After our afternoon walk, Pete needs to ice his ankle."

Franklin looked unprepared for collecting evidence because his hands were ungloved. Both deputies charged through the house, guns drawn, and then returned.

"No one's here," Lance said.

"We figured that part out," I said. "Someone came in here, through my locked door, mind you, and vandalized my belongings. Why?"

Franklin pulled out a notepad and pen. "Is anything missing?"

"Not that I saw," I said. "Who pays for the broken dishes and the slashed cushions?"

"Homeowners insurance may cover costs, but there's often a deductible." Franklin looked like he'd swallowed a cactus. "We'll take your statement and check entry points for prints. Does anyone have a grudge against you?"

"No one." I barred my arms across my chest. Anger and fear made my stomach queasy. I would not cry. Whoever did this wouldn't beat me. "No one's mad at me."

"She gives cookies to everyone she sees," Pete pointed out. "How could anyone be upset with River?"

"You must've riled someone with your questions about Chili," Lance said in a dismissive tone. "I warned you this would happen."

His smugness irritated me further. "You said it *might* happen. I haven't asked questions about Chili in days. I've given up on searching for him."

"Good. Maybe this was a warning," Lance said. "You'll be safer if you stay away from the Bolz brothers."

"Any other housebreakings on the island?" Pete asked matter-of-factly.

"Just this one." Franklin handed me a form. "Fill this statement out and sign it. I'll file it and we'll have a record of your incident."

Lance's phone rang. He stepped outside to answer, then stuck his head in a few minutes later. "Another call. I need to respond." He nodded to Franklin. "You good here?"

Franklin nodded. "I got this."

While Pete and I collaborated on the statement, Franklin donned gloves and checked for fingerprints on both doors, the lamp, and the paintings. Pete and I were printed for exclusion fingerprints, but Franklin used a kit from his car, so we didn't have to go to the station.

Finally, Pete and I were alone again. I looked at the mess, and the trembling in my stomach intensified. Someone entered my home, touched my things. Someone violated my privacy.

Did they think I was hiding a million dollars in my home?

Chapter Thirty-Eight

Cleanup on aisle four and five and six...My thoughts darted everywhere as I picked up the mess, threw out the broken items, and tidied my home. Pete tried to help, but his ankle and his bum arm limited his usefulness. Nothing I said made him sit down and rest. Finally, the living room, kitchen, and guest bath were in order. I darted back to the bedroom, scooped up my clean clothes that'd been thrown on the floor, and got them running through the washer, along with the muddy yellow blouse.

"Sit," I said when I walked back in. "I'm certainly gonna."

"This day put a new spin on the case," Pete said, placing the remaining throw pillows around him on the sectional and propping up his arm and leg.

I rested both aching feet on the coffee table. "How so?"

"We learned Chili is alive and scared. A million dollars is missing. Someone tossed your house. And last but not least, you lied to the police."

"I did not lie. Every word I spoke was the truth."

"Unlike the cops, I understand why you're no longer looking for Chili. Keeping silent about finding him and knowing about the missing money are lies of omission."

I covered a yawn with my hand. "Only if you want to get all technical about it."

"Why did you make that choice?"

How quickly the mighty oaks toppled, I thought. My response had been automatic, and if challenged, I'd do it again. I didn't consider myself above the law, but I'd reached the point where I trusted very few people. Lance Hamlyn and Gil Franklin didn't make the cut, even if they were cops.

"My loyalty is to Chili," I began slowly. "I don't want mob guys to kill him. We need to figure this out. We believe something is up with dockmaster Garnet Pierce and with Chili's hunting friend, Justin Adler. Chili didn't deny their involvement."

Pete met my level gaze. "He didn't confirm it either. I recall him saying Justin was a fair-weather friend. That's different from someone who tried to kill you or stole a million dollars."

"I've been thinking about that money all afternoon. Seems like someone would've spent the money, and there'd be tangible evidence of new wealth."

"Unless they were too smart to do that," Pete countered.

"Smart. There's evidence of brain and brawn throughout this case. Chili left two messages to tell his mother where he was. That took guts. Chili knows who beat him up, and he thinks it's the same person who beat his mother to death. Someone broke in here without leaving a trace on the doors or windows, and then made a huge mess."

"We're lucky we weren't home. Good chance we'd be more busted up if we encountered the killer."

I recoiled instinctively, and my head bounced off the sofa, adding to my disorientation. "You think the killer broke in my place?"

"Follow my logic. The mob laundered money on the island. They recruited several locals, namely Chili, Kale, and Estelle Bolz. It didn't end well, and the menace is still on Shell Island, as evidenced by our break-in. We locked this house when we left, which means the lock was picked. Which in turn implies a more serious bad guy. The path of reason circles back to the stolen money in my mind, so yes, I believe the killer tossed this place."

The killer? A fierce shudder ripped down my spine. "That's sobering."

"There's another possibility. The mob wants their stolen money back. What we don't know is who killed Estelle and beat up

Chili. The killer came here to discover what you know. The mob would've been here looking for the money."

My gaze fixed on a decorative snail across the room, frozen in time. I knew how he felt. "So, I should be happy the killer came instead of the mob? What if the killer is part of the mob?"

Pete groaned. "I'd be happy if we left on a cruise right now."

"Absence won't fix anything. And there's a good chance my house would look like Estelle's when we returned."

"Good point."

"This sucks."

"We'll get through this together."

"And my locks are no good?"

"You have deadbolts on all exterior doors which we didn't engage when we went out. Those slow down most burglars, skilled or not. You need a big dog."

"I've got a watch cat. Major warned us something was wrong."

"That he did."

"Okay. We'll keep the deadbolts engaged for added protection. Who are we protecting ourselves from? Garnet Pierce? Justin Adler? Or someone else?"

"We don't know."

"I need to search Garnet's house to learn more about her. In the old days, the marina master lived in the cottage near the head of the access road. We could slip over there when she goes to work in the morning and she'd never know."

"Just curious. What would you look for?"

"A million dollars for starters. Any sign she spent lots of money on her personal possessions. A large stash of guns or drugs."

"What would you do if you found those things?"

"Call the cops."

Pete gazed out the window, and so did I. Shadows were lengthening. I should start dinner soon. Just because my day had blown all to hell and back was no reason not to have a decent meal. Cooking dinner would help me feel grounded, and then I'd take that much-needed shower.

"Here's a random thought," Pete began slowly. "There's someone who's been in this from the start. Someone who knows your every move."

I poked his good arm. "Are you talking about me? Because there's no way I did any of this."

"Not you. Someone who keeps showing up, someone who bugs you for regular progress reports."

My blood chilled as I followed his logic. "Lance? You think a deputy did these terrible things? He swore an oath to protect and serve."

"He had access to information all along." Pete's voice roughened. "What do we really know about this guy, River? Who are his people?"

This suggestion seemed fantastical and impossible. Lance was a cop. A sworn good guy. Pete and Lance didn't get along because Lance was also attracted to me. Not because he was a crook. How could I talk Pete off this particular ledge? "He said he came here from Texas."

"I remember you mentioned that. Hold on a minute. Let's see what's online about him." Pete drew his phone from a pocket and punched in rapid keystrokes. "Hmm."

"What did you find?"

"It's what I didn't find. No social media footprint, and no one with his exact name shows up in the search engine. Over near Abilene, there's a small town of Hamlin, Texas, but it's spelled differently."

"Maybe it's a rule that cops can't be on social media. Try Deputy Gil Franklin."

Pete's thumbs tapped quickly on his phone. "He comes right up. So does Chili, your catering service, me, your friend Vivian Declan."

"What about Jude Ernest?"

A few clicks later, Pete nodded. "He's searchable. Got multiple people with that name, by the way."

"But nothing for Lance Hamlyn. That's strange."

"There may be an explanation, but in the meantime be careful around the deputy. His past is not an open book. It may be closed on purpose, or it may mean something else."

"He's a decent guy," I said.

"People under pressure do crazy things. I saw that out in California. And Chili said to trust no one."

"Supposing I believe you, and I don't, how can I even look Lance in the eye now? He's a cop. He'll know I'm suspicious of everyone, including him."

"You'd better pull it off," Pete said. "Your life depends upon it."

Chapter Thirty-Nine

In a refreshing break from mobs and killers, Pete accompanied me to Shell Island Elementary School to help with tutoring the next day. His friendly manner made him a natural with the fourth graders. He didn't get testy with the kid who couldn't stay seated. Instead, he leaned in and began whispering a story to the other kids. The antsy child sat down to listen.

I liked patience and ingenuity in a man. Those traits, and others, of course, were why I'd fallen in love with Pete. He was a big teddy bear of a man until he was a grizzly protecting his own. I didn't doubt that he'd fought with heart and soul for his California company, but whatever he'd done to stake his claim, they'd done more. Thank goodness he'd walked away from a life of confrontation and fear.

He caught my eye across the classroom, and I beamed at him. One of my kids tugged my sleeve, then all the little girls at my table giggled. My face heated, but I was happy. This was who I was and I was right where I was supposed to be.

Afterward, as the kids filed out and waved goodbye, I checked my phone messages. Three from Melanie Walker, the bride who wanted me to cater her wedding, one from Jude Ernest who wanted us to meet, and a hang-up. I set an electronic reminder to call Melanie, dismissed the hang-up, and decided it was time for Pete to meet Jude. I hit "call back" on the phone but Jude's call flipped to voicemail, and it was full of messages.

"How's your ankle today?" I asked as we strolled out of the building.

"Fine."

He limped and leaned on the cane, but he wouldn't admit any weakness. That was so different from my brother who, if he was allowed, would take the whole day off school for a splinter.

Ah well, guys had their own codes. My code was to help family and friends, and the missed call from Jude burned brightly in my thoughts. "One of my messages was from Kale's attorney, Jude Ernest. He didn't answer my return call. You feel up to a trip into the wilds of the island?"

Pete gazed around us, checking out the slotted cars. "Sure. We'll shoot for Garnet's place after visiting the attorney?"

His watchfulness heightened my fearfulness. Did he see a peaceful parking lot or an array of barriers for threats to hide? I hoped we both could relax our guard soon. "Yep. I feel Jude is a higher priority. Lucky for you I know a shortcut, so there's little hiking involved."

"Sounds good, though I could hike if needed."

We helped ourselves to water bottles from the cooler inside the van before we buckled up. I glanced at my behind-the-seat food cache on Pete's side, once again bulging with protein bars. "How about a quick snack?"

"Sure."

We each had a bar as we rolled through the congested part of the island. Finally, we were the only car on a lonely road. I turned down a fish camp road. The paving ran out about halfway down the road, so we bounced along on the dirt until I edged left into the tall grass.

"Are we cutting our own trail?" Pete asked.

"You'll see." I crept along in the grass, studying the grain for the access point in the woods. Nearly missed it, but I hung a sharp left between two pines. Pete clung to the armrest as we bounced and jostled down the grassy tract.

We drove a little farther, turned a bend, and a felled tree blocked the rough passageway. I slammed on the brakes. "This wasn't here before."

"No offense intended, hon, but is this the right way?"

"Yes. Jude showed me this exit last week. He must've wanted a barrier up on this side of his property as well as the front. That tree is too large for us to move or go around. Sorry, we have to hike the rest of the way."

"I can do it."

I shifted into park and cut the engine. "Of course you can, except I wish you didn't have to. I want your ankle to heal."

"I'll be fine.

The hiking was only about a quarter of a mile. Even so, I was glad we'd consumed water and energy bars before tromping through knee-high grass. At least this time Pete and I could check each other for ticks.

Pete's face was pale when we entered the clearing where the ramshackle cabin sat. I wanted to mother him, but he wouldn't relish that kind of attention out in public.

"Jude?" I called when no one answered my knock on the back door. "You here? It's River Holloway and Pete Merrick."

"I hear you," Jude said, hobbling out of the woods using a rifle as a cane. A scrap of fabric held up his left arm in a makeshift sling. "This your boyfriend?"

"Yes." I made the introductions.

The lawyer limped closer. "Looks like we attended the same school of hard knocks."

"Same mentality of guy came after both of us, looks like," Pete said. "I busted my arm warding off a knife attack. The bum ankle came from the other guy whacking the heck out of it with a bat. Gotta few broken ribs. How about you?"

"Nearly the same laundry list." Jude shrugged. "Sucks."

"Does."

I made a show of pretend wiping my hands clean. "Okay, now that we've finished the male bonding ritual, what happened to you, Jude? Did you press charges?"

"No charges, doll. Didn't know the masked guys that jumped me. Just hightailed it back here afterward."

"Was it the mob or someone else?"

"Kale rising from the dead and being in federal custody surprised the hell out of folks. My attackers encouraged me to tell Kale to keep his mouth shut."

"Good grief. Where'd they ambush you?"

"Did a pincer move on the highway a few miles up the main road. No other cars in sight, no security cameras to catch them."

"What about here? You got security cameras for protection?"

"You better believe it, and motion sensors too. That's how I knew to hide in the woods as you approached. If you'd'a brought a cop back here instead of your boyfriend, you wouldn't have seen me."

I whispered in his ear. "I have something private to share with you, but I don't want it recorded."

He returned the courtesy. "Keep your voice down and step to the tree line."

We moved in a group of three, and I leaned close to Jude. "Pete and I found Chili yesterday. He's alive. He told us that you're his point of contact now."

Jude's eyes gleamed. "Good boy. He knows which plants to eat, how to catch fish and game. He'll be all right."

"Chili won't come in until this is over. Nothing I said to him caused him to change his mind, except he was thrilled to hear his brother was alive."

Jude nodded. "Better for him to wait it out."

"He's living like someone two hundred years ago. I don't know how he's surviving."

"He's surviving because he has to. He wants his life back, and this is the only way to get it."

"Wouldn't he be safer in federal custody like Kale?"

"Unlike his brother, Chili isn't wanted for anything illegal."

"Is Kale talking to the feds?"

"I can't tell you that."

"How can this end unless all of the bad guys are caught?"

"These things happen on their own timetable, River."

"That sounds like the Uncle Jay I used to know." I scowled. "How'd you go from the laidback outdoorsy guy I knew to an ambulance chasing lawyer?"

"Different wilderness, different set of rules." He shrugged. "The suits, they didn't like my kind of people. All they wanted was to rake in the big bucks from corporate clients. I wanted to help ordinary people. Going after the accident crowd was expedient and profitable. Best of all, I didn't screw my clients."

I tried to see things from Jude's perspective. Chili was alive but hiding out, on purpose. Jude took a beating from someone who wanted Kale to keep silent. Bottom line, the bad guys must feel vulnerable.

"You need help out here?" I asked.

"I need you to be careful. These people are fighting for their lives and livelihoods. They take no prisoners. They killed Estelle because she wouldn't give up her boys."

"Or because she didn't give them the money. She couldn't because someone stole it from her." I recounted what Chili told me about the missing million dollars. "Look, it's good to see you, but you could've warned me to be careful over the phone. And someone tossed my place yesterday while we were with Chili."

"They are getting desperate, and either the cops or the crooks could be tapping your phone. I didn't want to risk saying the wrong thing on the phone. Besides, now I know Chili is safe and megabucks are missing. You didn't tell the cops about finding Chili?"

"No. I couldn't."

"Good girl. We'll have you thinking like a first-order conspiracy theorist in no time."

Estelle gave her life to protect her sons. I hadn't thought of it that way. "Why would they come after me? I don't know any details. I should be safe."

"No one is safe until this is over."

Chapter Forty

Sobered by my visit with Jude, I drove to Garnet's place. Her truck wasn't parked by the cottage on the property, which was a good sign. I turned to Pete. "See any cameras?"

"No."

"Okay. I'll knock on the door. If she answers, I'll ask her to recommend a fish supplier."

"Good cover. If she's not there and the door's locked, how do you plan on getting in?"

"I'm hoping she hides a key nearby like the rest of us do." I prayed my voice sounded calm. I didn't want Pete to know how nervous I was. "I'll be right back."

The house was built on a slab, so there were no stairs to climb. I tried the screen door. It was unlocked. Knocked on the wooden door. "Hello! Garnet, it's River Holloway."

No answer. I tried the knob. Locked. I turned around and shook my head. There was no porch full of furniture to search for a hidden key. Just sand and crabgrass in her yard. I circled the house, trying windows and the back door. All locked and the blinds were drawn.

"It's a triple no-go," I said as I climbed in the van. "Nobody home, no key, and no line of sight inside."

"A woman of secrets," Pete said. "We could go to the marina to see her."

My skin itched from walking in the tall grass at Jude's place. "Not yet. I need a shower, a change of clothes, and a better strategy."

*   *   *

Pete was in the shower when the doorbell rang. My stomach knotted as I realized who my unexpected company was. Deputy Lance Hamlyn.

I stepped out on the porch to greet him, pulling the door closed behind me. A gentle breeze rustled palmetto fronds and my freshly showered hair. "Lance," I said. "What's going on?"

He stood with his hands in his uniform pockets. "Thought we'd compare notes on the case."

"Frankly, I'm frustrated by the lack of progress," I said, for the first time acutely conscious of the gun he always wore strapped on his hip. "We don't know who killed Estelle. The only good news is that Kale is alive."

"He's in a lot of trouble."

"I can only imagine. But maybe he can redeem himself by helping the feds."

"Not a good plan. Everyone he's ever known will be in jeopardy if that happened."

"Since he knows everyone in the county, that'd be a tall order."

"He only asked to speak to you, River. You and that sleezy lawyer."

"Our conversations weren't private."

"I didn't mention this before but you need to know that the Bolz family is not who you think they are. We're now certain they're linked to organized crime. Estelle stole from the Ferarrelli cartel."

I drew in a quick breath. "I don't believe you."

"Believe what you like, but we have a money trail straight through the Bolz family that's undeniable."

My fingers curled into fists. His accusations made me see red. Chili said to trust no one. I clung to that thought. "No way."

"River, these people don't deserve your loyalty. They're criminals."

"This is news to me, and it sounds like a horror story. I've known the Bolzes for over twenty years."

"I wish you knew where they hid the stolen money," Lance said. "If the mob had their money, they'd go away."

"This is a lot to take in all at once," I said. "First you tell me my friends are in organized crime, then you say they stole from the mob. I don't believe you, and I don't know where any money is."

The door opened and shut behind me. Pete joined us on the porch, standing shoulder to shoulder with me. Water beads dripped from his hair, his shorts and shirt were twisted as if he hadn't dried off before donning them. His bare feet looked pale next to the bruising on his swollen ankle. He'd done too much today, and here he was again, rallying to my side.

Neither man made the effort to shake hands. Electricity crackled in the air. If Lance assumed Pete was weak because of his injuries, he'd be mistaken.

"She knows nothing about the Bolz's troubles, Hamlyn," Pete said. "Don't drag her into their mess. River wasn't involved in their illegal sideline."

"I believe that," Lance said, "but truth is subjective. When trouble came her way, Estelle Bolz contacted River and so did Kale. River's part of this by association, whether she wants to be or not."

Pete shifted his weight onto the balls of his feet. It wouldn't take much for him to punch Lance. He shouldn't hit anyone, but hitting a cop would be a disaster. I needed to defuse the situation. "I want justice for Estelle. Even if she led a double life, she didn't deserve to be beaten to death. No one does."

"The people who hurt her were sending a message," Lance said. "Cross them and that's what happens."

I shook my head fast. "I don't plan on crossing anyone."

"That's what I'm trying to tell you. If they believe you know something, whether you do or not, they'll come after you, and this guy, and your brother. This'd be a good time to take a vacation."

"I'm not leaving. This is my home. I refuse to live in fear. If that's the reason you stopped by, message received. You can go now."

Lance gave a curt nod my way. "One more thing. Chili's boat

turned up again."

"It did? I didn't know it was missing. The dockmaster told me you took it into evidence."

"Garnet lied. It was at the dock and then it wasn't. A boater towed *Reel Fine* to Bayside Marina this morning. Said it was drifting in the sound. I've had a crew down there fingerprinting the boat, but most of the muddy prints aboard were made by raccoons."

"Why would Garnet lie to me?" I asked.

"That's a very good question," Lance said. "I'll ask it as soon as I find her."

"She's missing?"

"She isn't at work or home, and her vehicle is gone."

"What about her phone? Can you track it?" I asked.

"Thought of that too. Her calls roll to voicemail. Her phone is turned off. Wherever she is, she isn't using her phone."

"Did she get beat up or fake her death?" I asked.

Lance turned to go, glancing at me over his shoulder. "I think she did what the Bolz brothers did—got the heck out of Dodge."

I stepped forward. "Is she part of it?"

"That remains to be seen. If you hear from her, let me know."

We watched him stroll away and drive off. "Now that was darn interesting," Pete said. "You didn't tell him about finding Chili, and he warned you that your friendships signify guilt by association to others."

"I'm not guilty."

Pete sighed. "He's right, you know. In the eyes of some, their truth is the only acceptable one."

"He didn't scare me, plus I can't afford a vacation. I have a luncheon for the Ladies of Distinction tomorrow, and I should get started on that pan of vegetable lasagna right after I finish our lunch."

"Sounds good to me, as long as we eat lasagna tonight."

Nothing untoward happened over the next twenty-four hours. The

Ladies of Distinction raved over my salad greens lightly dressed in my special lemon vinaigrette, and they darn near licked the pan of my veggie lasagna. The chocolate mint cookies were winners too. As Pete and I packed the empty warming trays and the empty tub of salad in the van, I noticed Pete looked at me in a different way.

Driving home, I couldn't take the brooding silence. "Did I do something to offend you?"

He sighed out a breath. "You did nothing wrong."

"Odd, because you flipped from a good mood to a dark place all of a sudden. Did you hurt your ankle again?"

"My ankle's fine. My arm's fine."

"But we're not fine, and I want to know why."

Pete gazed out the window as we rolled past cottages, condos, and the elementary school. "I just had an epiphany."

"About what?"

"About us. I don't think...I mean, what if...What I'm trying to say is...Look, I nearly messed this up before. I can't bear the thought of hurting you. What if I get all hepped up about another company?"

"Goodness. That's a lot to put on me while I'm driving. Hang on a second." I whipped down the short strip to the pier and parked. "Do you feel up to a walk?"

His face clouded but he nodded.

A strong wind snapped the nearby nautical flags as we exited the van. We strolled under the shelter, Pete looked more world weary with every step. Finally we reached our favorite bench and sat.

"Did I say something wrong?" he asked.

"You're fine, and I'm fine, but it doesn't seem like we're fine," I repeated. "What changed? I love you, Pete Merrick, and I want to know what's bothering you."

He stared glumly at the worn dock planks. "You're good at your job."

"So are you."

"It's not just the food, which is excellent, by the way. It's the people. They're so happy to see you, and they don't want you to leave when the event is over. You can't fake that kind of enthusiasm."

"I don't understand." My brow furrowed, the confusion I felt went bone deep. "You expected me to be bad at catering?"

"Not bad, per se, but I assumed your occupation was mobile and impersonal. My sincere apologies. I totally misunderstood your business model. You provide much more than a meal. Your clients love you."

"I've spent years building customer rapport. It's the reason I had second thoughts about job hopping from place to place."

"I heard you say that, yes, but I didn't understand until I went on today's catering job with you. My assumptions were wrong. I had our future mapped out, and now the map isn't relevant. I've always been the answer man. I made things happen, only now I'm struggling for answers."

"It's okay. We'll figure it out as we go. I have faith in us."

"I've walked in your shoes now," Pete said, "and I'll never take you or your business for granted again."

"Thank you." I took his hand in mine, blinking away the moisture in my eyes. "I appreciate the recognition."

"Let's go home." He squeezed my hand. "I'd rather show you how I feel than talk about my feelings."

I rose. "Yes."

We strolled down the pier, side by side. "About the case," Pete began, "I have an idea. Soon as it's good and dark, I'm heading to Bayside to take a peek at the marina security feed."

"Now we're talking. I'll join you, partner."

Chapter Forty-One

A single light glowed in the empty parking lot, along with muted footlights on the marina jetties. Though it was a mild night in the sixties, I shivered as I parked behind the marina office.

"Stay in the van," Pete said. "I won't be long."

"Forget it." He spoke as if he could run a marathon, but I knew better. Still, any mention of his physical limitations would make things worse. I huffed out a breath of frustration. "I'm not staying behind. We're partners. Besides while you copy the camera feed, I can search for other information."

"If we're caught here, you'll have more than the perception of guilt going against you."

"We're in this together. I need answers."

"All right, but I'll go first. We'll get in and out as quick as possible."

We eased from the van into the starlit night, and the briny salt marsh scent on the back side of the island filled my head. My heart thumped in my ears as we crept toward the door. Pete tried the knob and the door swung open.

As we entered, the hair on the back of my neck rose and I felt tingly all over. "Pete, I've got a bad feeling."

"Me too." He edged forward guided by starlight behind us, heading for the office, and tripped.

I steadied him, suddenly finding my footing uneven too. "What's wrong with the floor?"

Pete flicked on his cell phone flashlight. Chaos met my gaze in every direction. "It looks like a grenade went off in here."

"Someone tossed this place." He shone his light over the sales counter. "Cash register is missing." I tagged after him to the office. His light illuminated the desk. "Computer is gone too. No chance of us getting a copy of the camera feed."

I picked up a few of the scattered pages, wishing I'd brought my cell inside. "What are all these papers?"

Pete shone his light my way and glanced over my shoulder. "Invoices."

I dropped the papers. "I'm worried for Garnet. If someone tossed this place, she's not one of them."

"Unless she double-crossed them. With all those dock cameras, she had to know about the money laundering. If she wasn't part of it, maybe she blackmailed someone. One thing's for sure, she's not here."

"I wish we could find something to help us figure this out. Seems like every lead we follow is a dead end."

Pete scanned the room with his light. "You see something?" I asked.

"A whole lot of nothing," he said, urging me toward the door.

Pete paused halfway to the van. "I need another minute."

I hurried to sit in the driver's seat. Pete's door opened abruptly. He slid in, setting an object on the floorboard. "Let's get out of here. Now."

I cranked the engine and eased out the back way. It was rutted, not more than a dirt track really. "Where does this go?"

"Out of here. That's all we need to know."

"So, this was a bust. No Garnet and no video surveillance."

He grinned and hefted the item from the floorboard. "Didn't say that."

"What'd you get?"

"A state-of-the-art video camera."

"That gizmo? It doesn't look like much."

"Precisely. I would've passed it by if not for my recent experience with surveillance equipment. This camera is our trump card. Whoever installed this puppy didn't expect anyone to find it.

This unit wasn't connected to the batch camera feed. It stores images on a SD card inside."

My brows shot up. "We'll see who did this?"

"We'll see who came and went in front of this camera."

Chapter Forty-Two

We raced home to view the camera feed. Pete fired up his computer on the kitchen table, and I stood behind him, watching over his shoulder.

The camera's field of vision included a side angle of the parking lot and a view of anyone who stepped off the dock into the parking area. "Interesting," I said, gazing at the still photo on his laptop. "This wasn't set up to see traffic to the shop. This is all about the dock. What on earth?"

"I presume the other security cameras covered the shop and office. This camera was an afterthought. Someone got cold feet about current events and filmed the dock activity for protection."

"Or blackmail." I sat and drummed my fingers on the tabletop. "Maybe Garnet suspected her dock was being used for illegal purposes. She allowed the activity to occur, or maybe she was forced to allow it. They might've even paid her to look the other way. She could've gotten greedy and wanted more, hence the hidden camera."

"If blackmail was Garnet's motive, she had to know the odds of that working out for her weren't good. If she went after the mob, they would retaliate. They'd leave a bloody mess as a warning to anyone who dared to cross them because that's what happened to Estelle. We're dealing with someone else here."

"Who?"

"Once we see who stars on this video, we'll know if my hunch is correct."

My hackles rose. "You're not still thinking Lance, are you?"

"Whoever it is, I want to stop these thugs, and I want you as far from these people as possible."

He wouldn't meet my gaze. He *was* thinking Lance did this. "He's a cop. Sworn to uphold the law. He helped me with catering jobs."

"He insinuated himself into your business. He flattered you about your personal connections in the community so he'd know if you found anything about Chili. He isn't a friend, whether he's guilty of a crime or not."

"You believe I have a blind spot when it comes to Deputy Lance Hamlyn. You have an even stronger bias against him."

"It isn't personal. I have a strong bias against everyone until they gain my trust."

That admission stopped me. Floored me. "How do you live with those suspicions clouding your every thought, word, and deed? Isn't it hard surrounding yourself with negativity?"

"It's how I've survived this past year. Seems like you'd be grateful I'm alive instead of the other way around." He studied me with inscrutable eyes. "Why do you always stand up for Lance?"

"I love you, Pete, and I want so much for you, for us. Lance has been helpful in my business and in searching for Chili, so I trust him. I believe in the goodness of people."

"I don't trust the deputy, but it doesn't matter what we think. These images will tell the tale." Pete returned to scanning the file. The fuzzy image on the screen flickered. Pete reversed the feed to see the captured image. He made a note on a pad of paper. "What did you write?" I asked.

He slid the pad around to show me. "I made a note of the date, time, and description of the person."

My gaze stopped on the date. "That's two weeks ago. Before Chili vanished. Before Estelle died."

"Given the small size of this memory card and the length of time involved between visitors, it seems logical this marina is indeed a front for something. But for what? Is it money laundering or more than that?"

"Like what?"

"Guns or drugs as you previously suggested. Illegal immigration. Human trafficking."

I couldn't stomach the last two, not that guns or drug trafficking were any better. "Oh, let's hope not."

He didn't wait for a reply and continued viewing the feed at top speed. Chili was not in any of the frames. A stocky woman appeared multiple times. Going by the familiar-looking flannel shirt, it was Garnet. A man of average height appeared multiple times, sometimes in uniform. I got a sick feeling in my gut.

In one frame in which the uniform was in focus, the man's identity became certain. "We know this person," Pete said.

"I see Deputy Lance Hamlyn, same as you. His presence on the dock could mean any number of things. He investigated Chili's disappearance. Chili's boat went missing. It makes sense that he was on the dock looking into the matter."

"Could be," Pete admitted.

I searched the frozen frame of Lance on the screen. With his sunglasses on, I couldn't read his expression. "His hands are empty," I blurted out. "He isn't carrying the missing money."

Pete advanced to the next captured image. This time it was the dockmaster. "Neither is Garnet. Everyone is walking around emptyhanded. Doesn't mean they're innocent."

"Doesn't mean they're guilty either." More pics streamed past. A person flashed in one. "Hold up."

"You see something?" he asked.

"Yeah. Garnet went out on the dock. I didn't see her come back on the camera feed."

"Good point." Pete clicked backward through the images. "She walked down there two days ago, and she didn't return the same day or the next. Seems like someone would've noticed the office being closed." He clicked through the rest of the saved images. One was of a stranger carrying fishing gear to a boat and later returning with a mess of fish. Lance showed up twice more. The last image was of Pete approaching the camera.

"Garnet left Bayside Marina by boat most likely, if she's alive," Pete said. "Maybe she took a boat out to meet someone."

"You think she's dead?" I asked. "Wouldn't a body have turned up by now?"

"Not if she was weighted down or dumped offshore."

I retreated. "This is crazy. This kind of thing doesn't happen on Shell Island."

"Things change when the mob shows up."

"She could've boated to another marina or a private dock. She could've gone into hiding, same as Chili."

"Perhaps, but it feels like someone tying up loose ends," Pete said. "Whatever happened at the marina, Garnet had a bird's eye view from the office. Even if she didn't physically see people coming and going from the marina, the cameras did. With Kale Bolz faking his death six months ago, this money laundering has been going on at least that long, possibly for years as Chili indicated. How long has Deputy Hamlyn been on the island?"

"I'm not sure. I wasn't aware of him until he arrested Doug for stealing the sheriff's vehicle. He's been here at least three months."

"We know he has no social media presence, nor does he have online mentions. Who is this guy and why is he here?"

A reason popped into my head. "Maybe he's working undercover and Lance Hamlyn is a fake name."

"Are you still cooking up excuses for him?"

His accusation pushed my hot button and I rose. "This isn't about me sticking up for Lance. I provided a plausible answer to your questions."

"You did. I'm sorry I snapped at you. Seems like we trip over Hamlyn any way we go. I don't like how he inserted himself in your life."

I wrangled my emotions under control and sat down. "Noted."

"Where were we?"

He'd made a concession. So could I. "Based on the hidden camera photos and Garnet's disappearance, I've changed my mind. The images suggest Lance and Garnet are involved. If not, then one of them is likely the killer and the other is a victim. Seeing as how Lance is strutting about town and Garnet is not, the future looks bleak for the dockmaster."

He nodded his agreement.

Emboldened by our accord, I posited further, "We need to put that camera back. Who knows what else it may record."

"Right." Pete erased his image from the SD card. "I'll check property records to see who owns the dock."

I watched as he conducted the web search. A name cropped up on the tax assessor's site. "Southern Shores Corporation? Never heard of it."

Pete searched for the business online and then turned to me. "Lots of double talk and nothing about Southern Shores. It must be a shell corporation. Everything points to this place being a front. I wonder why Hamlyn didn't come across that fact?"

My phone rang again. I glanced at the display. Melanie Walker, my bride-to-be. "I need to take this. Melanie's called three times already today."

"Go ahead."

"The wedding's off," Melanie breathed fire in my ears. "That lowlife belly slider doesn't deserve to spend the rest of his life with me. I am too good for the likes of a salesman."

When she paused for a breath, I asked, "Is someone there with you? Should I call your Mom or a friend?"

"No, I don't want anybody to know he's cheating on me."

"Are you certain?"

"Yeah. His date posted their picture on social media."

Having been estranged from Pete last year, I knew the value of a phone call. "Have you talked to him? There could be a very good explanation."

"Why would I talk to a cheater?"

Her words sounded slurred. "Melanie, do you want me to come over?"

"No. I'm a mess. I don't want anyone to see me like this."

She didn't want family, friends, or me. I was out of options.

"How can I help you?"

"I wanted to make sure you knew so you didn't start ordering all the food."

Oh. That made sense. "Thank you for that. Are you sure I can't come over to sit with you?"

She swore, shrieked, and hung up on me.

"The wedding's off," I told Pete.

"Sounds like trouble all right. Are you taking her off the catering calendar?"

"Nope. I'm doing something better. I'm calling her mom in the clear light of day. She can get to the bottom of this. With Melanie's history of failed marriages, there might be an underlying reason."

"Be sure you add handholding to your resume."

Chapter Forty-Three

Jude Ernest called me later that night. I'd gone over to my commercial kitchen to test new recipes for Sunday's baby shower. I'd just about gotten my equilibrium back when the phone rang. I activated the speaker phone option.

"Kale's been transferred to a federal prison, but it's not too far away," Jude began. "He's asked to speak to you again, and the feds approved. You've been added to his visitor list."

"I'll head there first thing in the morning, if that's okay."

"Why wouldn't it be okay?" the lawyer asked gruffly.

"Like if there was any urgency to the request. I hoped I didn't need to make that drive in the dark."

"No urgency. The boy done wrong and he knows it. He'll be spending the next few years behind bars in Jesup."

"But he'll stay alive."

"Let's hope so." Jude cleared his throat as he gave me the rundown on visiting procedures. "You need two forms of government ID. No food allowed, and no purse unless it's see through and small. Also, you can't visit with him for more than an hour. I'll text you his Register Number. Visit the Correctional Institute website if you have more questions on what you can and can't bring."

"What about Pete?" I asked, glancing at my boyfriend who'd been helping me slice and dice.

"Kale didn't ask to see him, so his name isn't on the pre-approved visitor list. However, I'd feel better if he rode over and back with you."

Made sense. "I would too."

I ended the call and turned to Pete. "Looks like we have a road trip to Jesup tomorrow morning. Kale Bolz asked to see me again. You up for the drive?"

"Yes. We stay together until this is over. I don't trust anyone."

Kale looked good sitting across from me. His eyes were less haunted than before, and he seemed comfortable in his surroundings. Even so, I asked after his well-being. "You doing all right?" I began.

"Nice not to be constantly looking over my shoulder. Plenty of bad guys in here, but I figure if any knew the guys that want me dead, I'd be dead already. So, I'm grateful to be here. Maybe one day I'll see my brother again, but if I don't and I get dead, well, then I'll see my mom soon. It's win-win for me. No more living in limbo."

"That's the spirit." He sounded like the Kale I used to know. "You asked me to visit?"

"Yeah." He glanced around the room. "I wanted to confide in you before, but I couldn't. I was too scared."

"Because you'd been arrested?"

"Nah. Figured I had that coming." He paused for a breath. "Because I got locked up in the Riceland County Sheriff's jail."

He gave me a knowing look. I chewed my lip wondering what I was missing. "Is this conversation being taped?"

"Count on it."

"You'll have to be more specific about your fear. I don't understand."

"One of the deputies is dirty."

I couldn't tell him Pete and I had reached the same conclusion. "Oh?"

"Yeah. That's why I asked for a lawyer and got the feds involved so quickly. It will be hard for that cop to get me in here."

But not impossible. Nothing was impossible. "Can you tell me his name?"

"Nope. That's part of the deal I'm working on. The feds will give me a new identity far from here if I cooperate with them. I'm sure hoping that comes to pass."

"Okay. What does this have to do with me?"

"I figure Chili will contact his little sis at some point or another. I want you to remember this message and tell him."

"I'm listening."

"Tell him these exact words. 'Life's done treed me, and I'm sorry I left you and Mama in a bind. Don't let the vultures get you down, bro.' Can you remember that?"

I repeated the message back to him verbatim and he nodded. "This is goodbye?" I asked.

"I hope so. I mean, I'm sorry I won't see you again, but if all goes well, I get a do-over. Not too many of those in this life."

"I'm pulling for you, Kale. I hope you take advantage of whatever the feds can do for you."

"I may be dumb about book learning but I ain't walking around stupid. I'll manage. Don't forget my message to Chili."

I tapped the side of my head. "Got it. Take care."

On the drive home, I relayed the conversation I'd had with Kale to Pete. He grinned as soon as I mentioned dirty cop. "I knew it," he said. "There's our confirmation Lance Hamlyn is the dirty cop."

"True, except neither of us has proof. Lance looks guilty but other than his presence at the marina, we have no evidence of him doing anything wrong. There's a chance it could be someone else on the force. Riceland County has thirty-something deputies when you count up all the shifts."

"How many of them are outsiders?" Pete asked. "Not many, and I'll bet that the Bolz family troubles started not long after Hamlyn hit town."

I sighed as we sped down the dual highway, sun high overhead. "Those secret photos show him at the dock a lot, and he is always underfoot, seems like. I can't help but repeat this. He seems like a nice guy."

"That's what neighbors of serial killers say. You've had a couple of social interactions with him. He's shown you what he wants you to see. I have no trouble thinking of him as a dirty cop."

"I don't see how he looks at himself in the mirror every morning."

"People rationalize decisions they make. There's a chance the bad guys have leverage on him, and he's a pawn in their empire. Or, it could be he thinks of himself as an honest man, but I'm betting his choices led him down the wrong paths."

I absorbed those words. It took those hidden camera photos to change my mind about Lance's possible guilt, and we hadn't seen him do anything illegal. Pete distrusted Lance from the get-go. Jealousy, I'd assumed at the time, but Pete's bad guy instincts were truer than mine.

"If he's dirty, it explains why he appears so often on that secret marina camera," Pete continued. "It also explains why he's made it his business to stick close to you. He wants to make sure nothing traces back to him."

"I'll bet the mob is holding his family hostage. Surely it has to be something powerful like that to corrupt a lawman."

"Time will tell."

The bride-to-be's mother answered her phone on the first ring. "Melanie called last night and said the wedding's off," I began. "What do you want me to do?"

"Sit tight," Geneva said. "I'm on it."

The phone clicked in my ear. I turned to Pete. "That's how it's done. Geneva Walker wants Melanie to be someone else's problem. She'll get to the bottom of this quicker than a sheepshead can steal your bait."

Chapter Forty-Four

Two federal agents knocked on my front door late Saturday afternoon. The male of the pair spoke up, badge on display. "Ms. Holloway, we're with the FBI. I'm Special Agent Ken Hightower, and this is my partner, Special Agent Latisha Greene. May we come in?"

I hesitated, aware of Pete coming up behind me. "Is this about my visit to Kale?"

"Yes, but we'd prefer to talk with you in private," Hightower said.

"Anything you want to say to me can be said in front of my boyfriend Pete Merrick." Glancing up at Pete, I saw his gaze travel from the navy blue suits, to the nondescript sedan in the driveway, and the shiny badges. He nodded his okay, and it warmed my insides knowing I had backup. Even more so that I wasn't outnumbered for this meeting.

"Let's sit at the kitchen table," I said, opening the door. They followed me in, and I served iced tea and macadamia nut cookies. "What can I do for you?"

Hightower fixed me with a steady gaze. "Kale Bolz promised us intel on a drug trafficking case, but only if we moved him to a federal facility. We did that, he spoke to you, and now he's talking to us. We don't have a relationship with Mr. Bolz, so it's difficult to know if he's feeding us correct information."

To buy a moment of thought collecting, I bit into a cookie. "In all the years I've known him, Kale never told lies. He might omit information instead of saying something he didn't mean. He isn't a fan of conflict."

"Trust me, we got that message loud and clear."

"He's tellin' you the truth," I said loyally. "It must've been horrible for him to hide out in Florida when he was on the lam. He's always had a close relationship with his mother and brother. Being alone for that time took a toll on him."

"He's safe now and eating regular meals," Hightower continued. "We have an understanding about the criminal enterprise he joined but we need outside confirmation. That's why we're here. Kale is your friend. There's a reason he asked for you and not any of his other acquaintances."

"He trusts me," I said, feeling warm under the collar. "He's known me most of his life. He and his brother call me their little sister."

"In that case, where's the money, Sis?" Hightower asked.

I squirmed in my seat, not liking this line of questioning. "You heard our taped conversation. He didn't tell me anything about the missing money. I'm so out of the loop. I denied even the possibility of Chili, Kale, and Estelle being mixed up with bad people when a local cop suggested that was true. I didn't know they were desperate for money. They never let on that they were in need. Even so, I don't believe they stole a dime. I know nothing about missing money."

Agent Greene bit into one of my cookies. She closed her eyes in bliss. "These are delicious," she murmured.

"Thanks. I made them myself."

Hightower glared at the cookie plate and his partner before he turned to me. "What can you tell me about the island police force?"

"First off, they're sheriff deputies. None of the deputies assigned to the island only works on the island. They ride the whole county."

"But a select few spend most of their time only on Shell Island."

"That's right."

"How many of them have familiarity with boats and marinas?"

I shrugged. "The only cop I know personally is Deputy Lance Hamlyn, and I don't know what he knows about boats. I've met Gil Franklin, but I don't know him other than in his professional capacity."

"Hamlyn spent a lot of time at Bayside Marina," Hightower said.

"Is that a question?"

"It can be."

"Again, I don't keep track of him, but he visited the marina several times after Chili disappeared."

"You know this how?"

I wasn't going to admit to checking the secret video feed. "He told me."

Special Agent Hightower searched my face, making me wonder if he had some kind of omission radar. "Kale Bolz alleges Deputy Hamlyn is not on the up and up. He says the cop is dirty."

"Officers are sworn to uphold the law," I countered.

Hightower watched me a little too long. "You didn't leap to his defense as you did for Kale. We heard you knew Hamlyn well enough to go out to dinner with him."

Heat seared my neck. Good thing Pete already knew about those occasions. "We ate dinner together once because we joined forces to search for Kale's brother. Lance said people didn't open up to him. He thought my personality made conversation flow, but I had help with those interviews. My friend Viv Declan can get anyone to talk. She introduced me to folks at several bars over the course of two nights."

"Nights that you also spent in Hamlyn's company."

The weight of his gaze tugged at me. "That's right."

Another long silence followed. Pete stirred. "You're fishing for information. River told you what she knows. She's a busy lady, and she is prepping for a catering job tomorrow. Get to the point and go on your way."

"We agree you're easy to talk to," Hightower said. "And you're an excellent cookie baker according to my partner. We need you to meet with Deputy Hamlyn privately about the missing money."

"I don't like it," Pete said, his voice sour. "This sounds dangerous."

"It won't be. Hamlyn has no reason to suspect River of anything. He has a pattern of meeting regularly with her to discuss the case. We feel confident he'll ask River about her appointment with Kale this morning."

"I can't give him the message meant for Chili. That's really the only thing I learned from Kale."

"You learned more than that," Hightower said. "Kale expects a sweet deal for cooperating with the investigation. He met with you to say goodbye."

"That's true."

"Trust me, that'll be enough to put Hamlyn on guard. He'll push to see what Kale knows."

"I don't know any more than that."

"What's the point of getting River alone with this guy?" Pete groused. "It's an unnecessary risk. Set your trap for him with someone else."

"Can't do that. She's his only friend. He'll confide in her."

"That's not reason enough. If you were in River's shoes you wouldn't do it either."

Hightower glanced pointedly under the table at our feet. "My big toe wouldn't fit in River's tiny shoes, but that's not the point. This guy's against the wall. If he's a middleman as we suspect, he's got to recover that money. If he's an enforcer, he's got to kill Kale and Chili. The only way for him to gain access to either Bolz is through River. She's the key to building our case against him."

"No," Pete said.

"Yes," Greene said. She turned to me. "Once we clear this case, the Bolz brothers get their lives back. Otherwise, chances are you'll never see them again."

"Don't play on her sympathies," Pete said. "You're asking a civilian to do your job."

"Wait a minute," I said. "This is my life, I decide what I will or will not do."

"Thatta girl," Greene crowed. "Don't let the menfolk push you around."

"River, this is dangerous," Pete said. "Hamlyn's a cop. He carries a gun. One wrong move and he'll shoot you."

"He won't hurt me," I said. "Or he would've done it already."

"He's a desperate man," Pete said, taking my hand, "and so am I. We plan to have a future together. Chili and Kale are grown men. They knew what they were getting into. Their mess doesn't involve you."

I saw Pete's point, honestly, I did. But I also saw the agents' point. If I helped them, Kale and Chili had a way out. If I could help Kale and Chili have a future together, wasn't it worth a try? I loved Pete with all my heart, but Chili and Kale were brothers to me.

"You may not like this decision, Pete Merrick, but I've never turned my back on family or friends in my life. Chili and Kale need my help now. I want to help them, but I'm not stupid. I need assurances and a plan."

"Yes!" Greene said. "I love this woman and her cookies."

"Let's talk strategy. Where should you meet him?" Hightower dug into the cookies with a hearty grin.

I remembered the remote location where Lance met me last time. "I know just the place."

Pete groaned.

Chapter Forty-Five

Lance called at noon while I was packing the van for the baby shower. "River, we need to talk. It's about the case."

"Did you find Chili?" I asked, knowing the feds were probably listening to every word. "Is he okay?"

"Not on the phone. We need to talk in person."

"You sound different," I said, meaning it. "Are you okay?"

"Fine," he snapped. "Meet at the same place as before. Twenty minutes."

I went from being elated that I'd guessed right about the location to realizing that wasn't enough time to get everyone in place, even though the feds were already out there setting up. Luckily I had a built-in excuse. "Can't. I've got an event at two. It will have to be after the event. Four thirty or five-ish."

"This is important. Can't you take a few minutes and come right now?"

"No, I can't. My catering reputation is on the line with every job. If you want to meet before then, come over here now or sneak into the back of the Parish Hall later."

He swore. "Call me when you're cleaning up. I'll tell you where, and River?"

"What?"

"Lose the boyfriend."

"Forget it. Pete's coming with me."

"No," he said tersely. "This is a private conversation."

I gripped the phone tighter. I'd also been instructed to keep him on the line as long as possible. "Lance, is something wrong?"

"Yes. Something is very wrong."

The call ended. I glanced over at Pete. "The feds are right. He's rattled."

"He should be. The feds are closing in. No way will he come out of this without a truckload of dirt on him."

I placed tubs from the refrigerator on the cart, along with boxes of glass vases for the unicorn pretzels. "My catering job bought the feds all day to get set up at the Christmas Tree farm."

Pete added another tub on the cart. "Hightower texted this morning that everything is ready. They mounted a miniature video camera on the little office shack out there. Make sure Hamlyn talks to you in the same place again."

"I'll remember."

"I'll be hiding in the trees with the feds. I don't trust Hamlyn not to do something stupid."

"Let's hope he's on his best behavior."

"He better be."

For all my tough talk earlier, I was a nervous wreck by four thirty as I turned into the Christmas tree farm lane. Lance's police SUV was parked in the same spot. Not wanting to buck tradition, I parked in the same place as last time too and stood in front of my van.

Lance strode my way with prowling steps, his hands fisted at his sides. "What did he say?"

"Who?" I asked, doing my best to stay calm. I had trusted this man, but those dock surveillance photos suggested I shouldn't. It was up to me to discover his true agenda.

"Kale Bolz," Lance snarled. "My fed contact told me you spoke to him yesterday."

"Calm down. He gave me a message for his brother, in case I ever see Chili again. That's why I was so excited that you called." I managed a tight smile. "I hope you have good news about Chili."

"Forget him. That man is a ghost."

My heart stuttered as I searched his face, emotions on my

sleeve. "He's dead?"

"Might as well be. There's no trace of him."

I let out a shaky breath. "Oh. Figure of speech, then. I'm disappointed. I'd hoped this would be over, that our lives could go back to normal."

Lance's face glowed redder than usual. "What else did Kale tell you?"

"Not much. The message for his brother. He's trying to make a deal with the feds. That was it."

"What kind of deal?"

"Information for sentencing help, as I understand it."

"Tell me."

"He didn't share his information with me. It must be related to his disappearance and missing money keeps coming up."

"A whole lot of missing money. Who's his handler?"

The still air blanketed me with evergreen scent, making it hard to breathe. "I don't understand."

"Handler, as in who is working him to get the information."

"I'm not sure. I spoke with agents Hightower and Greene afterward."

He stepped closer, looming over me, his aftershave blocking the evergreen scent. "What'd they want?"

"You're making me nervous. Calm down. I'll tell you what I know, but it isn't much. They asked if Kale was a liar. I told them he wasn't."

Lance swore and stabbed his fingers through his hair. Because my senses were on hyperalert, I noticed two things. His manicured fingernails were long for a guy. There were also scrapes on his knuckles.

"This is not good," Lance said.

His battered hand. Why hadn't I noticed that before? He wore gloves a lot, and when he didn't he kept his hands in his pockets or out of sight. His knuckles looked like Jimmy Brown's a few days after he got into a fight on the school bus.

Lance had hit something. Or someone. My breath hitched.

Estelle. He'd beat Estelle. Was his hand the proof we needed that he was a killer?

"It's good for Kale," I said, amazed at how calm I sounded. "He made mistakes, and now he can minimize the penalties for his problems."

"He's gonna ruin everything." Lance turned from me and strode a few steps away. Then he circled back. "Word for word, what message did he have for Chili?"

"It was a private message," I said, fingernails biting into my palms.

"Tell. Me. Or I'll run you in for withholding evidence."

"You're forcing me to betray a confidence? I thought you wanted to be my friend."

"My job's on the line. What did he say?"

"They don't make sense to me." I repeated the lines rotely, feeling like a weasel for caving, but the feds already knew what Kale said. "Do you know what they mean?"

"They spell trouble."

"You understand it?"

"Better than you think." He glanced around the clearing again and then back at the hut. His gaze narrowed. "Damn it."

Before I could utter another word, he yanked me to his chest. In the flurry of movement, I saw scrapes on the knuckles on his other hand. A sudden realization sickened me. The feds were right and so was Pete. Lance beat Estelle to death and nearly killed Chili with his fists.

"I'll kill her," Lance shouted. "Come out right now."

Chapter Forty-Six

"What are you doing, Lance?" I struggled against his tight hold on me. "This isn't funny."

"Not meant to be funny. You're my hostage. The feds put you up to this, didn't they?"

"You're not making sense. You called this meeting and determined the place. Put the gun away. You're scaring me."

The thumping of my heart nearly deafened me. I had to keep him talking. The feds needed a confession from Lance. Even though I was scared, I had to hold it together to help Chili and Kale.

"Either you've lost your mind or you killed Estelle and hurt Chili," I said, pushing against his arm to no avail. "Let me go."

He loosened his grip on me but didn't let me go. "I can't. You know too much."

"I knew nothing until you grabbed me just now. I trusted you."

"You're playing a dangerous game. I tried to warn you off, twice, with the kitchen fire and the home invasion, but you don't give up." He took a deep breath and groaned. "God, why do you have to smell like cookies?"

I grimaced at the knowledge he'd done those things to me. "I baked cookies this morning for the baby shower. Let me go. I've done nothing to hurt you, and I told you everything I know."

"They suspect me don't they?" His hot breath prickled my neck.

My brain froze. That's the only reason I could think of for not spinning some tale. I couldn't tell him the feds were hiding in the woods or he'd shoot me. Conversely, I couldn't lie without him hearing it in my voice.

"Never mind, your silence speaks volumes. What do they have on me?" He jerked my arm.

I bit my lip against the rising fear. If I could just get him talking. "Stop. That hurts. The feds suspect everyone. Even me. They don't know any of us. They don't trust Kale."

"He fingered me?"

"He said a crooked cop was involved. I thought that was a lie. I told myself it wasn't you because I trusted you. And yet here we stand with you calling me a hostage. Turns out you're the liar."

"It wasn't supposed to be like this. I wanted you for myself, but you weren't interested."

I glared at him. "I have a boyfriend. I told you that from the beginning of our acquaintance. Look, whatever you've done, you can come clean and start over."

"Doesn't work that way for cops. I'm screwed. Those feds are using you. Are you wearing a wire? Is that how they plan to take me down?"

"No wire," I said.

"Prove it. Take off your shirt."

Outrage simmered in my blood. "I will not take off my shirt."

He swore again and patted me down, front and back. He also checked out my midriff and looked down my top. "Nice tatas. You're right. No wire."

"Told you."

"I don't get it," he said. "Why'd you come out here?"

I leaned against my van because my knees threatened to buckle. "You asked me to come. You set the location. You said it was about the case. I came because I care about Chili. What's the deal, Lance? What are you and the Bolzes into?"

He relaxed and leaned beside me. "I need that money. The money will make everything right."

"I don't have any money. I told you that already. What is this truly about, Lance? How can I help you?"

"No one can help, unless they have the money. Shell Island

was supposed to be an easy gig. We bought the marina, kept most of the boating traffic away, and moved money here for cleaning and then offshore."

"Who's we?"

He didn't answer. "If you're the dirty cop Kale referred to, I know you have to kill me. Satisfy my curiosity. Who do you work for? Are you in the mob?"

"I don't want to kill you, but it has to be done. My wife and kids depend upon me doing my job."

"You're married?"

He winced, then gave a terse nod. "Sixteen years. Four kids."

"You tried to date me."

"As a cover but I like you more than I should."

This kept getting better and better. My opinion of him kept sinking. "Would you have slept with me as a cover?"

"Yeah, so what?"

"You aren't the man of honor I believed you were. Unless you were coerced. Are they holding your family hostage?"

"My brother-in-law runs the cartel. I literally married the mob. Thought I knew what I was doing. Big mistake."

"Love screws with your head."

"Love and power. Ultimately it became about power as my wife advanced in the ranks. Unless I do what they say, I'll never see my kids again. As it is, I'm lucky to see them twice a year."

"Killing people, destroying families, that's wrong."

"You're a welcome breath of fresh air. I wish I'd met you before Isabella. For you, River, I would've been a good man. For Isabella, I'm hired muscle and an occasional toss in the hay when she tires of her regular playmates."

"What's Isabella's maiden name?"

"Ferarrelli. It still is. She refused to take my last name when we married. That should've been an omen of things to come."

"You live in Mexico?"

"I live wherever they tell me to live. None of that matters now. Without that missing money, I'm a dead man. This organization thrives on getting the job done."

"Are you really a cop?"

Lance shrugged. "I'm wearing the uniform and carrying a gun. The Ferarrelli machine is good at constructing solid backgrounds. Even the feds believed it."

"Have you solved any cases since you've been here?" I asked.

"Yes, of course. Nearly a hundred, if you must know. I really got into my role."

"Did you look for Chili?"

His silence was damning. Realization dawned with icy certainty. He never officially looked for Chili. He didn't investigate Estelle's death either.

A wave of nausea and dizziness hit, along with total revulsion for Lance Hamlyn.

He gave me an appraising look, and I feared it was the end of me. Information, my brain reminded me. This was about gathering information. "How'd the laundry operation work?"

"Like a charm, for a while at least. I left five-gallon buckets of drug money in Chili's boat. He and Kale hauled the money to Estelle who washed everything through her dry-cleaning business and deposited the cash in our accounts. In late fall, we received a double batch of money. I moved the money to a new drop spot, but the Bolzes claimed they never saw it."

"Sounds like quite a system. How long did it run?"

"They had it up and running before I arrived eight months ago."

An uneasy silence settled around us. I couldn't take it. I had to say something, anything to stay alive. "What happens now?"

"Now I shoot you and leave your body in a creek full of alligators."

His icy tone was as cold as his eyes. "You don't have to do that. You can choose to be a better man."

"Not happening. You never should've agreed to help Estelle Bolz. Her dirt rubbed off on you. There's a different set of rules for dirty people."

I couldn't wrap my head around the choices Estelle had made. "What rule is that?"

"He who has the biggest gun makes all the rules."

"I don't want to die."

"End of the road. Any last words?"

Chapter Forty-Seven

"Hands in the air, Deputy Hamlyn," Special Agent Hightower yelled from the tree line. "FBI. We have you surrounded."

Lance pivoted to the sound of the voice, and I used that moment of distraction to slip around the side of the van, and then raced behind the shack. With every step I wondered if I'd catch a bullet in the back.

"No way," Lance said. "I don't know who you are, but you're messing with the wrong guy." He must've noticed my disappearance. "River!" he shouted.

I darted into the trees behind the shack. Pete caught me by the third tree. I lunged into his arms, sobbing and shaking and relieved I'd survived.

"You did good, River," Pete said over and over again until I calmed.

I wiped my wet cheeks with the back of my hand. "He was about to kill me."

"But he didn't. You got what the feds needed. Hamlyn is in federal custody now. He won't see the light of day for a very long time."

I eased into the comfort he offered, absorbing his strength and tenderness.

It didn't take long for the feds to place Lance in a black SUV and drive away. We watched the team remove the hidden cameras. Soon they departed too. I thought about driving Pete and me home, but my hands wouldn't stop shaking.

The differences between Pete and Lance were staggering. Pete had high moral character, integrity, ethics, compassion, and commitment. He followed through on what he said he'd do. Lance, well, Lance was the opposite of all that. Truth rang in his voice when he said if he'd met me before his wife he'd have been a good man. It dawned on me how lucky I was that I hadn't had to make bad choices in order to survive.

"What're you thinking?" Pete asked, gripping my hand.

"Everything and nothing. About how we got to where we're standing."

"We drove here."

I shot him a wry smile. "Deeper than that. We're standing on top of the decisions we made. Each choice had a consequence and pointed us in this direction. It's all connected."

"Don't go getting soft over Lance. He doesn't deserve your sympathy."

"I'm thrilled he didn't shoot me. I just wondered what I would do if life dealt me a bad hand."

"One of the main differences between your life and Lance's is that you kept going when speedbumps came your way. You always found a way to support your family. You moved in with your mother when she was ill, and you didn't complain about it or worry about making ends meet. You went out and did what you needed to do."

"Of course I did."

"Lance didn't do that. He took shortcuts, he was lazy, and he fell in with the wrong crowd. He gambled with his fate. Now he pays for those choices."

"He killed Estelle. Once I got a good look at his hands today, I knew what'd happened. He threatened Kale, who then faked his death. He beat Chili to within an inch of his life too. Then he turned his fists on a defenseless older woman. He's a monster in my book."

"The feds agree with you."

"But will they cut a deal with him to get someone higher up on the drug food chain?"

"It's a possibility."

"That'd be wrong. Estelle's life meant something. He should pay for his actions."

"It's out of our hands. At least we know the truth, and there's no way Lance will return to the police force. The citizens of Riceland County won't feel his fists ever again."

I shuddered, but at least this time I was successful in grabbing my keys out of my pocket.

Pete reached for the keys. "I'll drive. Your hands are shaking worse than mine."

"I'm happy to let you drive, but why are you shaking?"

He drew me into an embrace. "You're kidding, right? The woman I love with all my heart met with a stone-cold killer. The feds had to restrain me. I tried to charge headlong into this clearing and tackle him when he grabbed your arm."

"You did? That's the sweetest thing you've ever said to me, Pete."

He kissed me. "River, when will you wear my ring and agree to be my wife?"

"Soon."

Geneva Walker called me at seven that evening, and she was with Melanie on speaker phone. "My daughter has something to say to you," Geneva said to start the conversation.

"Good evening to you both," I said. "What can I do for you?"

"I apologize for the calls," Melanie said. "Mom and Malcom explained that he'd been tapped to take the big boss's daughter out when she visited their branch of the company. It wasn't a date. He escorted her so she wouldn't have to eat alone."

"That's good to know."

"And," Melanie said, "if you haven't booked my date with anyone else, I still want you to cater my wedding."

"I'll be glad to, Melanie."

"Whew, glad that's over," Melanie said. "Mom said we can't afford to lose you."

"Your mom is a smart woman."

Special agents Hightower and Greene called midafternoon the next day and asked to see us. Everything went better with food, so I invited them for an early dinner at five.

Pete surprised me by offering to do burgers on the grill. I made an easy strawberry pie, baked sweet potato fries, and whipped up a perfect batch of coleslaw.

Pete made margaritas for everyone, though I noticed Hightower didn't touch his. While the grill and oven were doing their thing, we gathered on the back porch. The deep blue sky overhead gave the illusion everything was picture perfect. It hadn't been that way for me. Yesterday, I'd gotten a lot closer to the action than I liked.

I kept looking for the cat but Major hadn't been around all day.

"Lance survive the initial interview?" I asked Agent Hightower after he and his partner arrived.

"Didn't get to ask him anything. Lawyered up at first breath."

"Oh. That's not helpful."

"We have our ways. Lance Hamlyn is no match for the FBI."

"What about the missing money?" I asked. "You have any idea where it is?"

"No. We hoped you had ideas."

"I'm just now understanding the bigger picture, but I don't see why they needed Estelle's dry-cleaning shop when they already had a perfect business cover in the marina. They had the facility to themselves. It would be easy to fake invoices for goods and services from there and pass the dirty money through the bank."

"We believe they started out with the marina laundering the drug money, then they set up Estelle to also run money through her business," Hightower said. "Once they had both systems in place, they sent Lance to keep an eye on the process and enforce the cartel's wishes. When the double shipment of money vanished, Lance jumped all over the Bolz family. In his eyes, they were expendable."

"Why didn't he jump all over Garnet at the marina? Why target the Bolzes?"

"The dockmaster is his cousin by marriage. From what we can gather, he trusted her completely. Now she's elsewhere, and a million dollars is missing. With no leads here for the money, the mob will go after her for it."

I shuddered. "I wouldn't want to be Garnet when the mob enforcers find her."

"If she's smart, she'll find an island in another country and lay low for the rest of her life."

"Is that likely?" Pete asked as he flipped a burger.

"Sadly, no. Between you and me, she's most likely to end up a Jane Doe homicide elsewhere. We may never know her fate."

"How dirty was my friend Estelle Bolz?" I asked.

"She laundered mob money, that's illegal."

"How'd she get involved with these people? I don't understand her stooping to their level. She supported her family with a small business, for goodness sake."

"We subpoenaed her bank records," Hightower said. "She made regular deposits in her personal checking account of $3,000 a month for the last three years, so she was on their payroll that long. Other than Social Security, that was what she lived on. What income she netted from the dry cleaners, paid the bills there. She had very little personal income from the dry cleaners."

"I thought her shop was rock solid and profitable. Since it wasn't, I believe Estelle kept it open so that her staff had jobs."

"It might've seemed successful from the outside, but her shaky finances from the previous five years indicate Estelle had done everything short of selling her blood to pay her bills. We think Estelle was targeted because she had the kind of business they needed to expand the money laundering operation, and she desperately needed money."

"I feel awful about her situation. If I'd known, I would've moved her in here with us. Why didn't Chili and Kale help her? I don't understand this at all."

"We'll never know, unless her sons tell the story, and there's a chance they may not know all of it. Pride is a terrible burden to seniors, as is independence. Odds are, Estelle did everything she could to maintain both."

I glanced at the lengthening shadows in my yard. How many more people in my life were just barely making it? Jude Ernest for one. I needed to make sure he got more meals each week, but he'd protest my help. That was his way.

"We have your written statement, and once the federal prosecutor is ready to file the case, you'll hear from us again."

"How is it a federal case with the money still missing?" I asked.

"Estelle's financial records document money laundering occurred at her cleaners. We're hoping Hamlyn will roll on the enforcers that tore up Estelle's house. If he does, we have a shot at the biggest guns in the drug ring. We're also hopeful to learn more once we get deeper into the marina finances. We took their computers and cameras, even found a hidden trail cam on our second pass through there."

"Let me see if I understand the logistics," I said, keeping my smile to myself about the trail cam we'd returned to the marina. "The mob funneled cash through the marina to a regional bank, and from there the money transferred to different financial institutions until it landed in offshore accounts. When they needed more money processed, they brought Estelle's dry cleaners into the fold."

"Since Estelle kept the books for her business, no one was the wiser when her net receipts increased to a few hundred dollars a day on a regular basis, and then jumped to nearly two thousand a week," Hightower said. "We estimate that over $100,000 passed through her dry cleaners. She hadn't filed her taxes for last year yet. Those hefty bank deposits into her new business account at that regional bank would've triggered an audit. The mob probably intended to sideline Estelle soon. That's their pattern, to involve local business owners and then bug out when the activity comes under scrutiny."

"Poor Estelle." I tried to piece more of it together. "But why did Kale fake his death if he was barely involved in the money laundering?"

"He said Hamlyn came to him and demanded the missing money or he'd kill him."

"That's scary. Why didn't he tell someone?"

"He probably told his mom," Pete chimed in. "He wouldn't have trusted the cops."

"If either of them confided in Jude Ernest or me, we could've found a better way to deal with this," I said. "Estelle might still be alive."

"And you and Jude might be dead," Hightower said. "Kale did what he had to do to protect the ones he loved."

"What happens to him now?" I asked.

Greene smiled benignly. "He's our guest for a while longer."

"And if Chili surfaces?" I persisted.

"We want to talk to him too. Someone took that money. We think it was Garnet, but we have no proof either way."

Chapter Forty-Eight

"Someone took that money."

Those words resonated in my ear all evening and into the next morning. Over coffee on the back porch, Pete and I continued the conversation. "Kale and Chili didn't steal the money. They're not bad people," I said, eying the big black cat that rested near me on the bench. Major showed up last night after the agents left and he showed no sign of leaving here again.

"People under stress do things you wouldn't expect," Pete added.

"I know them. If they found a billfold in the street without ID, they'd take it to the nearest business. They wouldn't help themselves to anything inside it."

"A million dollars is a huge temptation. Think about what you would do with a million dollars."

I went to take a sip of coffee, but my cup was empty. I set it down. "Me? I'd buy a new van and help get Doug set up in business. I'd help seniors with their bills. I'd set up a soup kitchen somewhere so that everyone who was hungry would have food. I'd repair Estelle's house because what those men did was wrong. I'd figure out a way to get Jude back on his feet."

"What about a new house? Trips overseas?"

"I don't need those things. If I had a million dollars I'd spend nearly all of it helping people. But I might hire a few people to help me do the cooking for giving away free food. No way could I do that and keep Holloway Catering afloat."

"You're a good person, River. I wouldn't be so charitable if I had a million-dollar windfall. I'd plan the best wedding and honeymoon trip ever and bank the rest for all the kids we're going to have. Bottom line, I'd invest the money in our future."

"That's lovely," I said, meaning it. "But Kale and Chili. If they had a million dollars, they'd probably buy a hunting preserve and live there with Jude. We'd never hear from them again."

"Wonder how Hamlyn got the money to the marina," Pete said. "Did he meet a boat offshore?"

"We'll never know, but that sounds reasonable to me."

"Garnet kept a low profile, and even though we suspected her, we had no proof of her association with the mob. Wonder what she'd do with a million dollars? I haven't a clue."

"Which makes me think she took the money," Pete said. "Think about it. Lance is in jail, Estelle's dead, Kale is singing for the feds, and Chili's off the grid. Garnet is the last woman standing."

"Except she's one of them." The cat's purring was so soothing I had to work hard to string my words together. "Why would she need the money? She probably got a higher cut than Estelle, probably had more money than she could spend without blowing her cover."

"Some people never have enough money. She could've felt slighted at some point along the way and figured she would take her due. In any event, we're speculating. We may never know what happened to the money. Though her banking records for the last three and a half years indicate a huge rise in her deposits. She must've been skimming money from the marina too."

"It doesn't feel finished," I said. "The ending is messy with the money at large."

"We got a bad cop off the street and both Bolz brothers are alive. That counts as a win in my book," Pete said. "The case is over, and we'll never see any of those people again."

Easy for him to say. The loose ends still flapped in the ocean breeze. I didn't like how unsettled I felt. There was no storm brewing on the horizon. The sky was bright and clear, despite my clanging intuition. Where are you, Garnet?

That unsettled feeling wouldn't leave me alone. The next day I told Pete, "I want to find Chili again to give him an update."

Pete and I drove to Jude's house to ask about Chili, only Jude wasn't home either.

"Chili's been here," Pete said, pointing out a small object.

The rusted mint tin sat on the porch under the railing. I grabbed the box of secrets and inside lay a small scrap of paper. "Previous coordinates," it read.

I whooped with delight and took Pete's hand for the hike back to the van. Before I cranked the vehicle, I turned to Pete. "I wonder if Chili left us a message out there. Will we ever find out what happened to that money or Garnet?"

"Garnet's body never turned up, so there's a possibility she's still alive. She's missing. The money's missing. I think she took it, but what do I know? Since the FBI found out she'd been skimming from the mob, it's fair to assume the mob did too. Either organization could've recovered the money," Pete said, pausing for a moment. "There's a good chance we'll never know."

"Hmm. Estelle used me to hunt for Chili. Kale gave me a message for his brother, only I didn't see Chili after that."

"You gave Jude the message," Pete reminded me.

"I did, and he must've known what it meant." Realization dawned. "They used me. All of them. I fell into the little sister trap, trying to help them, and they used the misdirection to get away."

Fortunately Pete hadn't cleared the cache in his phone and the GPS coordinates were still there from before. I drove to the other end of the island and found my pull-in spot. We loaded up with water and protein bars and set off to our fallen log.

But when we arrived, there was no flashing sign that said, "River look here." As before I sat on the fallen tree to rest. I searched the nearby trees with my eyes. "We hiked out here for nothing."

Pete had been sitting quietly, but then he grinned. "Look. Up there."

I glanced where he was pointing, the stout pine next to the fallen log, and up high a small plastic box was nailed to the tree. I fetched it and opened the box, withdrawing a note wrapped around a hunk of bills. I handed Pete the money and opened the note.

"It's Chili's handwriting," I said eagerly reading aloud.

Thanks for everything, L'il Sis. You've always been family to us, and we thank you for welcoming us into your life. You made this island bearable. Uncle Jay loaned me this money. Use it to bury Mama in Kale's unused grave. Put her birth date, death date, and Mother of Chili and Kale on her headstone. Don't look for us. Uncle Jay and I are taking off and laying low until Kale gets out of prison. Uncle Jay knows the right people for us to start over with new identities, so that's what we're doing. Use whatever's leftover on your wedding. I regret I won't be there to watch you walk down the aisle. Chili. PS we did not steal the money nor do we have it."

Pete met my gaze. "There's probably ten grand here in hundreds. That's one heck of a memorial tombstone."

"Wow," I said. "Chili's okay. He's with Uncle Jay. You were right earlier. We'll never see these people again."

"Does it matter?" Pete asked. "You have me and your brother and the cat."

"You're right. I'm not alone. But this dance with the mob cost them dearly. Nothing can replace Chili and Kale's mom."

"Chili and Jude and Kale will be fine. People underestimate small town folk all the time. They think we don't have half a brain to think with. We are just as smart as they are, if not smarter, because we know what's important. Family is important. Money makes things easier, but if you trust the right people, your heart will always be full."

I stared at Pete. He'd never mentioned his personal philosophy before, and it warmed my heart that he believed the same things I did. He took his time coming to the realization he needed me in his life, but he'd come home, and that was the important part.

As for me, I'd been so busy helping my friends that I hadn't given Pete the attention he deserved. My friends were safe now and so was I. That missing money could stay missing for all I cared.

"I trust you completely," I said, looking deep into his eyes and smiling.

He stared back. "Does this mean what I think it means?"

"It does."

"I've been carrying this with me since Valentine's Day when I asked you the first time." He reached into his pocket for my engagement ring. "River Holloway, will you be my wife?"

Emotion choked my throat. I tried to speak and not a sound would come out. I nodded. He slipped the diamond ring on my finger and drew me into his arms.

"Thank you," he said. "I stumbled down the wrong road, trying to build an impressive resumé and get rich, but the effort nearly cost me the treasure I hold most dear. You."

"We've been tempered by life," I said. "We learned from our mistakes."

"We're a helluva team."

As we sealed our promise with a kiss, a song filled my heart. Not a song with words, but one of joy and peace. While I was sad about Estelle, her sons and Jude were starting over now that the dirty cop was in custody. The truly important thing was I'd found my way back to trusting Pete with my heart. He would be careful with it from now on, I believed that with every fiber of my being.

I wasn't perfect, far from it, but I did my best every day to help others. Pete and I had committed to each other. There'd be storms, but the sun would always appear. I'd wintered plenty of storms to date and they'd strengthened my character. I was the caring, helpful daughter my parents had raised. They'd be proud of me for helping the Bolzes, for finding my own happiness, and for guiding my brother into maturity.

Light glittered on my ring. Life was good, and the future shone diamond bright.

River's Delicious Sea Bass

<u>Ingredients</u>
4 servings of sea bass (about 4-7 ounces each)
8 ounces of baby bella mushrooms, sliced
A "bunch" of scallions, bulbs sliced diagonally
Ginger root, peeled and thinly sliced
Garlic cloves, thinly sliced
2 lemons, sliced in thin circles
Salt and pepper to taste
Parchment Paper

<u>Butter Mix</u>
4 tbsp softened butter
2-3 tbsp honey
2 tbsp rice wine vinegar
3 tbsp tamari sauce, shoyu sauce, or coconut aminos

Heat oven or grill at 375 degrees.

Begin by whisking together the butter mixture until smooth. This can be done ahead of time and refrigerated. Tear off 4 pieces of parchment paper, each one a foot long. Next, salt and pepper the fish.

Lay the parchment paper pieces on the counter. Onto the center of each sheet, layer ginger and garlic slices first, then equally distribute the scallions and mushrooms, and top the stack with sea bass. Add about 3 TBSP of the butter mix to each stack, then place lemon slices on the fish. Fold each parchment paper into a sealed pouch shape and place on a baking dish. Cook for 12-14 minutes.

River Cakes a.k.a. Crab Cakes

Ingredients
1 pound crab meat
1 large egg
1 tsp Tabasco sauce
1 tbsp lime juice
¼ tsp Old Bay seasoning
3 tbsp mayonnaise
Scant handful of flour*
½ stick of butter*

Mix all ingredients except butter. Shape into hamburger-sized patties. Place in large frying pan with melted butter. Cover. Cook over medium heat until bottom browns, about five minutes. Flip and cook again until bottom browns. Enjoy!

*For those with dietary restrictions, other flours and fats may be substituted.

Luscious Lemon Meringue Pie

<u>Pie Crust from Scratch</u>
1 ½ cup all-purpose flour
½ tsp salt
1 tsp sugar
1 stick butter, softened or sliced thinly
¼ cup cold water

Mix dry ingredients together. Cut in butter. Stir in water until dough is crumbly but not dry. Chill pastry for 15 minutes before rolling it out and fitting to a 9-inch pie pan. Cover crust with parchment paper and add dry beans or rice on top to keep crust from bowing during cooking. Bake in a 400-degree oven for 5-10 minutes, until lightly browned. Cool 15 minutes and remove parchment paper and rice or beans. The crust is ready for filling and further cooking.

<u>Lemon Filling</u>
6 tbsp cornstarch
1 ½ cup sugar
¼ tsp salt
½ cup cold water
½ cup fresh lemon juice
1 ½ cup boiling water
3 tbsp butter, softened
3 egg yolks (reserve whites for meringue)
2 tsp lemon zest

Select a thick-walled saucepan. In the pan, mix cornstarch, sugar, and salt. Sequentially stir in the cold water, and lemon juice, followed by the boiling water. Cook over medium-low heat, stirring constantly, until mixture boils. Once thickened (about 5 minutes), remove from heat, and stir in butter until it melts.

In a heatproof bowl, beat the egg yolks. Slowly beat in ¼ cup of the cornstarch mix, and then stir this back into the filling in the saucepan. Add the lemon zest. Stir and cook until thickened, about another minute. Remove from heat and cool for 15 minutes.

Meringue
5 egg whites
½ tsp cream of tartar
Pinch of salt
½ cup superfine sugar
1 tsp vanilla

Pour egg whites into a heatproof bowl over simmering water and beat until foamy. Mix in cream of tartar and salt and beat until soft peaks form. Add the fine sugar a little at a time, beating after each addition.

Assembly
Pour filling in cooled pie crust and top with meringue.
Use a kitchen knife to create decorative swirls atop the meringue.

Bake at 350 degrees until lightly browned, about 10 minutes. Cool pie on a wire rack. Serve slightly warm or at room temperature. Do not refrigerate. Store in a draft-free place.

MAGGIE TOUSSAINT

Southern author Maggie Toussaint evolved into a mystery author after getting her feet damp in romantic suspense and dystopian fiction, with twenty fiction novels and two nonfiction novels to her credit. A three-time finalist for Georgia Author of the Year, her work won three Silver Falchions, the Readers' Choice, and the EPIC Awards. She's past president of Southeast chapter of Mystery Writers of America and an officer of Lowcountry Sisters In Crime. She lives in coastal Georgia, where secrets, heritage, and ancient oaks cast long shadows. Visit her at maggietoussaint.com.

**The Seafood Capers Mystery Series
by Maggie Toussaint**

SEAS THE DAY (#1)

Henery Press Mystery Books

And finally, before you go...
Here are a few other mysteries
you might enjoy:

PUMPKINS IN PARADISE

Kathi Daley

A Tj Jensen Mystery (#1)

Between volunteering for the annual pumpkin festival and coaching her girls to the state soccer finals, high school teacher Tj Jensen finds her good friend Zachary Collins dead in his favorite chair.

When the handsome new deputy closes the case without so much as a "why" or "how," Tj turns her attention from chili cook-offs and pumpkin carving to complex puzzles, prophetic riddles, and a decades-old secret she seems destined to unravel.

Available at booksellers nationwide and online

Visit www.henerypress.com for details

PILLOW STALK

Diane Vallere

A Madison Night Mystery (#1)

Interior Decorator Madison Night might look like a throwback to the sixties, but as business owner and landlord, she proves that independent women can have it all. But when a killer targets women dressed in her signature style—estate sale vintage to play up her resemblance to fave actress Doris Day—what makes her unique might make her dead.

The local detective connects the new crime to a twenty-year old cold case, and Madison's long-trusted contractor emerges as the leading suspect. As the body count piles up, Madison uncovers a Soviet spy, a campaign to destroy all Doris Day movies, and six minutes of film that will change her life forever.

Available at booksellers nationwide and online

Visit www.henerypress.com for details

CPSIA information can be obtained
at www.ICGtesting.com
Printed in the USA
LVHW042349130420
653369LV00014B/1064